DAUGHTER

of the

STORM

Tina Callaghan

POOLBEG

Published 2019
by Poolbeg Press Ltd
123 Grange Hill, Baldoyle
Dublin 13, Ireland
E-mail: poolbeg@poolbeg.com
www.poolbeg.com

A catalogue record for this book is available from the British Library.

ISBN 978-1-78199-786-4

Typeset by Poolbeg in Sabon 11/14.5

www.poolbeg.com

About the Author

Tina Callaghan is a writer of speculative fiction. Her stories involve elements of history, mythology and the supernatural, although she mostly just makes it up as she goes along. Her short stories have appeared in anthologies alongside horror and science-fiction greats Stephen King, Dean Koontz, Ray Bradbury and Robert Bloch. Her first novel *Dark Wood Dark Water* was shortlisted for the Young Adult Book of the Year in the An Post Irish Book Awards.

She lives in County Wexford with her partner Joe and lots of pets.

Praise for *Daughter of the Storm*

'Atmospheric, evocative, menacing, surprising – you can smell the sea, sense the danger and share the fear. This book is a cracking read, definitely one to be devoured'
Helen Moorhouse, author of *Ever This Day*

'Devastating as it is beautiful, *Daughter of the Storm* is a compelling and chilling exploration of generational grief and love'
Dr. Sarah Cleary, horror academic and Horror Expo Ireland Creative Director.

Praise for *Dark Wood, Dark Water*

'A story Stephen King would have written if he'd grown up in Ireland' Peadar Ó Guilín, author of *The Call*

'Chilling, atmospheric and with an effortlessly vivid sense of place, this novel sustains the intrigue from the first page to the last. A genuinely impressive debut from a storytelling talent to watch. And read' F.G. Cottam, author of *The Colony*

'A sublime fantasy horror grounded in dark and sinister local folklore' Ruth Frances Long, author of the *Dubh Linn* series

'A moody, atmospheric and entertaining tale'
Joseph Delaney, author of *The Wardstone Chronicles*

'An impressive, ambitious and entertaining debut'
Ginger Nuts of Horror review

Acknowledgements

With love, I thank those who support me in the slightly mad endeavour of making up stories, particularly my dear friends and family, as well as my publisher Paula Campbell and editor Gaye Shortland, who I count among them.

For those who wish to create or enjoy a story in any medium, don't let anything stop you. It's the best feeling in the world, akin to love in all its glorious forms.

For Joe

From 'Memorable Accidents and Unheard of Transactions' published in 1693, held in the British Library. The book contains 'An Account of Several Strange Events: As the Deposing of Tyrants, Lamentable Shipwrecks, Dismal Misfortunes, Stratagems of War, Perilous Adventures ... and Select Historical Events.'

Rocks that jutted out into the sea, lifted up the Vessel to the Clouds, letting her fall on a sudden upon the Cliffs with such violence that she could not hold out long. You might have heard her already cracking on all sides, some parts of her falling off the rest; and at last, this great Mass of Wood being for a while thus dreadfully shaken and toss'd from Wave to Rock, was dash'd to pieces with a horrible noise. The Poop bore the first shock, and accordingly was the first part that bulg'd. To no purpose they cut down the Masts and threw overboard the Guns, and all that lay in their way; all their precautions were in vain, for the ship struck upon the Rocks so often and so rudely, that at last she open'd under the Gunners Room. The Water then entring in abundance, began to gain the first Deck, and to fill the Gunners Room, it advanced even to the great Cabbin, and in a moment after it reach'd to their Girdles that were upon the second Deck, and still ascending insensibly, our ship at last sunk quite down into the Sea, till the Keel reach'd the bottom, the body of the Vessel remained some time immovable. It would be a hard task to represent the astonishment, terror and consternation that seiz'd up on every Heart on the Ship; Nothing now was heard but cries, sighs and groans: Some prostrate upon the deck implor'd the assistance of Heaven: Others were throwing into the sea Barrels, empty Casks, Sailyards and pieces of Boards, to aid them in making their escape. After the violence of the crying was over, they that remain'd on the Vessel began to think of saving themselves.

One

Lia watched the ferry lumbering towards the slipway where she waited. She hoisted her rucksack on her shoulders and clutched her ticket. The October air was cool and the sea and sky grey. Her jacket should have been enough to keep her warm, but a chill ran through her.

From the moment she had first bought the plane ticket to Ireland and the connecting train and bus tickets online, to actually sneaking out of the house with a hastily packed bag, she had been full of confidence. She was only a nuisance to her mother in New York – Jasmine was trying to get her life back in order since 'the tragedy', as she insisted on calling it, but that didn't mean that Lia was ready to do the same. But, instead of leaving her alone to spend the summer thinking and just walking around as she wanted to, Jasmine kept trying to take her places, buy her new clothes, new laptop, new friends. There was even talk of a puppy, but by then Lia had made up her mind to go. She had to get away from all the … everything that was going on in her childhood home.

The brownstone was lovely, her friends were lovely, the city was lovely. Even her original plans of going to NYU were lovely. The only teeny-tiny problem was that she didn't want lovely. She wanted bleak, grey, stark and lonely to suit her mood. She wanted answers too.

One evening, after an unusually bitter row with her mother over college, Lia was sitting on the side of her bed with her new laptop open beside her when a thought arrived unannounced, as though someone else had spoken it clearly into her ear.

Where can I find bleak, lonely and grey, plus answers?

She already had one answer. The island off the Irish coast that was her father's homeplace. She booked the tickets there and then before she could change her mind. It would be better for Jasmine not to have to argue all the time. They could both do what they needed to get better, if they were apart for a while.

Out beyond the ferry, where it was hard to tell the sea from the sky, lay the island. If she squinted, she could make out a shadow that might be it. Clearer were the two sea stacks known as the Chimneys. The ferry website had pictures of them. They were quite famous, it seemed.

She followed a couple weighed down by shopping bags up the ramp. She guessed that October wasn't the best time for tourists. She wasn't a tourist of course.

The journey was slow and Lia watched the island come closer, both fascinated and somehow fearful. In fact, the sight of it was a shock. On the ferry website, the island had been lit up with sunlight, although still pretty rocky. Though she had been looking for bleak and lonely, those pictures hadn't prepared her for frightening cliffs, edged with white waves, and a grey mist that pulled the island back into the blurry horizon.

When they were quite close to the Chimneys another text

from her mom that she wasn't going to answer arrived. Lia had texted once to say she was safe and just needed a break with friends. She had sent a selfie so that Jasmine wouldn't think she had been kidnapped and coerced into texting that she was fine.

She glanced up and found that the ferry was giving a wide berth to the Chimneys. Even so, they were spectacular. Looming towers of black rock and limestone, streaked with bird poop, much bigger than she had expected. As she watched, a lump of rock tumbled from the top of one and crashed into the sea. The movement sent up a flock of gulls, a brief flash of sunlight catching their undersides, blindingly white against the darkening sky.

Lia took a quick picture, then noticed her phone had no service. She held it up again, watching for bars, but nothing happened.

'Once you're past the Chimneys, that thing is no good to you.'

She looked around, startled. A lady was sitting on a bench, shopping bags piled around her feet, her face soft and powdery.

'I'm sorry?'

'Your phone. There's no service on the island.'

Lia stared at her, appalled.

The lady chuckled.

'Sorry – I'm not laughing at you, dear. You just looked so shocked. I know you young folk like your phones. But everyone has a landline if you want to call someone. As long as the weather doesn't knock out the wires on the mainland. Or you can post a letter of course, at the shop – my shop. I'm the postmistress. AJ the ferryman takes the post across.'

Lia looked up at AJ in the wheelhouse. He was younger than she expected, and he briefly met her gaze with a blank expression that could have been hiding everything or nothing.

The lady went on. 'He's an islander, though he doesn't live

on the island anymore. He's got mainland blood of course – his mother Kitty is a mainlander.'

Lia didn't know how she was expected to respond to that.

'But maybe you won't be staying long enough to want to post anything?' the lady enquired.

Lia shrugged and said, 'Maybe'.

The lady nodded and looked out towards the bow.

'We'll be landing soon,' she said.

Lia followed her gaze and saw the little harbour, the houses of the village clustered behind, backed by a semicircle of low hills. She watched intently as they grew closer.

The lady was standing now, waiting for departure, many bags hanging from white fingers. A man – presumably her husband – came up and took some from her, nodding to Lia. He looked piratical, with unruly dark eyebrows, shot through with white.

'Do you have anywhere to stay tonight or is there a tent in that bag?' the lady asked.

'I'm here to see someone,' Lia said.

'Oh?'

Lia hesitated, but she had to find him somehow or spend the night under a tree. Not that there were any proper trees that she could see on the wind-stripped rock ahead – just stunted twisted little things.

'It's Harry Crowe.'

'How do you know Harry?'

This was from the husband, suddenly staring at her with sea-green eyes.

'He's ... yeah, he's my uncle.'

They shared a look but there was no time for more as the ferry ground its ramp onto the stone slipway.

'Bye then, dear.'

Letting her husband go ahead down the ramp, the lady glanced back.

'We'll be in the shop if you need anything. That house there, with the red door.'

She hurried after her husband and Lia followed slowly behind, realising that she should have asked for directions. On the way down the ramp, she read the same notice that held a prominent place on the mainland.

Ferry operation subject to weather.

Suddenly feeling an aloneness that was very different to what she had been looking for, Lia sat on a bollard until the ferry eased away from the pier and made its way out to sea, bearing a few new passengers. When it had gone around the Chimneys, she stood up, turned towards the village, hitched her rucksack higher and went up the slipway. What else was there to do?

She considered calling to the red door, which she now saw doubled as the name of the shop, to ask for directions but something about the look the two had exchanged made her nervous. She looked around for a likely stranger to ask.

Down below her, fishermen were working on boats in the small, sheltered harbour, doing whatever fishermen do. They all looked too busy to ask.

A guy was close by, with a camera raised to his face. She looked to see what he might be photographing, but it all looked the same colour grey to her. Then she raised her gaze and saw two big white-and-yellow birds flying towards the Chimneys. A birdwatcher. Hopefully harmless.

Lia walked towards where the birdwatcher was standing on a spongy expanse of moss and grass leading to a small cliff. Below him was a beach, part sand, part shingle. It probably looked pretty in the summer.

'Hi,' she said, still a small distance away, not wanting to startle him.

He turned sharply, snapping a picture as he did.

'Oh, did you get me?' Lia said. She was conscious that her

hair was a mess and she needed a touch of the lip gloss that she had shoved in a pocket of her bag.

'Think so.' He made no effort to look or to delete it. Instead, he just looked at her.

His eyes were some sort of blue, but dark. He actually looked quite nice. He wasn't smiling, but he didn't look annoyed.

She stepped towards him, her hand out.

'I'm Lia Crowe. I'm looking for my Uncle Harry.'

His eyebrows drew together but he took her hand. His was warm.

'Oh. Isn't he meeting you?'

Lia made a face. 'He doesn't know I'm here.'

'Oh?' he said again, letting her hand go.

Lia bit the inside of her lip.

'The Rest is up that way,' he said.

'The Rest?'

'Don't you know the name of your uncle's pub?'

'I know he has a pub but I don't know its name.' No one at home had spoken much about the island.

'The Robin's Rest.'

'Thank you. Nice to meet you …' She looked at him enquiringly.

'Ed Wray. Nice to meet you too. I'll print the picture for you. If you'll be around for a few days?'

'Oh – yes. I will.'

Lia walked away, feeling him watching her. When she stepped off the grass onto the road, she glanced back. He was facing the sea, the camera held up and following the flight of another bird. She made a face at herself and walked on in the direction he had indicated.

She had just reached the point where she thought she must surely have gone too far and was starting to worry, when the road curved back towards the sea and there it was. It was a charming stone building with sash windows and a multi-coloured roof, made up of mismatched slates, presumably replaced piecemeal after storms. All at once, Lia's nerves twanged and she felt her stomach flip. Her legs felt wobbly. She turned around and stared at the road back to the village. It wasn't really very far, although the pub seemed quite isolated. She walked back to the corner and saw that lights were coming on in the village. There was probably somewhere there she could rent a room.

She heard a noise and turned back towards the pub. A window had been closed and the pub's lights were on. The scent of a fire rose from the chimney and drifted towards her, pushed by the ever-present salt air from the sea. Lia had never felt farther from home.

She hitched the rucksack straighter on her shoulders and walked towards the pub. As she rounded the curve in the narrow road she saw another house in the distance, almost entirely sunk into the oncoming darkness. 'House' was too small a word for it. It loomed on the horizon, looking disconnected from the earth, almost as though it were riding on its own black shadows. It made her shiver and hurry towards the door of the pub. She had time to notice the name burned into a piece of wood, alongside a carving of a robin about to land, its feathers ruffled and feet out to grab onto a branch, but she didn't linger.

She was in a small hallway with a door to the left and another to the right. She chose left. It opened onto a small snug. Four old men were sitting at the bar. One thumped his fist on the bar, punctuating some important point in his argument. The conversation stopped and four weather-beaten faces turned towards her. They stared for a second before turning back to their drinks, but the conversation, when it restarted, seemed without the passion that had generated the fist-thump. Lia backed out, closing the door quietly.

The right-hand door opened into a large lounge, where a fire burned in the hearth and a tall man was stooped over it, throwing on more turf and logs. When he had filled it to his satisfaction, he dusted his hands off and turned around. The resemblance to her father was uncanny. The two hadn't been twins but, born within the same year, they might as well have been. Lia's dad had been paler than this man, his hair more red than chestnut-brown, and he'd been a couple of inches shorter in height. This man, surely her Uncle Harry, was handsome.

'Hi, can I help you?'

He had a much stronger Irish twang than her dad, who must have lost most of his in the city.

'Hi,' she said, the words she had planned on the journey evaporating.

'Hello there.' He seemed to hesitate. 'It's a bit late in the evening, and the year, to be hiking. Do you have anyone with you?'

He sounded slightly wary, or just cautious. But not hostile. She shook her head.

'Well, you've missed the last ferry back. I suppose you can stay here, although the spare rooms are closed up. Unless you're camping?'

Again that hesitant note.

'I'd like to stay, please ... Uncle Harry.'

He came quickly towards her. With a hand that smelled of turf, he tilted her face to the light.

'Lia?'

She nodded and he grabbed her to him, hugging her as best he could with her rucksack in the way.

'Good God, Lia, don't you know your mother is going crazy trying to track you down?'

'She called you?'

He nodded. 'This morning. But I didn't for a minute think you'd come here. But when I saw that hair ...' He touched her hair, a lighter chestnut-brown than his. 'It's the same as my mother's,' he said, with wonder in his voice.

He fell silent for a few moments, holding her shoulders, gazing at her.

'Anyway, what the hell are you doing here? Jasmine is beside herself.' He shook his head and repeated himself. 'She said you'd come here – I told her I couldn't see why you would. But here you are.'

'I … I just needed some space, after … you know.'

His stern expression softened a little. 'I do know. I'm fond of space myself.'

His stern expression softened a little. 'I do know. I'm fond of space myself.'

That's right, Lia thought. Her dad had said that Harry had been married a long time ago but wasn't any longer. No kids either. She wondered briefly if he was gay.

'Will you tell Jasmine I'm here?' she asked.

'Of course. I have to. When will I tell her you'll be home? Now that you're here, you can stay a week or two if you want. It'd be nice to get to know my only niece.'

He went behind the bar to wash his hands and fill the kettle, before coming back out to her and taking the heavy bag from her shoulders.

'I'm not going back,' Lia said.

'What? Now we don't want talk like that. What age are you? Fifteen?'

'Sixteen. And I've finished school – I skipped a year and graduated before the summer.'

'Good for you – but you're still just a girl. You need to be at home, going to college or something.'

'I don't want either of those things. Jasmine wants me to go to college. I'm not ready.'

He looked at her, eyes narrowed slightly. He had the same colour eyes as her too, more hazel than green.

11

'She mentioned there might have been a row along those lines,' he said. 'Look, how about we figure it out after we feed you? I roasted a nice lump of beef earlier. It's there if you're hungry.'

Lia felt the tension leave her. He must have noticed her shoulders relaxing because he suddenly smiled, and it was as if her father was standing in front of her.

'C'mon now, Lia, everything will be alright. We'll get it sorted, eh?'

He slung an arm around her shoulders and tucked her into him.

'First things first. Grub.'

He showed her the kitchen, put together a plate of beef and jacket potatoes with gravy for her, along with a glass of cold milk. With an apology, and an instruction to make herself at home, he hurried back out to his customers.

She emptied the plate. She hadn't been aware of how hungry she was. Then, feeling nervous at being alone in a stranger's kitchen, she stacked the crockery in an old dishwasher, its front more smoky-yellow than white.

She looked around. She could see that the small kitchen was used both to supply the pub and for Harry's personal life. There were cases of soft-drink bottles stacked in the corner, and many books in various stages of being read, judging by the scraps of paper sticking out of them as bookmarks. She looked at one, a thick tome about Russian oligarchs, his place marked with a drinks-company invoice. It seemed that, as tidy as her father had been, his older brother was the opposite. After the perfection of the New York brownstone that she knew as home, she found the room charming – 'dirty enough to be happy, clean enough to be healthy'. The words echoed in her mind. She had often heard her father say them. Had he in fact been tidy, or was it just Jasmine's rules and a steady stream of cleaners that had made the brownstone perfect?

Lia felt lost again, and swallowed tears for her father. Was it possible that he had been unhappy all along, only nobody noticed? Why else would he have come back here to do what he had done?

There were old photographs in frames on the dresser, almost lost among books, crockery and more paperwork. She stared at the brothers, arms slung around each other's shoulders. Carefully, she picked one up. It was no more than a snap and had tilted sideways in the frame. They looked the same, handsome, her father redder of hair and skin, Harry darker and more tanned.

'We were best friends. I miss him like crazy.' Harry, having come into the room unnoticed, took the picture from her and touched his brother's face, frozen in time.

Lia felt her swallowed tears rise and nodded.

'Me too.'

He put the picture back and took her into his arms. She rested her head against his chest and breathed in a scent that was both familiar and strange, the scent of her father and of an unknown man to whom she was linked by blood and, it seemed, sorrow.

Lia went outside while Harry called Jasmine. She didn't want to hear her mother's upset through the phone. It would make her waver in her decision to stay away. She had decisions to make about her next step and where she would go but she wasn't ready for that yet. Despite the rows, she loved her mom, although they were very different people. Jasmine was tough, cool and glamorous, but Lia had started to see vulnerabilities in her, a fragility either revealed by her husband's death or created by it. If Lia heard tears in her voice, she might give in to Jasmine's way of thinking. Fights were easier than sadness.

She sat on a bench at the back of the pub. The moon was rising, a little over half full, and orange. Lia listened to the soft sound of waves at the bottom of the cliff, and to the occasional call of some night bird. Despite her anxiety, she felt her eyelids grow heavy. It had been a long day and she had travelled between her familiar world in the city to one entirely different. She felt drained.

In an effort to wake up, she walked to the end of the garden, the path lit by small ground-level solar lights. Dark as it was, once she was beyond the reach of the pub's lights, the rising moon was enough to show her the shadowy outline of the big house she had seen earlier. It created a kind of blank dark, deeper than the natural night, like a hole in the sky.

'Lia?'

She turned quickly and saw Harry framed in the warm light of the pub's open back door. As she walked towards him she saw that his face looked shadowed and thought the worst.

'What did she say?'

'A lot, but she settled down a bit after she got it off her chest. She's just worried about you.'

'I know.'

'She said you could stay for a while though. If it's OK with me.'

Lia searched his face. His expression was severe.

'What ... what did you say?'

He came out, letting the door swing shut behind him.

'The island can be a pretty tough place to live in the winter. There's almost no one here your age, or close to it. The pub won't be crazy busy the way it is in the summer, but I'll have to be here all the time anyway. Rose helps out but only part-time. Rose Tierney. You'll meet her. There won't be much for you to do. You might end up being on your own a lot. Plus, we often end up using a generator for power and the phones get knocked out. The TV in the bar is the only one I have and it's always tuned to sports. I only go across about once a month and the ferry is infrequent once the weather comes in.'

'That's a lot of reasons against.'

'It is. And I have a lot of company during the summer and there's always the local custom in the winter, but other than work I've been used to keeping to myself. There aren't many women's touches around here, although Rose slips things in once in a while. I've got used to being by myself and I forget to have things nice.'

''K.' Lia sat down on the bench, feeling unexpected tears spring to her eyes.

Harry sat beside her and sighed heavily. He stared at his upturned palms for a second before wiping them on his thighs.

'But then here you are, looking so much like Will and wanting to know why he ...' He cleared his throat. 'I don't know. Maybe you deserve to stay for a while. Maybe it's your right.'

Lia looked up at him. His brow was furrowed.

'You won't regret it, I promise,' she said. 'I'll help out and be no trouble.'

'I hope I won't regret it. There's enough of that to be getting on with as it is.'

'Thank you. Thank you, Uncle Harry.'

'Oh, just Harry, please. I'm not used to that uncle stuff. And you seem to call your mother by her first name.'

'OK.' She smiled. 'Although with Jasmine it's because she sometimes wants people to think I'm her sister, not her daughter.'

He laughed and patted her awkwardly on the knee before getting up.

'Don't stay out here too long. The night air isn't good for you. It's not too cold yet, but it's still nearly winter.'

She stood too. 'I'm coming in now. I'm really tired. Bedtime, I guess.'

Smiling, he threw an arm around her and they went in together.

The side door of the Robin's Rest opened, letting out the smell of the fire and a gale of laughter, followed by Harry's shout for last orders. Andrew Murphy shut the door behind him and the four men stood in the quiet night. Two lit cigarettes but no one spoke. The night sky was clear, the moon casting shadows. They had no difficulty making their way along the familiar path that led to the cliffs.

Andrew stood on the very edge and stared down into the white-tipped waves gently breaking against the rocks. The calm sea could be seen a long way out, so bright was the sky. He looked back up along the jagged coast of the island, his eyes drawn, as always, to the dark shape of the Hall. His own land cut over and back between the Hall and Dan Wray's farm.

The Hall towered over everything. The trees had all grown small and bent under the onslaught of the wind which was strangely absent so far this year. The house stood with windows watching seaward and in towards the island. He could just make out the large twin stone birds on the parapets.

He often wondered what sort of people had built the place. Everyone on the island knew what the history books said, but none of the dusty tomes described the nature of people who would build an ugly, frightening block to sit on the edge of the world, often wrapped in the fogs that crept in from the sea. His shoulders tightened. Even when it was hidden from view, it could be felt in the stiffening of hairs on the back of the neck, in the sudden goose bumps that rose as though a spider had run across his flesh. *Somebody walked over my grave.* It was an expression few on the island used. It felt too close to the truth.

He became aware that someone had spoken. He turned his attention to his companions, still feeling the presence of the house just outside his peripheral vision.

'We're heading home, Andy,' said Evan.

'See you tomorrow,' said Jim.

He nodded. They left, patting his shoulder as they went by.

Brendan remained.

'You OK, Andrew?' he asked.

'Sure I am,' Andrew said curtly. 'What makes you ask?'

'I just thought you seemed ...'

'*Seemed what?*'

'Nothing. Night.'

'Goodnight, Brendan.'

He stared after Brendan. Usually he tolerated his attentions, which had been constant over the years. Felt sorry for him. Tonight he was short on patience.

He stood still and looked out to sea. This was the very spot where Harry and Will Crowe used to sit as boys, dangling their legs over the grassy edge into the world of air, sea and rocks. Not twins but born in the same year, different but alike. They hung around with Andrew and the others but were closer to each other than to anyone else.

Andrew's wife Kitty wasn't an islander, but a cousin of one – she had come to visit, met him and never went home. Will had gone travelling and shocked everyone by marrying and staying abroad. Harry most of all. Despite being the publican and a man people looked up to, once Will left there was a sort of distance in Harry, as if his brother had taken some part of him away. He was the only one without a wife or children. Apart from Brendan of course who had never had any interest in women. Harry used to enjoy a woman's company, during the summer at least, but these last years he had kept to himself.

And now, Will's daughter was here, the closest blood relative Harry had, looking for her own answers, staying in the pub. Not a summer person but not a full-blood islander either. If she was her mother's daughter, from what he remembered of the woman the one time they met, two weeks would be enough for her. But if she was a Crowe through and through? He didn't know.

There were no other children on the island. The small school stood empty.

All of the summer people had gone back to their lives and the small row of pastel-coloured houses on the outskirts of the village stood in cold silence.

During the summer, the days on the island seemed to last forever. The nights were a brief few hours where the dark never reached full penetration. The stars out here were clearer than anywhere he had ever seen them. On a night like this, a waxing moon made the world a bright monochrome.

He realised he was closer to the edge, staring down into the dark drop to the sea. Trying to answer silent questions. The waves below muttered against the sharp rocks. Answers didn't come.

And neither did the storms. The official start of winter was a couple of weeks away. There hadn't been a sight of the heavy storm clouds that were every year drawn to the island, to spend themselves in wildness and abandon before they reached the mainland to drop a few sprinkles of reviving rain.

Andrew turned away from the cliff edge and stared at the shadow of the house. He thought he saw some movement above the stone birds, almost as though some other night hunter had come to rest on one of their granite heads. He squinted to see better, but it was much too far away. Primitive nerves that lived at the base of his brain made him turn and head back to the Robin's Rest. Kitty would be along in the truck – the only vehicle on the island – to collect him any minute. She had gone to spend the evening with a friend in the village and would collect him on the way back.

Rose glared at him when he came back inside, shutting out the night. She wanted people to go home, not come back in. He wasn't alone though. There was the usual crew of customers who liked to stay as late as they could. Out here on the island, there was no one to enforce the law of closing

18

times except Harry. Rose was great and knew how to give as good as she got, but the boys wouldn't shift for her. She grudgingly gave him a Captain Morgan and orange to finish the night and he half listened to the quiet chat of the stragglers.

Harry came back into the snug and laid his hands wide apart on the counter. One of the more sober lads gave his mate a dig.

'Just going now, Harry, no bother.'

And there was no bother. They drained their glasses and were off.

Rose replaced the glare with a smile, stacked the last glasses in the dishwasher and was out the door two minutes after the last customers. Andrew raised a hand in farewell to Harry and blessed himself quickly as he passed the big window that faced the Hall.

Kitty was waiting, half asleep. She said hello and set off the minute he settled in the passenger seat. As always, she pressed harder on the accelerator as she passed the Hall, never acknowledging the habit.

Andrew looked out the side window as they passed between the Hall and the last farm before their own – Dan Wray's house. There was a light on upstairs. Probably Ed, reading or brooding. The boy didn't want the farm. He didn't really want to stay on the island. Andrew could see it in him. In a way, Ed reminded him of Will. There was something unsettled in him. The island needed Ed but Andrew wanted the land that would become Ed's when Dan finally drank himself to death. It was a knotty problem, but one he had to put aside while Dan refused to sell to him. He was ready if he ever changed his mind though. Or if he dropped dead and Ed wanted rid of the farm.

Kitty braked sharply on the gravel outside their house, stalling the truck. The pain of the fibromyalgia made her tired and grumpy. Inside, her eyes closing, she went straight to bed, and disappeared into an exhausted sleep. The night before she had barely slept at all with the pain.

Andrew dropped his clothes on a chair and drew the curtains against the night. His thoughts were dark and, with his wife in a dead sleep that was no comfort to him, he drew the covers over his head like a child, finally drifting to sleep and into a nightmare.

Two

We with our lives are like islands in the sea, or like trees in the forest. The maple and the pine may whisper to each other with their leaves ... but the trees also commingle their roots in the darkness underground, and the islands also hang together through the ocean's bottom.

William James, 'The Confidences of a "Psychical Researcher"', 1909

Lia pushed the sash window up and leaned out. The late-autumn air was fresh and filled with the scent of the sea. For the first time since she lost her dad, she felt like there might light somewhere behind the clouds. She hadn't reached that place yet, but she sensed it. She knew deep inside her that, for the moment at least, this was where she was meant to be.

She couldn't see the village, but the acoustics of the water brought the sound of it to her and it was unmistakeably the song of a working harbour. Men called to each other. There was laughter and the cry of gulls. The musical jangle of boats moving, and of human business going on.

She took a deep breath and ducked back into the room. It was a simple but pleasant room, with a lot of wood. Harry meant what he said about no woman's touches, but she liked his style all the same.

She took a fast shower and used the little hairdryer she found in a drawer to put some discipline into her chestnut tangles. Lip gloss and mascara were enough. She was still tanned from the long summer walking around the city trying to avoid her mother. Dressed in jeans, shirt, sweater and boots, she felt ready to face the day.

She went downstairs and followed her nose to the kitchen. There was evidence that Harry had eaten a fried breakfast. She found a Post-it note stuck to the fridge door.

Eat what you like. I'll be back soon. H

She smiled at his scrawl and filled a bowl with cereal, eating it as she walked around the kitchen, looking at the rest of the pictures and knick-knacks. She discovered a funny whimsy that she presumed had to be Harry's. Big tough man though he appeared to be, he had a surprising number of hand-carved animals tucked into corners. She found rabbits, foxes and one gorgeous little badger.

She rinsed out her bowl and left it and the spoon to dry on the drainer. On the window beside the back door she found a tiny carved robin, feathers fluffed up around his neck, eyes half closed. It recalled the carving of the robin above the pub door and she suddenly realised that these must be Harry's own work. She saw him, as clear as a memory, sitting here alone, carving exquisite little creatures while the rain rattled against the windows. She didn't know yet if he was a happy man, but she wouldn't be surprised to find that he was a lonely one, even if he didn't know it himself. It made her sad. Her parents had fought a lot and ignored each other a lot in their last years together, but Lia remembered a time of their happiness. Was the sadness after worth the happiness that came first? She didn't know. Harry had chosen his path, or had it thrust upon him by island life, but she wasn't ready to choose yet. Despite her refusal to go to college this fall, there were things she wanted to do. They were out of sight because she needed to be here, to figure things out, but they would come into focus sometime.

She took out her phone to text this to her mother, wanting

to reassure her for the first time about her future, but swore under her breath when she saw that there wasn't even one bar. She glanced at the landline phone, but that was a bit too personal yet. She left the cell phone on the dresser next to a small fox and, pausing only to fetch her jacket, went out the back door. Harry had left it on the latch, so she did the same.

The daylight didn't make the big house any more attractive, but Lia wanted a walk and, besides, she was curious about it. Did anyone live there?

She began to walk in that direction. Mist drifted around the base of the house like gossamer skirts. It looked lonely out there.

She could hear seagulls fighting over food, their raucous calls ringing the melody of the sea. Crows, almost her namesakes, were everywhere, as they were all over the world, hardly noticed except when they flocked together to roost. Little birds were flitting around the misshapen hedgerows, which had been trained by the wind to lean away from the sea. Out there though, near the house, there seemed to be nothing moving.

The narrow road was edged by stone walls and even though the sun only broke through the grey clouds occasionally, there was a sense of warmth coming from the old stones. A little flock of goldfinches kept ahead of her, landing and taking flight as she walked. Watching them, and the sea visible across the strip of coarse, spongy grass, she soon came to the gates of the house.

She looked at it with almost a sense of shock, as it filled her senses.

The long avenue was straight and flat, both it and the house itself unadorned and exposed to the wind. The tall gates were secured with a shiny lock but anyone could climb the stone wall back along the road and go through the field to the house. She looked back. It would be easy.

Her goldfinch friends were sitting in silence in a scrubby bush growing from the wall. As she watched, they rose in a colourful cloud and fled silently across the field away from the house. When she turned back to the house, she realised how still the day had become. The clouds had overwhelmed the sun and the small breeze had dropped. Lia held herself still and listened. Somewhere, almost below audible level, there was a deep hum, like an engine running. It was as though she had put her ear to the ground to hear a train approaching. Yet there was something biological about it. Not an engine or a train. More like the sound a doctor might hear through a stethoscope. A hum of blood rushing around the body, pumped by a great heart.

'Hey.'

The voice broke the surface of the bubble and sound came rushing back in. Lia jumped and turned. It was Ed Wray. He was wearing the same jeans and boots but had a rain jacket on. His camera hung from his neck. She guessed it was a permanent fixture.

'Hi – you scared me.'

'Sorry, I know. I was thinking of coughing but that seemed weird.'

She laughed. After their few minutes of acquaintance from the evening before, she already knew that he was weird. He seemed friendlier today however, because he grinned back at her.

'Well, Lia Crowe, how are you today?'

'I'm fine, thanks.'

'Harry let you stay so. You didn't give him a heart attack turning up out of the blue like that?'

She shook her head. 'I think it might take a lot to give Harry a heart attack.'

He nodded. 'You might be right.'

For a moment, Lia didn't know what to say next. She

wasn't that used to boys' company. Since she had petitioned to move up a year, she had lost touch with the boys in her former class. The older boys thought of her as a kid and a damaged one at that. The girl that studies all the time because she can't get over the death of her father.

She turned slightly towards the gates and felt Ed take a step closer. Together they stared at the house.

'So what do you think of the Hall?'

'The Hall? I don't know. It's strange. What's its name?'

'I forget. Everyone just calls it the Hall.'

He raised the camera, clicking several times before turning to face her. She was tall, but he was taller. His hair was dusty black and, as she had noticed the day before, he had an unusual eye colour. She had to stop herself from studying his eyes. That colour. It was a stormy dark blue.

'Look there,' he said. 'It's a buzzard.'

She followed his gaze and saw a huge bird slowly flapping across the sky, its furred legs dangling.

'There's lots of them now. They became extinct in Ireland over a century ago but have gradually reappeared, and they're doing well. I love them, even though they prey on nests.'

He took a few pictures of the bird, following its progress over them. When it reached the edge of the land on which the Hall sat, it veered off and swept towards a farmhouse.

'That's our place over there. You're welcome to come for tea or something. There's only me and my father, but he's not home much.'

'Thanks.'

There was an awkward silence.

He had crinkly lines around his eyes.

'Well, I'm usually there,' he said. 'If you wanted to see the pictures or anything. I haven't printed the one of you yet.'

He was tanned, but a flush rose in his cheeks.

'I was a mess probably anyway,' she said.

'No. You looked … you were grand.'

He hadn't said anything effusive, but she felt herself blush all the same.

''K.'

'So – see ya.'

He turned and crossed the road, hopping the stone wall with ease. Lia stared after him. She didn't know what had just happened, but something had. He looked a couple of years older than her, maybe eighteen. She shook her head and started back towards home, thinking about the colour of his eyes, forgetting the Hall.

A huge white seagull was sitting on the roof of the pub. It stared at her with a cold eye, unafraid. She studied it, taking in the snowy white of its plumage and the yellow of its hard beak. Without any warning, it spread its wings, swooped and fell towards the water below, curving upwards at the last moment to wheel across the masts and flying bridges of the boats in the harbour. It called as it flew and Lia thought she could stay there forever, with the sound of the birds and the rattle of buoys and bells.

She took in a deep breath of the sea air and entered the pub under the watchful gaze of the robin on the sign.

Harry was sitting outside the bar, studying invoices. He looked up when she came in. 'Morning, you're in time for tea.' He started to get up.

'No, you stay there. I've got it.'

She went behind the bar and got out two mugs and made steaming dark tea, the way he had the night before. She joined him on the public side of the bar.

She wrapped her hands around the mug. She hadn't realised how cold her fingers were.

'So, is your curiosity satisfied?'

'Not in the least.' She grinned at him. 'What's the story with the Hall out on the cliffs?'

'No story, just a derelict old place. It's dangerous, so you shouldn't go near it. One more storm could bring it all crashing in. How did you know it's called the Hall?'

'I met a guy. Ed Wray? He gave me directions to the pub last night and he was taking pictures out there this morning.'

'Ed and his camera.'

'He looks about my age, sort of.'

'Ed? He's eighteen.' He peered at her over his mug. 'Why? Do you like him?'

'No, of course not. Shut up.'

He grinned.

'Maybe I do. Is he a psycho or anything?'

'Ed's alright. A bit of a dreamer, but the world needs dreamers, or so I hear. Just don't go getting me into trouble with your mother with some holiday romance.' He paused and raised an eyebrow. 'Or some running-away-from-home romance.'

'Hey,' she said, but she smiled back at him. 'Anyway, about the Hall. It looks fairly solid from the gate.' She saw his look. 'But I won't go too close, I promise.'

'Don't, good girl. No one does. It really is dangerous. We expect every winter to be its last.' He turned around on his stool and gazed out at the Hall, visible through the big window. 'Winter is nearly here. We usually have storms before now. A couple in October, then regularly until the end of January, maybe into February.'

'All through winter?'

He shook his head. 'Frequent, not constant. But nothing so far this year.'

'That's good, isn't it?'

He dragged his gaze from the window and put another spoonful of sugar in his mug, stirring vigorously.

'Yeah, course it is, good for the farmers and the fishermen.'

'Is that how most people make their living here?'

'It's mostly small farms and tourism now. The big trawlers do most of the fishing and they go to the mainland to unload. Farther out, the Spanish boats do their work, factory ships, trying their best to empty the sea. But there are still local fishermen. They supply a lot of the restaurants on the coast.' He nodded his head in the direction of the mainland.

'They moor here in the harbour?'

'Yeah, most of them. Every year now it seems that we lose another family of fishermen. Rose's husband Frank sold his boat last year and turned the shed into a craft store. Rose sells knick-knacks to the tourists and works here part-time. It's an easier life for them now that they're older.' He took a big swallow of his tea.

'Better to be a publican then?'

'Sure is. Dealing with drunks is easier than battling winter storms any day or night.'

'So maybe you can teach me how to be a bartender?'

'We'll see,' he said with a grin that lit up his eyes.

'Oh – *we'll see*. I know what that means.'

They smiled at each other in a companionable way and Lia marvelled at the way they had so quickly fallen into being comfortable.

In the late afternoon, Ed came in from the yard to make dinner. He was a few minutes early, so he plugged the camera into his laptop at the kitchen table and uploaded the pictures to a new folder. Behind him, the oven was pre-heating. He had a chicken ready to roast for dinner. He wasn't a fancy cook, but he was better than his father and someone had to feed them. It was only a matter of bunging the chicken in the oven and peeling the spuds.

There were days, and many of them, when he decided that he'd had enough, and he was going to leave the island behind. Those were often the days when storms seemed likely, when the birds were hiding in their safe places and the sun was doing likewise behind the lowering clouds.

There wasn't enough money to go to college, but he knew he would make it away from the island, even without a degree. But then he would come across his father leaning on a wall that he was supposed to be fixing, tears running down his broken-veined face and snot hanging off his beaky nose.

Ed missed his mother, but in a different way. She had wanted very little from life and it made his stomach burn to think she hadn't even had that very little. Instead, she had a husband who became someone different with drink in him. She had borne her bruises with no complaint, but Ed was left with the anger that she should have had. He didn't blame her when she couldn't protect him from his father's fists. He knew she wasn't strong enough to protect either of them. He vowed that he would protect them instead and many times he had come between his father's fist and his mother's face. Once the cancer came, and both he and his father realised that there was nothing either of them could do to save her, the violence stopped, although the drinking didn't.

Ed had to give him that much, whenever he found him crying. The old man had at least stopped when she was sick, when she was dying. Despite the years of suffering her husband's blows in silence, the cancer made her cry aloud, calling for her own mother in the depths of the pain. The doctors finally gave her enough morphine to quieten her, to make her sleep. Then, on Good Friday, her sleep became so deep that she wouldn't ever wake from it again.

Ed had stopped calling his father 'Dad' when she died. If he had any reason to call him anything, he called him Dan. His father hardly noticed because he was too busy drinking more than ever. He drank so much that Ed managed the farm whatever way he could and had fed them what felt like a million roast chickens over the last year.

Despite everything, when he found the old man crying it made him sad. Somewhere inside there must have been love of some kind, corrupted by alcohol but originally true. It was this lingering hope that made him stay.

Once he had got his growth spurt at fourteen and farm work had filled out his chest and shoulders, the old man didn't hit him anymore. In the deepest hours of the night, when the wind was howling outside and the old man wasn't in the house, he let the anger rise up in him, tasting like blood in his mouth and making him burn with the desire to give his father all the pain that he had ever inflicted on his mother. In those dark moments and hours, he would gladly have killed his father. With the storm pressing against the glass, he watched for some movement in the night. Something about the violence of the elements stirred fury and vengeance in his heart.

When the wind died down, often with the coming of the dawn, he would go downstairs wearily to find the old man slumped over the table, wetting his sleeve with tears. Ed knew that the tears were mostly of self-pity, but there was that something in there that was about more than indulgence. There was real sorrow. So, he stayed. They barely spoke, but he stayed. He knew it wouldn't last forever. Nothing did.

He loved his birds and the pictures he took of them. To him, they felt like a silent moment at the heart of a symphony. His vague impossible dream was to make a living from that still moment. The new pictures were part of a plan. A year of island birds, to make beautiful colour plates. He didn't want captions or explanations. The birds would speak for themselves, as they always did.

He moved slowly through the pictures from the morning and afternoon, discarding those that were bad or ordinary. He took a lot and discarded a lot. He had caught a lovely one of the goldfinches in flight. He paused before moving to the next frame. He knew what it would be.

She had been so still, staring at the Hall. Even on a mostly dull day, her chestnut hair shone. The picture showed this image of her, exactly as he saw it in his mind's eye. Slender, still, facing away, somehow lonely with the Hall looming in front of her.

The photograph was ambiguous. Was she staring in wonder or loss? She could have been a girl leaving a place she loved, never to return. Or a girl taking a last look at somewhere she never wished to see again after that moment. It had the mystery that he found in his best photographs. He could never tell if the picture made him feel sad or happy. Those were the ones that he knew would last and perhaps get him somewhere other than here.

He hadn't taken any pictures of her face when she turned but when they were looking at the buzzard he had caught her staring up, her throat exposed. The picture was no good, taken at a bad angle, as he was trying to hide that he was taking it at all, but he didn't delete it. He didn't know why, but he didn't. He went back to the first picture of her, from last night. She had a quizzical look on her face. She was beautiful. A mystery.

'What are you lazing about for? Half the day's gone already.'

Ed jumped and slammed down the lid on his laptop. He shoved the chicken in the oven and dumped spuds in the sink for peeling. He felt his father behind him. He peeled the potatoes in silence.

The old man grabbed his arm, hard fingers digging in, pulling him around. He was close enough for Ed to clearly see the veins and black pores on his nose and smell his breath, oddly sweet.

'You think you're better than me with your pictures and your bloody birds, don't you? Think you can get away from the island just like your mother wanted to.'

He stripped his lips back, showing his strong yellow teeth, with the gap where a cow had struck him with her head. Despite the effects of the weather and the drink, he had somehow aged well. Ed's mother had always said that he was much older than he looked. Birthdays were not celebrated, not since Ed was small, and he had no idea what age his father was.

'She didn't go anywhere and you're not going to either.'

His right hand swung around and struck Ed a hard blow across the cheek, catching his eye, rocking his head. The old man pulled back his hand, this time making a fist. Ed shoved his own hand forward and the old man paused and looked down.

The potato knife was pressed to his stomach.

'Back off,' Ed said, in a voice that sounded like a stranger's. Older, deeper.

The old man was still for a second, his bloodshot eyes flickering. Then he laughed. He turned and walked out of the kitchen, not knowing how close the laughter had brought his son to driving the knife into his gut. Not the slap or the threatened fist, but the laugh.

Ed took a breath and let it out with a hiss. He stared at the untidy kitchen and heard the television come on in the sitting room. He turned around to the sink, and with visions of birds' wings and chestnut hair filling his mind's eye against a backdrop of pulsing red anger, he blindly went on peeling.

Three

Are the days of winter sunshine just as sad for you, too?
When it is misty, in the evenings, and I am out walking by
myself, it seems to me that the rain is falling through my
heart and causing it to crumble into ruins.

Gustave Flaubert, *November,* **1842**

After dinner, Lia pulled on her jacket and went out under the robin. She had been used to being alone in the city, with both parents working. She knew how to keep herself safe. Here, although there seemed to be nothing to be afraid of, it was all entirely new. The sun was gone but the sky still bore the last traces of a moody, rusty colour. Darkness was sweeping in.

She went back inside and stuck her head into the lounge where Harry was now pulling a pint.

'I'm going to take a little walk down to the harbour, Harry, OK?'

He looked up and seemed to hesitate. 'Fine.' He paused. 'But don't wander off anywhere else – and don't be too long, d'you hear? It's getting dark.'

'OK.'

Outside, she rolled her eyes. She might as well be back with her mother in New York. Harry had slipped into the parental role like he was born to it.

She turned towards the harbour, walking slowly, taking in

the sound of the fishing-boat engines rumbling and the shouts of fishermen returning to their safe haven. Four boats had come home and there was good-natured ribbing going on between the crews. She couldn't make out everything they were saying as their accents were thicker than either Harry's or Rose's. She leaned on the harbour wall and watched as they secured the trawlers. The heavy clouds brought night closer and one fat drop of rain struck her hand. She thought she would have to run for cover, but after two or three more drops, the clouds held on to their heavy cargo.

Most of the men glanced at Lia as they passed. She nodded hello to them, smiling. They were surprisingly shy, dipping their heads as they passed her, whether old or young.

'What do you think?'

Lia jumped.

Ed was leaning on the wall a few feet away.

'That's twice today you scared me.'

'Sorry.'

'I'm not normally jumpy, you know, when people don't sneak up on me.'

'Last time, I promise. Probably.'

'Probably?'

'You concentrate when you're looking at stuff. It's not really my fault if you don't notice me sneaking up on you.'

Lia laughed and he smiled at her.

She turned around and leaned her back against the wall.

'So what happens around here after dark?'

There was a small silence. Lia bit her lip. She hadn't meant it in any weird way.

'People go home, or to the pub, or visit their neighbours.'

Lia felt herself relax. He could have picked up on what she said and embarrassed her about it, but he had chosen to be kind. She liked him for it.

'We could go for a walk if you like,' he said. 'There's a path with lights along the cliffs. I mean, I could show you where to go, if you wanted.'

Lia hesitated. 'Is it far?'

'No, it's just a bit beyond the village.' He pointed in the opposite direction to the pub. 'There's a bench with a nice view of the Chimneys during the day.'

She nodded.

'Look, it's no problem if you need some space.'

'No, it's fine,' she said. 'Let's go.'

Rose blew Frank a kiss and shut the door. Frank settled down with his new book, a juicy crime novel. When it hadn't gripped him after the first few pages, he put it on the arm of the chair and just sat for a moment. He didn't fancy watching TV. He thought about a cup of tea, but Rose had forgotten to buy biscuits. He clasped his hands together and closed his eyes. Maybe forty winks would be nice.

His mind started whispering about money and bills. The summer had been OK, and they had enough fuel for the winter, if it wasn't too long or hard. Life was much softer now that he was off the boat, but the household bills were still there, hanging over them. Like everyone, coming into the winter meant buying food and fuel in bulk in case they were cut off from the mainland.

He opened his eyes, sighing, then stood up and looked out the window. The village was bright with the lights from the houses and the big sodium lights around the dock. He stared at the fishing boats and felt the longing that had never left him, the longing for the sea.

Turning away, Frank looked around the tidy sitting room. Rose was a great cook and housekeeper. He did his best not to make the place too untidy. After he sold the boat, he had tried to help out around the house, but Rose would have none of it. She shooed him away, saying that she had kept house through years of being married to a fisherman and raising three children and she didn't want him under her feet now. She had smiled as she shooed him though.

Becky was their only child still on the island. This was Rose's night to visit her, even though they had seen each other every day since Becky announced her pregnancy. He didn't mind. The women could talk about whatever women talked about when men weren't around. Becky's Matt was away on one of the big trawlers that stayed at sea for weeks on end. Otherwise, he and his son-in-law might have gone for a pint.

He glanced at the clock above the mantelpiece. Not too late. Rose wouldn't be home for another couple of hours. Maybe a pint and a game of darts in the Rest. He fetched his jacket and tied his shoes carefully, leaving his slippers by the fire.

He scrawled a note on the whiteboard in the kitchen below *Call Declan on Wednesday.* Their youngest had his final exam to qualify as an accountant on Wednesday. Frank wrote *Gone to pub back soon.* He thought for a moment before adding two kisses.

Outside, there was a moon behind the fog, lighting the grey in a strange way, like a shifting veil. It gave Frank a shiver. He remembered too many nights on the boat, when everyone was tired and it seemed like the sea beneath the boat was alive, not just with fish, but alive in itself, a sentient beast carrying the boat on its back, but a beast which at any moment might turn and swallow them whole.

Shut up thinking, Frank.

The voice was familiar. It was the quiet voice that spoke to him during silences and storms, the one which knew better than he did.

'OK,' he said aloud and turned from his contemplation of the eerie moon-fog.

No one else was out. Frank wondered if he had eaten

something funny, because he had an unsettled feeling in his stomach. He heard a seagull fluttering its wings to his right. Something moved in the small garden of the house to his left. He found himself glancing about with unease.

He listened for the voice which would tell him if anything was wrong. The voice was absent but instead he felt the hairs stand up on the back of his neck. He stopped in a circle of light and pushed up his sleeve. His skin had roughened with huge goose bumps. A cold breeze slid over him, even though the goose bumps had come first.

The path was covered in crunchy gravel and led, as Ed had said, to a black wrought-iron bench sheltering under some gnarled, scrawny trees. They sat down on opposite ends of the seat.

'The Chimneys are out there. Look. You can see them clearly on a bright night.'

She could see their shadowy looming shapes.

'You didn't answer my question.'

Startled, she looked at him. 'What question?'

'I asked you what you thought, when you were looking at the harbour and the lads coming in.'

'Oh. It's all great. So different to what I'm used to. I like it.'

He nodded.

'It's probably pretty wild later in the winter though, I guess,' she said.

'We've usually had a couple of storms by now. It's been a funny few months.'

'You sound like you miss the storms.'

'It's not that. It's just … the weather has been a bit weird. The island has felt strange or something.' He shook his head. 'Don't mind me, I'm just rambling. Are you cold?'

'A bit.'

'Do you want to go back?'

She looked out over the water. 'Not yet.'

She turned slightly towards him. His eyes were shadowed, but she knew he was looking at her. She'd had a couple of boyfriends in New York, each for a few months only, before she skipped a year. Her mother had checked each boy out over a scary dinner. It had all been perfectly innocent, mostly just kissing. She thought that Ed wanted to kiss her, even though she couldn't see his face properly.

Then he stood up, looking past her into the dark. He stared for a moment, before grabbing her hand and pulling her up, close to him. She felt the tension in his body and followed his gaze. She could see nothing outside of the pool of light, but she suddenly felt vulnerable in the bright circle with the night pressing in on them.

Ed gripped her hand tighter. He took two steps backward before turning them both and heading back towards the village. Lia wanted to ask what he had seen, but she was aware of darkness behind her and she was afraid to speak, in case her words broke the precious glow of light around them.

They were nearly off the path when Lia looked over her shoulder. The lights and the bench seemed to mark the boundary of the places where people walked. Ed tugged her hand but before she turned back she saw a wisp of white, like a floating edge of lace, as though the light had caught the tail of a dress.

Frank had been walking on into the fog, trying to shake the eerie feeling off. Still his skin crawled and the feeling that there was someone or something behind him grew. He spun about, hurting his bad knee, but there was nothing to see except the silent village. Up the slight hill and around the corner, the Robin's Rest was waiting, like landfall after a bad night at sea. Between him and it (*safety, between him and safety*) lay a no man's land, a deep pool of black night. Putting a foot into that dark sink would be like stepping off the boat into the cold sea. He thought about turning back and going up the hill to his daughter's house. *I said I'd just call in for a cup of tea.* They wouldn't mind this once.

Something clicked behind him, like metal on a damp cobblestone. This time he didn't turn around but every muscle in his body tightened for flight. He tasted rust in his mouth as though he had clamped his teeth on his tongue. *If I smile now, my teeth will be red.*

Once when he was a boy, he had been searching for mushrooms in the small fields behind the village. He already had a bag half full when he sensed a presence behind him. Old Tom's billy goat was staring at him, its horned head slightly lowered. The beast was uphill of him and he suddenly felt very small. Its yellow eyes were the wrong shape and chunky strings of its coat hung loose from its bony shoulders and hips. They stood silently, the goat waiting for some signal to come for him, and Frank trying to hold in his pee. The beast suddenly reared on its hind legs and then threw itself down the slope at Frank, its head lowered for impact. Frank remembered the sound of his own scream and the warmth of the pee running down his leg, but he could no longer remember the name of the man who had hauled him sideways out of the path of the goat.

He remembered someone tall fending off the billy goat with a walking stick. There was no one left to ask about the man, but he often appeared in Frank's dreams, even now.

Suddenly, with his muscles tense again and the pressure of urine in his bladder, Frank realised that the voice he heard in times of trouble, when the wind was in the wrong direction, or some other calamity loomed, was the voice of the man who had saved him from the goat.

And there, on the edge of the dark, he both smelt the goat again and heard the voice of the man. He was screaming something at Frank but he couldn't make out what he was saying. Everything was far away. Picturing the Robin's Rest as his goal, he stepped forward into the darkness because he couldn't go back.

He walked into deep cold shadows and felt the darkness swarm up his legs. His bladder let go and he felt the warmth of urine down his leg once more before cold sank into his bones. Like being swept underwater, he didn't know which way was up. He turned twice but felt blind and encased. Then the moment from the past came again. He had been waiting for it to arrive all his life since the day of the goat. The beast fell upon him.

Rose set the cup on the coffee table in front of her daughter. Becky's discomfort was growing along with her bump. Rose sat beside her, giving her hand a pat.

'Let the tea cool a minute, love. Are you feeling any better?'

Becky shook her head. 'I don't know what's wrong with me. It's like I have pregnant-woman vapours or something.' She looked at the uncurtained window and put her hands on her belly.

'You're just nervous because Matt's away. He'll be back in plenty of time and me and your dad are here if you need anything.'

Becky nodded slowly but her mouth stayed turned down at the corners.

'Did you feel like this when you were pregnant with us? With me?' she asked.

'Every woman feels nervous, especially the first time.' Rose took her daughter's hand.

This was not the time to remind her that she had loved being pregnant, that it had made her feel content and warm and somehow perfect. She knew that not everyone felt that way. Poor Becky's feet and ankles were swollen and she was still feeling sick most days. Normally a cheery girl, the pregnancy had set her emotions swirling. Rose and Matt had had their bad moments, but she had to admit he was perfect for her daughter. He wasn't from the island, but he was of the sea, so he understood the island. Plus, his solid bulk seemed to settle Becky's nerves and Rose wished he could be here. He was working extra hard so that he could afford to be off for a few weeks after the birth. If they had known it was going to be so hard on Becky to be without him at this stage, they might have made a different choice. But, after all, Rose was on hand to take care of her.

'And count your blessings. Your father was thrilled when you were born, but men didn't have much to do with the whole thing in those days. Matt can't wait to do everything for you and the baby. Even if he is like a bull in a china shop.'

Becky laughed and covered her mouth. 'Stop it, you're terrible,' she said.

Rose smiled, glad to have got her to laugh. Matt had broken two of her nice cups the first time he came for tea, when he and Becky had started going out. He was built for the dangerous life of a deep-sea fisherman, not for the kitchen of a small cottage, neither hers nor her daughter's.

'He's doing a good job on the house though,' Rose said. 'It's really coming together and I'll have your curtains and cushions ready by the weekend.'

Becky looked again towards the featureless dark at the window and Rose mentally berated herself for bringing her attention back to it. The dark pressing against the window felt like the malevolent gaze of something unseen. Even if the rest of the curtains weren't ready before the weekend, she vowed to bring the one for that window tomorrow. At least the windows to the side of the house showed the lights of the pub, just visible beyond a fold in the hill. None of the windows were huge. The island storms were too wild to have big windows and this cottage had to bear the brunt of the gales. It was one of the reasons it had been going for a song. The American daughter of an island woman who had emigrated to the States years back had come 'home' to find her roots and built it. In love with the impressive view over the island, which included the Hall, against all advice she had built it on family land to the windward side of one of the small hills that sheltered the village and harbour. The rest of the island was open to the Atlantic gales, resulting in sparse bushes and trees, all leaning away from the wind, looking like they were seeking the safety of the harbour, in flight from a pursuant peril. The islanders had shaken their heads and let her go ahead. She was half-islander, after all, and entitled to build on family land. She had endured a single winter in the cottage, put it up for sale in the spring and left.

Rose shivered and passed the cup of tea to Becky. She sat, holding her own cup in both hands, suddenly feeling cold.

She put her cup down too firmly on the table and stood up, rubbing her hands together.

'It's getting colder. Let's have the fire on. I never feel that the central heating is as good as a fire. Besides, it'll cheer us up.'

She fetched the bucket of coal from the small utility room and made up a fire. Becky turned the TV on to watch a reality singing show that they both liked, apparently joining Rose in her efforts to change the mood by turning up the sound. It blocked the press of dark silence from outside.

After she lit the fire, Rose rooted around in the still unpacked boxes in the baby's room until she found a colourful cot blanket. Smiling at Becky, she draped it over the curtain pole and pinned it with two clothes pegs. The thick wool covered the glass and Rose saw her daughter's shoulders relax slightly. She smiled and started to brew fresh tea.

When the show was over Becky was feeling better, and

sleepy. Rose helped her into bed, put more coal on the fire, put the fireguard in place and quietly let herself out into the night.

The wind was slow in coming this year. She wished it would arrive, because it would drive Matt home. Instead, it felt like the whole of nature was holding its breath. She shivered again and turned for home.

Harry looked at the clock again. The pub was busy but he hadn't been able to miss the night drawing in against the windows. He was full of unease. His insides rumbled as they always did when he was worried. Lia didn't know the island yet. She shouldn't be out there after dark. He was sorry now that he let her go.

He was considering putting one of the more sober lads in charge of the bar while he ran to the harbour when she popped her head in from the hallway.

'I'm back, Harry.'

He just stopped himself from grabbing her into his arms.

'Lia, you don't know the island. It's too dark to be out.'

'Sorry, I stayed around the village. In the lights.'

He drew and released a breath and forced himself to smile. He didn't want to make a big deal of it.

'Good girl.'

'I'm going to bed now if that's OK. The travel is catching up on me again.'

'Great. I mean, of course. See you in the morning.'

He walked quickly back to the bar to finish pulling a pint of Guinness. His heart was pounding in his neck and wrists. He took another deep breath and made himself focus on a story that Dan was telling him, stammering less after a few drinks.

Feeling grateful to shut her own door against the night, Rose called out to Frank. *'I'm home!'*

She locked the door and slid the bolt across for good measure. They used the bolt for when the wind changed direction, which happened seldom, but rattled the door on its hinges when it did. She laughed at herself, feeling silly. Becky had her big husband to lean on, but Rose had her own harbour. Frank might not be as big a man as Matt, but he was always there for her, especially now that he had given up the boat.

She put the kettle on. 'I'm making tea!' she called out.

She automatically tidied as she left the kitchen, straightening a pair of boots at the back door, picking up the newspaper from where Frank had dropped it earlier.

He was sitting in his chair in front of the TV.

'You know, Frank, I think we should bring Becky to stay with us, at least until Matt gets back. She's too isolated out there in case something happens.'

She touched the buzz-cut remains of his silver hair, feeling a surge of affection for the one age spot on his bald patch. She leaned down to drop a light kiss on it.

'Rose?'

'Yes, dear?'

He didn't answer, causing her stomach to flip. Something was wrong. She hurried around the chair and bent down to him. His eyes, a faded blue, surrounded by the wrinkles of a thousand days at sea, moved to look into her own grey ones.

'What's wrong, Frank? Do you have a pain?'

He didn't answer, just looked at her. She began to fear that he'd had a stroke.

'Frank? What's wrong?'

He gripped her hand, grinding her fingers together. His eyes came a little more into focus.

'No. I'm grand. Grand. Just need to go to bed.'

She went to help him out of the deep chair but he stood abruptly, making her stumble backwards. He grabbed her arm to hold her upright and she again felt his iron grip. He pulled her close, his face almost touching hers.

'Rose,' he said.

She nearly fell again when he let her go.

He left the room.

She stared after him, her mind blank. She heard the bed creak upstairs as he climbed in. Not knowing what else to do, she took out Becky's curtains to finish, no matter how long it took her.

Dan lingered at the bar, hoping someone would buy him a drink. When no one did, he hitched his jeans and headed out. As it had been for the last month, the night was still. It struck him, standing under the robin, that it wasn't calm exactly. He could hear the sea and there was a light breeze off the water. But it felt like the island itself was holding its breath. He cursed. Now he was getting romantic ideas like that idiot son of his. And like Patty. His Patty. Tears flowed easily from his watery eyes. He wiped his face on his shirtsleeve and a thought occurred to him, as though another voice had spoken.

Go visit Patty in the graveyard.

He looked around to see if there was someone beside him. He was alone, although he could hear voices from the bar.

'Go see her,' he whispered to himself. 'Alright. Alright, I will. Just for a minute.'

He set off. There was enough moonlight to show the silhouette of the Hall against the sky. Another fanciful thought came to him. In the dark, it looked like a winged creature, hunched and ready to drop from its perch onto an unsuspecting victim. The stillness of the island was like that of the mouse which had suddenly become aware that it was being hunted and had frozen in place.

A night bird called from the direction of the graveyard and

Dan tore his gaze from the Hall and turned down the lane to where the islanders were laid to their rest. The tiny church, once part of the Hall's estate, had fallen into disrepair. A priest had to come over from the mainland now when the weather was good, to say Mass in the community hall, or to bury the dead. In the winter, the old women gathered to pray instead, reading the Gospel and doing what they could without a priest to say Mass.

Many of the gravestones were leaning, and some had fallen. Dan picked his way through them, using their shoulders to keep himself upright. He gave up trying to walk around graves and walked across them until he found her.

The stone was plain and simply said **Patricia Wray** and her date of birth and death. He hadn't had the money for more words. He stumbled forward and sat with his back to the stone.

He frowned and pulled at his lip, but he couldn't think of what to say to her.

'You can't hear me anyway, can you, girl? Stupid.'

He picked a fistful of the limestone pebbles that covered the grave and threw them at the back of the next headstone. They made an unpleasant noise clattering against the marble. It seemed to echo behind him. He felt an uneasy shiver work its way up his spine and suddenly wondered what was behind him in the dark.

Graves. Behind Patty was old Mrs. Talbot, with Bert and Mary Fitzgerald beside her. Behind them was the grave of the last priest that had lived on the island, Father Rossiter. His grave had a tall Celtic cross on it. Tall enough for someone to stand behind without being seen. Behind that was a low wall that separated the graveyard from the cliff and the rocks below.

Sitting still, Dan became aware again of the sound of the sea behind and below. There were caverns and blowholes in many places along the ragged coast and now he could hear the low boom of the sea, always moving, however calm the surface looked, filling the caves and moving back out, only to always and ever return. Using Patty's stone as support, he stood up and faced in the direction of the hidden water.

He found his way across a few graves until he reached the wall, casting a wide-eyed look at the back of the priest's cross as he passed. He leaned on the wall and looked out, trying to see. When he couldn't, he closed his eyes and listened. He had often heard his father say that the sea had a voice, if you knew how to keep your ears open. Dan swayed a little with the rhythm of the waves and, after a while, it did seem as though the water was speaking in low, deep tones.

It was calling him. He knew it was. He opened his eyes, not sure if he had been asleep. The thought that the waves were calling him made him shake. All he had to do was climb the wall and take two, maybe three steps before he would be wrapped in those waves and carried out to sea, forever moving, helpless flotsam, with no farm, no confusing son, no tears of guilt and loneliness. He took the first step on the springy grass that clung to clifftop before realising that he had climbed the wall after all. He flung himself backward and scrambled over it, stumbling into Father Rossiter's cross. He clung to it like it was a long-lost brother. His heart was thundering, the blood rushing in the same rhythm as the pull and thrust of the sea below.

When he had caught his breath, he stumbled back through the graveyard and up the lane. With the scrubby bushes leaning away from the sea wind, it looked like there was a stream of men walking alongside him. By the time he reached the road, he was in a shuffling run. He stopped, almost falling. He was drunk and it was dark and he had been in a graveyard. Plenty of reason to get the willies. Except he knew only too well that it would be better to get home out of the night and lock the door behind him. He turned towards home and felt a powerful gust of wind pass over his head. His heart stuttered and he broke into a run, this time fear making him run in earnest.

When he reached his own door, he was making little whimpering sounds, but he couldn't stop. He was fumbling with the key when the door opened and Ed reached out, grabbing his collar and pulling him in.

The sound of the door slamming behind him, locking out the night, was music sweet enough to make him feel a surge of love for the boy. He couldn't express such a thing, so he coughed and nodded and went up the narrow stairs.

He closed the curtains before he got under the covers.

Four

I am longing to be with you, and by the sea, where we can talk together freely and build our castles in the air.

Bram Stoker, *Dracula*, 1897

Lia pulled on a jacket, feeling her stomach fizz.

'Go on, you two, enjoy yourselves,' Rose said.

'You sure, Rose? Frank won't mind giving you up for a few hours?'

Rose's brows, black shot through with silver, drew together.

'He's in a bad mood anyway. Go on, off with you before I change my mind and go across shopping.'

The islanders referred to crossing to the mainland as 'going across'. Lia liked it. It was casual but she knew there were times when it wasn't – when 'going across' was impossible.

Harry grinned and ushered her out the door.

The sun had made its way through yesterday's grey shroud and the sea was sprinkled with glitter. The boat was little, with a small cabin and a big outboard engine. She put on a life jacket and tried to take everything in at once. Harry cast off and the little boat puttered out of the harbour.

Once clear of the dock, Harry let the boat's speed build. Soon, Lia's hair was flying behind her and she let out a yell of joy at the sensation. Harry laughed and they sped out to sea. Looking back, the island seemed tiny. The mainland was still covered in fog and it looked like the island was the only piece of land in a world of water.

They went far enough out to see a big freighter travelling to France, leaving a white wake behind it. Harry turned the boat into the oncoming waves created by the ship's passage and they rode the swell. It felt like they were passing over the back of a large animal, rising and falling with the undulations of its body.

When the ship was gone, they turned back and the island gradually grew larger until it filled Lia's gaze. Her uncle took the boat slowly along the coastline, staying out far enough to avoid hidden rocks. She wished she had a camera.

This made her think of Ed, but she tried to put him out of her mind quickly. She still didn't know why he had dumped her home without ceremony after they had almost kissed on the bench. Whatever he had seen had either spooked him or made him angry, because he barely spoke to her after that, except to say goodnight gruffly as he left. She had watched him through the window before he disappeared into the darkness beyond the pub's lights.

She made a face and concentrated on the cliffs again.

'This is the worst part,' Harry was saying. 'It's a ship's graveyard. Even now there's at least one wreck every year. The pub is up there, though you can't see it.'

He slowed almost to a stop and she looked into the water where he pointed. The water was clear enough to see the tops of what looked like towering mountain peaks just beneath the surface. The jagged stone looked like the teeth of some creature waiting for prey.

As though he had heard her thoughts, Harry spoke quietly.

'We call them the Devil's Teeth. When the tide is low, you can just about see the tops poking out.'

'Do people survive the wrecks?'

He glanced at her.

'Now, I mean,' she said. 'Not in the olden days.'

'If a boat founders in weather on a high sea, especially at this point, there's no way to reach it or any survivors. Even if the lifeboat can get here in time, they can't risk coming in here in rough seas. And the proximity to the cliffs makes it just as dangerous for the helicopter.'

Lia shuddered. 'So lots of people have died here?'

He nodded, his face tight and tense. 'Not all of them are found either. The sea doesn't often give up her dead around the island.'

'Harry, that's horrible.'

He looked at her, his face suddenly sad. 'Sorry, Lia.'

'Isn't there something you could do? Shouldn't there be a lighthouse or something?'

'There's been talk of it this long while but nothing much happens.' He pointed to the farthest visible outcrop of the island. 'They laid a foundation over there in recent years, but it didn't get any further than that. It was a bad summer and they had a lot of problems. They talked around and around about funding and regulations and such, but I think they just gave up. They'll probably get around to doing it – one of these years. In the meantime, people continue to die. While the big vessels steer well clear, the pleasure boats and sailboats still come to grief.'

She shivered at the thought.

Harry gave her a long look. 'Look, Lia, I'm sorry. We islanders are accustomed to the harsh realities of life here. It's a tough place to live and people have bad luck around here. I shouldn't have shown you that. Bad enough what happened to your dad.'

Lia put her hand on his. 'It's a part of me though, right?'

'Aren't you a city girl then?'

'Maybe I'm a city girl and an islander. I can be both, can't I?'

He didn't answer straight away. In the end he said, 'Just, please, make sure you keep yourself safe. I'd never forgive myself if anything happened to you.'

'I'll be fine. Honestly,' she said.

He nodded, still looking worried, rubbing his palms against his legs in a gesture she had often seen him repeat, perhaps without realising that he was doing it.

'C'mon then, Ms. Islander, I want to show you the caves.'

She stayed close to him as he opened up the engine again, taking them away from the Devil's Teeth.

Lia gasped when she saw the network of caves cut into the rock by thousands of years of waves crashing against the limestone.

'When the wind is up, the water crashes into the caves and shoots up through them. There are "blowholes" at the top where the water and foam flies out. It's dangerous because the holes are hidden in the grass. You could step into one and disappear into the cave and leave no trace above. At least when it's stormy you can make out where they are if you go slowly.'

Lia heard a low moan like an animal in pain.

'It's the sound of wind moving through the cave. Like a trombone. When the wind is up but not in full storm, you can hear the sound rise until it's like a scream.'

'That's pretty creepy,' she said with a shudder. 'But cool,' she added. She didn't want him to think she was afraid. And she wasn't. Mostly. She swallowed and braced herself to ask one of the questions she had come to the island to find an answer to.

'Where did it happen, Harry?'

'I didn't bring you out here for that. I just wanted to give you an idea of the place.'

'I need to see it.'

'Not today, Lia. I can't ...' He made a choking sound and cleared his throat, looking out to sea.

Lia stared at the dark mouths of the caves. Her parents had been on a temporary separation. He had then taken off somewhere -- they didn't know where. The first news they heard of him was when a stranger rang to say that he was dead.

A wave of guilt swept over her. She hadn't deeply considered what her mother would feel when she disappeared, only to turn up on the island too. She needed to apologise but she wasn't ready yet. She supposed she understood why Harry might not be ready to talk about his brother yet either.

But even though she had gone the wrong way about everything, she knew it was right for her to be here, to say goodbye. Her father couldn't tell her why he had done it, but all her research on the topic told her that it was impossible for those left behind to feel what their lost loved one had felt, to take that final, terrible step.

Having rounded the entire island, they approached the harbour from the opposite side, passing between the sea stacks and the island itself.

'I'm glad you got to see the Chimneys,' he said. 'I'm not sure they'll survive another winter. They've been losing bits for the last few years.'

Lia gazed at the rock-towers as they passed.

The harbour came into view and she saw how pretty the village was on a sunlit day, in stark contrast to the rugged coast.

She had a whole bunch of feelings that she needed to sort through and she felt strangely tired, although it was still only mid-morning.

A tall figure was leaning on the harbour wall and her stomach gave a little flip. Ed. She didn't know what to say to him. He hopped over the wall and caught the rope that Harry threw to him. When the boat was secured, he held out a hand to help her out but Harry quickly got out and reached for her hand to steady her.

Ed's cheeks reddened and he shoved his hands in the pockets of his grey fleece.

'Are you coming, Lia?' Harry said.

'I'll catch up to you.'

He grinned at her as he left and she knew he was going to tease her later.

'Hi,' Ed said, drawing her attention back to him.

'Hey. So what was that last night?'

He made a face. 'Yeah, sorry about that. I thought I saw something. Got spooked. Not very macho, I suppose. I thought I'd better get you home safely anyway in case Harry decided to kill me.'

'Harry is too busy laughing at me to have time to kill you.'

He laughed and his shoulders relaxed. 'I have a pretty vivid imagination at times. It helps with taking pictures, but maybe not with trying to look cool in front of pretty girls.'

He flushed again, and Lia felt her own cheeks get hot. Her stomach gave that funny little flip again.

Ed cleared his throat. 'So, how about going for a proper walk some time? There's a few great places for views and stuff.'

'I'd love that,' she said.

His face lit up.

She had only meant that she wanted to explore the island, but she had to admit to herself that the thought of spending time with him was exciting.

They stared at each other awkwardly for a second, half smiling.

'I'd better go,' she said. 'Harry is deliberately walking very slowly.'

'OK.' He cleared his throat. 'How would twelve tomorrow suit you?'

Lia reached for her phone before remembering again that they couldn't text. 'Fine. Where will we meet?'

'How about the bench? We can go around the island in that direction. You can protect me if I get the heebie-jeebies again.'

Lia laughed. 'OK, it's a deal.'

She could feel him watching her as she caught up with Harry. She willed herself not to look back.

'So, how come me and Ed are the only young people on the island?' she asked Harry. 'Where are all the kids?'

'On the mainland. It's for school. It's too hard to get kids across in the winter, so people moved over. They come back for the summer but they're always gone again by the start of September. There used to be a teacher here, but not for a long time now. It's mostly just us old folks here now.'

He had told her on arrival that there were almost no people her age on the island but up to now she hadn't registered the fact that there were no kids at all about. None playing on the small strand, no bored young teens hanging around outside the shop. And the silence. There was a curious backdrop of a soft stillness made up of waves and birdcall, but no sounds of children laughing or shouting.

'But that means that eventually there'll be no one here.'

He tucked her arm into his. 'There'll always be someone.'

Becky woke very late with sunshine on her face. Having her mother with her when she went to bed always helped her to sleep.

She hadn't wanted the cottage when Matt brought her to see it first. She didn't like its isolation and she knew it would be very exposed in winter. But Matt, as a mainlander and deep-sea fisherman, shrugged off warnings about winter winds and she was won over by his enthusiasm. He had so many plans and he had already put them into action. The house was not finished, but it was finished enough for comfort until the baby was a few months old. Then he planned to build on an extension and a toughened glass atrium for watching the sea and the weather. The way he explained it made it sound wonderful. Sometimes she just liked to listen to the sound of his gruff voice, softening with dreams and hopes for their future together. In those moments, she felt as though she was already sitting in a soft chair in golden sunlight.

She sighed and rolled into a sitting position. With Matt at sea, the house seemed empty. She knew that her mother was right. The baby was coming soon and she was nervous because her man was away. She knew this, even though some deep part of her was afraid of something she couldn't put a name to.

It was a feeling that came to her most often at night, but now, sitting in the sunshine on her own bed, it rose in her like bitter sap. Her skin roughened with goose bumps and she covered her belly with both arms, wrapping up the baby. He (she was sure it was a boy) moved once and lay still. She had the curious idea that he was holding his breath.

To shake off the feeling, she stood up, feeling a low ache in her back. Not bothering with slippers, she moved slowly around. She washed and dressed in leggings, a long jumper and her squishy Uggs. She checked her reflection and laughed at the sight. She was round and cosy, not at all like her usual self. It came from letting her mother feed her too much. The baby gave a sudden powerful kick.

'OK, baby, I'm having breakfast now. Hold your horses.'

She liked being in the kitchen. It was the warmest room in the house and where she and Matt liked to sit and chat. She sat where she could see the view, and glance at Matt 's crossbow. It was a hangover from his teenage years, when he'd actually won prizes for its use. She didn't like it, except when he was away. He had shown her how to use it. She didn't like that either, because she felt a curious enjoyment in using the powerful weapon – at the careful aim, the minor adjustments, the pull and tension, the release, the satisfaction of a good result. She didn't want to enjoy using it. She was just glad she could and that she could look at it in its bracket on the wall, more an ornament now than anything.

If she had to, she would use it.

She rubbed her belly gently. 'I would if it meant protecting you, little man.'

She put her mother's blackberry jam on toast and slices of cheddar on top. After two cups of tea, and another two slices of toast, she washed the stickiness off her hands, slipped keys and cash in a bumbag whose strap now had to run along the top of her bump, and headed out.

The walk did her good, blowing out the cobwebs and the fears of the night. She watched the ferry coming in empty and thought briefly about going across. The baby moved and she imagined the motion of the boat and decided the shop would do. She popped her head in at her parents' place, but no one was home, so she went and bought fruit and onions, chatting to Mrs. Glenn about her daughter who was an accountant in Dublin. They had been at school together. She waited until fresh bread came up from the ferry – an onion sandwich felt about right for lunch.

Then she set out for the walkway to the bench. She would sit on the bench for a while in the sun before heading home.

But there was already someone there. As she drew closer, she realised it was her father.

Matt looked up.

'What?' he said.

Christy turned his head, eyebrows raised.

'Did you call me?' Matt asked.

Christy shook his head.

Matt went to the side and looked across the sea. He had never thought the sea to be featureless – he loved it in all of its many moods. Just now, as he stood there, with the echo of someone calling his name, the sea suddenly filled him with a nameless terror. He couldn't see land. He looked down, knowing that there were huge deeps beneath the boat. He made his living pulling fish from the water, but he realised that he knew little of what went on in the grey depths. He was thousands of miles from the world's deepest chasms in the sea floor, but looking down made him feel that he was perched above a long tunnel that led down, down, down to complete, infinite darkness.

His father and grandfather had fished before him. He had been on boats in his mother's womb and as a new baby. His whole life was boats, fishing and the sea. This period working for someone else was for Becky and the baby, but in the back of his mind, where it had always been, was the dream of fixing up his own boat, and some day making a fleet.

And yet, looking at the expanse of water between him and the island, between him and Becky and home, his only wish was to turn the damn boat and close the distance. He looked around. The others had stopped working and were staring out to sea.

A fog bank was coming towards them, thick and fast-moving. It hadn't been forecast but it was filling the sea on the port side. The men were silent as it swept in over the boat and settled on them like a mantle. Matt couldn't see his hand in front of his face. No one moved. The fog made Matt 's chest wheeze. His face was damp with it.

Someone spoke quietly, a whispered question. Someone else told him to shut up. Still no one moved.

After a few minutes the fog started to change. It didn't lift or blow over. It shredded like candy floss, turning into wisps that floated into nothing. Matt found himself staring at the others. The captain was in the door of the wheelhouse. He was pale, despite his weather-beaten face.

Gradually, the men returned to their work, shrugging their shoulders.

The sea. You can never tell what she'll bring.

Matt's thoughts were overlapping, again as though someone was speaking to him. His own voice agreeing with the silent consensus.

Yeah, the sea, just the sea. Crazy things happen.

And the voice of the other. *Something is wrong. Crazy things happen.*

The thoughts dovetailed and shredded into wisps like the fog.

Matt shrugged his shoulders and got back to work.

'Hi, Dad.'

Becky sat on the bench with a sigh and put her shopping on the ground.

'Dad?'

Her father was staring at the Chimneys. She touched his shoulder and flinched when he swung towards her, his eyes very blue, his face somehow twisted.

'God, Dad, you scared me. Are you OK?'

The twisted expression faded, but she saw that his pupils had shrunk to pinpoints. There was an odd smell coming from him.

'Dad, you're not well.'

He smiled suddenly. 'Not well? I've never felt better. I've walked the whole island this morning. Full of energy.'

Becky remembered a couple of her fellow students at college. Pinpoint pupils and manic energy. Not from any natural source. But her dad?

'Are you on some new tablets, Dad?'

'No. I'm stopping taking anything. Don't need it. I feel great!'

She studied him, frowning. Was his hair darker today? The silver he had been sporting was less in evidence. It looked like there was fuzzy new growth on his bald patch. When she put aside the slightly scary look he had on his face when she startled him, he looked well, his skin tighter, younger. She shook her head and put her hand on her belly. This baby had a few weeks to go, but he was definitely messing with her head lately.

Her father followed the movement of her hand to her belly. She had got used to people touching her bump without permission, as though it wasn't actually her body, her personal space, but her father never had. He had treated her like a china doll since she broke the news, but their relationship was a traditional father-daughter one. He didn't like intimate details of the pregnancy or of women's business, as he called it, although she knew he couldn't wait for this grandchild.

Now though, he was staring at her hand on her bump, his strange eyes like blue lasers. She felt a flight urge but quashed it. This was her dad.

He put his hand out. It moved with treacle slowness and the baby started to kick and turn inside her. Adrenalin rushed through her body, making the baby move frantically.

Her father's scarred and tanned hand came to rest on her belly. Instantly, the baby seemed to freeze inside her. In the early days of feeling movement, she had been frequently frightened by lack of movement, worrying that something was wrong. This stillness was deeper than that. Coldness rushed over her and she knew, just knew, that something was badly wrong.

Her father took his hand away and stood.

'Bye, pet,' he said, though his voice was remote.

He walked away in the opposite direction to the village, striding straight-backed with no stiffness.

Becky didn't move, feeling frozen to the bench. She put both arms around the bump, and felt the baby start to move again. This time it was different. Wrong. She felt a gush of liquid and looked down, expecting her water to have broken. The baby was coming early.

It wasn't water. She stared at her clothes, suddenly darkened, not able to take it in. Then another gush came and, with it, pain. *Oh my God,* she thought, *it's blood. I'm bleeding.* But bleeding wasn't the word for this. This was a different word, one that she was afraid to acknowledge. Her mind kept shouting no at her, but it had to be faced. *Haemorrhage.*

She looked at her father, still visible on the headland, and opened her mouth to call to him. The sound that came from her was a keening sound that belonged in some desperate place, filled with loneliness and pain. She felt a spasm in her belly and felt the blood come again. She finally understood that she was in that place and this time she raised her voice in a scream.

Five

Despair has its own calms.

Bram Stoker, Dracula, 1897

They didn't get as far as the bench but bumped into each other in the village.

Lia had been waving at the woman from the ferry, aka Mrs. Glenn, postmistress and joint owner of the Red Door. Mrs. Glenn had paused in polishing the brass fittings on the door and Lia could see the thoughts crossing her face as plainly as though she had said them out loud. She was going to come over.

'Hey, Lia!'

'Ed, hi!'

Mrs. Glenn subsided and returned to polishing, but Lia was aware that she was still keeping tabs on them.

'You ready? I brought sandwiches. Chicken.' He tapped his small backpack. 'I thought we might get hungry exploring.'

She smiled at him. 'Good thinking.'

'Cool. Come on then, before Mrs. Glenn changes her mind and comes over to ask four thousand questions.'

Lia laughed and walked by his side towards the cliffs.

There they followed a winding path along the clifftop, with Lia peering over the edge at the sea below. She saw that there were ways made down to a sandy beach, much bigger than the strip beside the harbour. Although the paths down were steep, someone had set occasional steps into the side of the cliff at the worst parts.

'There's a safe way down from the back of the harbour, but kids like climbing down here. There were a few broken arms until we put the steps in. It's not as bad as it looks. Do you want to go down?'

'Not now. Let's go on. I want to see everything in one go today.'

'Cool,' he said again.

She pretended to look at the beach again so that he wouldn't see her smile. It was nice that he was a bit awkward. It was a good sign that he liked her.

Moving on, they reached the gravel path that led to the bench.

They had just stepped onto it when a scream split the air.

Lia grabbed Ed's arm. He took her hand, much as he done the last time they were here, and ran towards the bench, with Lia flying beside him.

The woman's legs were covered in blood. Lia could smell it, like iron, or pennies.

Ed let go of her hand and crouched by the woman.

'Becky, we're here. It's OK.'

Lia took her hand and squeezed it.

'We're going to get help,' Ed said.

He stood up and met Lia's eyes. There was instant communication, something she hadn't felt since she was best friends with Stacey in the eighth grade. She nodded and he took off running for the village.

Lia changed her position to sit beside the woman on the bench.

'Becky, is it? I'm Lia, Harry Crowe's niece. I'm going to stay with you. Ed will bring back help.'

Becky nodded tightly.

Lia took her hand again and held it in both of hers. The hand was icy.

Becky didn't speak, but breathed, her eyes unfocused. Lia felt every contraction through her fingers. Becky didn't move other than to shut her eyes for each one. She looked like a woman holding onto something too heavy for her, knowing that she couldn't let go. Lia realised that she was concentrating on holding the baby inside her and wondered if it was possible. She wished harder for Ed to come back with help.

If she had to, she would crouch between the woman's legs and catch the baby, but whatever was happening it was far from normal. She squeezed Becky's hand in encouragement.

Hold on, just hold on to it. Just for another little while.

Time passed with nothing but the sound of Becky's breathing, and gulls started to gather, riding updrafts from the cliff. Lia watched them. They were all huge and to her eyes they suddenly looked more predatory than the buzzard she had seen with Ed. They wheeled and circled like vultures.

A rook landed on the gravel path, its head tilted and its black eye shining. It looked like it was about to ask a question. It hopped closer but Lia was afraid to break Becky's concentration by waving it away. Indifferent to her, the rook hopped again, coming close enough to put its feet in the blood. It turned its head on one side, looking down. If it put its beak in the blood, Lia thought, she would scream or get sick. What if it did more than that? What if it started to jab at them with its huge grey beak? She clamped her teeth on her bottom lip and lightly kicked at the gravel under the bench, skidding a couple of pieces towards the bird.

It hopped back one step and studied her. Behind it, a huge

gull with a grey back landed in the grass beside the path. Its eyes were disconcertingly yellow. Lia watched them and Becky kept breathing and clenching her hand.

Suddenly, the birds took flight and Lia felt the wind created by their wings.

Ed was racing along the path towards them. Behind him Mrs. Glenn and another woman were hurrying along with two men Lia didn't know.

'OK?' Ed gasped, putting a hand on Lia's shoulder.

She nodded.

Mrs. Glenn arrived and took Becky's hand from Lia, squeezing onto the bench, making Lia give up her spot. She began to talk to Becky in a practical, motherly way, reassuring and lecturing all at once. There was a conversation between the others.

Lia moved to stand close to Ed, never as glad to see anyone in her life. With no shyness at all, he put his arm around her shoulders and she held on to him.

'Mrs. Glenn called the air ambulance – it's on the way,' he said.

The other woman came over to them.

'Hello, Lia – I'm Sheila. You did very well. We can manage now, so you and Ed can go if you want to.'

Lia looked at Ed and communication passed between them again. She shook her head.

'We'll stay if that's OK. We'll keep out of the way, but if you want us to run back for anything, we will.'

'Alright, dear.'

After that, no one spoke to them. They stood out of the way, listening to the cheery chatter that the ladies kept up with Becky, who seemed oblivious. The men stood to one side in silence, waiting to be of use – neither of them looked at the little group of women.

Ed heard it first and squeezed her shoulders, looking out to sea. She saw it, like a bird in the distance, then heard the engine. The men shifted, prepared for action. They went to the edge and waved. The helicopter passed over their heads and came to rest on the clifftop behind them. The island men ran along the path to go to it, but before they even reached the end two first responders appeared, carrying a stretcher between them.

Soon Becky was secured and they began to carry her back along the path. As they passed, Lia heard Becky speak, a muttering repetition of what sounded like a name.

The helicopter took off and turned towards the mainland. Lia took a deep shuddering breath and was glad of Ed's arm. He gave her a shaky smile.

'Well, that was a lot of things to be going on with,' Mrs. Glenn said. 'Are you two alright?'

Lia nodded.

'Right so, we'd better get back. They're getting another helicopter to find Matt. Hopefully he'll be in time.'

She hurried away, head close to Sheila's in a way that reminded Lia of the rook.

'Matt? Her husband?' Lia asked.

Ed nodded.

Back at the bench, Lia noticed the small bag of shopping. It was covered in blood. She carefully checked inside and seeing only bread, fruit and veg, she lifted it by one clean handle and dropped it into the small bin a short distance from the bench.

Ed stayed by her side. Then he took her hand as though they had been doing it forever. Lia turned into his embrace and they stood there, holding each other in silence.

He smelled good. Natural with a hint of deodorant. He felt good to lean against. She took a deep breath, feeling like she hadn't been getting enough oxygen for ages.

'She must have been calling for Matt,' she said.

He moved his head against her hair. 'When?'

She put a little space between them, feeling the gap like a chill breeze.

'When they were taking her to the helicopter, she was saying something over and over. I thought she was saying a different name, but I guess it must have been Matt.'

'Her mother maybe?'

'No.' She thought for a moment, listening to the echo of Becky's voice, repeating a name through pale lips. '*Dad.* I think she was saying Dad.'

They hung around for a little while, not sure what to do.

The two men came back with buckets of water and began to wash and scrub away the blood under the bench. They worked in silence and Ed drew Lia away.

'Do you want to go home?'

Lia shook her head. 'Would you mind if we kept going?'

He smiled his sudden smile. 'C'mon then.'

They walked on in silence.

Lia still felt shaky. She tried to concentrate on the spectacular view of the Chimneys.

'Fascinating, aren't they?' she said, stopping to stare at them.

'Not for much longer, they say. They're crumbling.'

'The birds will miss them.'

'Me too. I have quite a record of them. Been taking shots for years.'

'That's cool.'

They walked on.

'I've been meaning to ask you something,' she said after a while.

He raised his eyebrows, which she now recognised as his way of asking a question.

'When we met, when you gave me directions to the Robin's Rest, you were weird. Sorry. Why were you?'

'I was surprised first, because not many people come across this time of year, especially a girl on her own. And then once you said who you were, I didn't really know what to say.'

'Because of my father?'

He nodded. 'Why did you come?'

She hesitated.

'Look, it's fine,' he said. 'You don't have to say. Everyone has their own stuff to deal with.'

'I don't mind telling you. At least, I think I don't.' She made a face. 'My parents were on a kind of trial separation. But they weren't going to get divorced.' She heard the rising tone in her voice and sighed. 'Maybe they were. But anyway, he disappeared. I'm like him in a way. I like to walk by myself to think sometimes. Mom likes people around her all the time. She wants me to be like her, instead of Dad.'

'Maybe she just wants to make sure she doesn't lose you.'

Lia stopped, caught between a desire to hit him or run back the way they had come. That was just too personal. It made her feel even angrier because he just stood there waiting for her reaction, giving her space. Why did he have to be so calm and nice?

He reached for her hand and took it. Her stomach gave a little flip. The bitter anger didn't go away, but it went away from him. They walked on.

'Maybe,' she said quietly. 'Anyway, we didn't know where he'd gone and then we heard that they'd found him.'

'Yes.'

She squeezed his hand and looked at the view rather than his kind eyes.

'Do you know where it happened? Where he did it?' she asked.

'Yeah.'

'Will you take me?'

'If you want.'

'I do,' she said, not knowing if that was true. 'Where is it?'

He seemed to hesitate. 'It's a good way round.'

After a while, Lia felt the coastline begin to curve. The Chimneys were no longer in sight.

'See the tracks leading down?' Ed said, pointing at a view of a cliff face. 'Islanders use them to fish. Most people like to catch a few mackerel or pollock in the season, even though the boats come in. There are tracks like these all around the island. They're tricky if you don't know them. I've seen people from across getting stuck, afraid to keep going and afraid to turn back. There's a few places where the rock leans out and it looks like there's no way down. The old fellas never get stuck. Even my dad, with drink in him.'

'Does he drink a lot?'

'Mm,' he said.

They rounded a point and Lia felt the difference. With the change in direction, they were facing away from the mainland and out to the open sea. The breeze was in her face, snatching at her breath. The water now stretched out like endless ocean, making them tiny and helpless in comparison. He must have sensed something of what she was feeling because he stopped and silently shared the moment with her.

Lia had been to California. It would have been impossible not to feel the impact of the Pacific, a blue that went on forever. This was different. The water seemed less benevolent. She had seen the Pacific in calm weather and in breezy. It had been sedate in one and brisk and fresh in the other. This water was grey and silver where the peeping sun caught it. It gave an impression of something waiting in the cold depths. She looked back at the island. It made her think of a prison. If the weather dictated, they were all trapped on this odd platform in the middle of an unfriendly sea.

Her phone binged, making her jump. Out of habit, she had shoved it in her pocket, although it had proved worse than useless on the island.

She pulled it out, as more notifications came in.

'Sometimes there's a bit of service out around here. Don't move in case you lose it,' Ed said.

'Do you mind if I look?'

'Go ahead.'

He sat down on a rock with his long legs stuck out in front of him, not watching her. She wanted to sit as well but was afraid to budge.

She scanned the messages from her social media accounts quickly then moved on to the rest. There were 17 missed calls from her mother and some more from Chelsea and Deb, as well as texts and voicemails. She felt sick. She hadn't really thought about anyone at home since she left. Not really. Now, her phone showed her evidence that she had hurt people who cared about her. She couldn't bear to listen to the voice messages, but the texts were clear enough.

After a lot of frantic messages for her to call, the texts from her friends became less frequent, ending with a few terse words from Chelsea.

Your mother told us where you are. Thanks for letting everyone worry. Deb is pretty mad, so you needn't bother texting her for a while. I'm mad too tbh. But look, text if you need me. Ch xx

Lia's eyes blurred, making her blink hard. Her mother's messages were worse because she wasn't good with the phone when she was stressed or in a hurry. The texts were full of typos and autocorrects but her message came across loud and clear. She was furious. And worried. Then angry again. Finally, in a clear text from earlier that morning, she seemed calmer.

Harry will make sure you're safe. Stay as long as you need to. Please remember that I love you and only want the best for you. I am coping in my own way and I know that you have

to do the same. Call me when you're ready. Your mom xx

This last made the tears come. Jasmine always signed off texts, even to her daughter, as J. To see her call herself *mom* was a shock. Lia started to type a reply but didn't know what to say. Eventually, she typed OK with two kisses and put the phone in her pocket.

'I'm guessing some of that was your mother?' Ed said, his voice low.

She nodded and made some sort of noise conveying yes.

'It's none of my business but, if I could talk to my mother, I would.'

She turned around and sat down beside him.

'I'm not ready.'

'That's OK,' he said.

'I need to talk to my dad first, if that makes sense.'

She wasn't sure it did, but he nodded. He was staring at her, his own eyes slightly red. When he dropped his gaze to her lips, she felt heat as though he had kissed her. She closed her eyes, feeling a last tear escape from her lashes. Instead of kissing her, he softly wiped the tear away.

'Let's go then. We've a long way to go before we get to the place. We don't want to be stumbling around on the cliffs in the dark.'

Lia opened her eyes and watched him walk away, shoulders hunched. She scrambled to her feet and hurried after him. Her phone remained silent as she shoved it back in her pocket.

Ed pointed out several bird species as they walked, telling her a little about each. She was grateful to him for the distraction. He took her hand to steady her as she climbed down from a stile over a dry stone wall and didn't let go. It was cold out here on what felt like the edge of the world, so she was glad of the warmth of his hand and tried not to think about how it made her feel warm inside too.

71

Some of the walled fields still had grazing sheep and a few goats, hardy animals that didn't mind the weather. Ed pointed out a few donkeys in a distant field.

'People out here don't bother with cars – Andrew has his truck of course which he lords over the rest of us.' He grinned. 'That's Andrew. We manage fine with donkeys and carts. They carry what needs to be carried and don't need petrol! And the tourists like them. Harry has one he uses mostly for transporting barrels up from the harbour. Have you seen her yet?'

Lia shook her head.

Ed went on. 'She's usually with Jim's two for company. We don't have one since our last one died so we borrow from Jim if needs be. They're great.'

As if in agreement, one raised its big head and hee-hawed, making them both laugh. As there were none close enough to pat, they moved on.

She was watching the motion of the sea when Ed squeezed her hand.

'Look.'

Ahead she could see a flat grey area. When they reached it, Ed stepped up onto the surface.

'It's where they were going to build the lighthouse. There should have been one here for, like, centuries, but it never happened. They got as far as the foundation this time and just left it. We really need it though. There are hidden rocks everywhere around the island. You'd really have to know the area to find the safe channels for a boat.'

Lia walked around, looking at the concrete base.

'It feels weird, finding something industrial out here.'

He nodded. 'Yeah, it's out of place. Like it belongs to another world.' He paused. 'Are you hungry? Do you want to stop?'

Lia shook her head and was about to answer when there

was a sudden booming noise.

'It's the caves underneath,' Ed said. 'We're almost at them. Once we get past here, the ground gets a bit more tricky.'

'Harry showed me from the boat. Blowholes, right?'

'Yeah. They're mostly quiet when the weather is calm like this. That must have been a surge. In the winter, even standing here, you'd be splattered with salty foam. It's actually pretty cool.'

'Was it here ... that it happened?'

'No. We'll be nearly back when we get there.'

'OK,' Lia said, trying to relax.

'Are you sure you want to go on? We could cut through the fields.'

'No. Thanks but no. I've come this far, right?'

'Right.'

They moved on. Lia could hear the waves below now. Even with a calm sea, water was churning down there, cutting its way through the rock. The thought made her shiver. Earlier, she had thought that she would like to stay here forever, but now she saw that there were many sides to this place. The words sprang to her lips before she could stop them.

'Why would anyone live here? It's isolated and dangerous and scary.'

He cast her a haunted look but didn't answer.

'Sorry,' she said.

'It's OK.' He put his hands in his pockets.

She really was sorry she had asked. She didn't know what to say.

'People live under volcanos,' he said, surprising her. 'If it's home, people just sort of stay there. It's what you know, even if it is scary.' He gave her a half smile. 'People just do all sorts of crazy stuff.'

'That's true,' Lia said.

'Besides, you haven't seen it in the spring. It's beautiful

then. Everything is all blue and green and there are loads of rare wild flowers on the headlands. Botanists go mad about them. And there's whale-watching. We get humpback whales out here. Dolphins and porpoises too. And there's the birds of course.'

'Are you going to stay forever?'

He shoved his hands deeper into his pockets and shrugged. 'Dunno. I think about leaving. A lot. I haven't decided yet.'

He looked up.

'It's the Hall.'

Lia felt the shock of seeing the Hall in her gut. She had a queasy feeling and prayed that she wasn't going to get sick in front of Ed. The feeling passed quickly, leaving her surprised that she had experienced it at all.

The Hall was undoubtedly magnificent. It loomed and dominated, but it had a kind of beauty, like a crusty old aunt who was once young and proud, formal and prickly. Unlike the imaginary aunt, however, Lia didn't feel that the house had a kind heart beneath its old and elegant exterior. The closer they got, the more she imagined that she heard its dark heart beating, like she did before. She knew it was probably an echo of the sea in the caves, but she couldn't shake the idea.

In silent consent, neither of them spoke as they passed nor even with the Hall at their backs.

When Lia at last spoke, her voice came in a whisper.

'That place is so creepy.'

'Yes,' Ed said.

She looked at his face for any signs of humour but there weren't any. In fact, he looked a little pale under his tan.

'I thought ... I thought I could hear a heartbeat for a minute.'

'You have good ears,' Ed said. 'It's the helicopter.'

He pointed out to sea and she saw it, like a bird in the

distance.

She realised that the beat of its engine could have been the heartbeat she had heard or felt. Was there a helicopter around the first day she thought she felt the heartbeat of the house? She hadn't seen one.

'Are they only bringing Matt in now?' she asked.

'Hard to know. Maybe. He might have been pretty far away. Or they could be off on another mission.'

'I wonder if he made it in time for the baby.'

'I wouldn't think so,' Ed said. 'But as long as everyone is OK, it won't matter.'

They were nearly at the pub.

Lia halted.

'Did we miss the place?' she asked.

'No,' Ed said. 'We're here.'

'Here?'

Ed nodded, looking miserable.

'Yeah. Up there by the pub.'

'That's why Harry wouldn't say where it happened. Because it's here.'

'Yeah.'

She took a deep breath. 'Will you please tell me what you know? We were told there were witnesses.'

He nodded. 'Look, let's sit here a minute.' He sat on a log that had been left for tourists to rest on to watch the sea.

She looked towards the pub, but there was no sign of life. She sat down beside him.

He struggled to find words, but eventually they came.

'So, you know, he, your dad I mean, came back to the island a couple of weeks before it happened.'

'Oh,' Lia said. 'We didn't know when.'

'Sorry. Well, he seemed fine as far as I could see. I used to see him going for walks, looking at the water and stuff, but I wouldn't have been hanging out with them or anything.'

'Harry and Dad?'

'And my father and a few of the other older men. I suppose they were all friends years ago. A kind of gang. I think your dad was the only one who had left for good. And then he was back.'

She nodded. She didn't want to interrupt the flow again.

'Some people said there was an argument between the men in the past and that's why he left, but it must have been long forgotten because for a while your dad was always with one of them, or a few of them, having a drink or whatever. Except I did still see him the odd time out around the island, on his own early in the morning, when I was taking pictures.'

He coughed and put his hand in his jacket pocket.

'I took this one of him.'

Lia took the picture he offered her, holding it carefully by the edges. She wasn't sure she wanted to look at it, but when she did she realised that she wouldn't have recognised her father in it. He was at a distance from the camera, a silhouette against a brightening sky. If she had been pressed, she might have said that the figure was Harry, or even Ed himself. There was something in the set of the shoulders, some air of determination and tension.

She held the picture out to him, but he shook his head.

'Keep it. Anyway, the day after that, he came out of the pub in the evening. It was still bright and the pub was busy. I guess he gave his friends the slip. He followed the cliff path. No one knows how long he was outside before it happened.' He paused, staring at the grass between his feet. 'Evan and Jim stepped outside for a fag and saw him. They called him but he didn't seem to hear. And that's when he ran at the cliff edge and jumped.'

'Show me, Ed. Please.'

He stood up and offered her his hand.

She took it but let go quickly.

This was it. He led her along the grass until they stepped onto the worn path. They followed the path to the cliff edge. She could see that it was a place that had long been worn down, so that the grass no longer grew there.

'It seems that your dad and Harry used to sit here when they were kids.'

'I want to see,' she said.

He grabbed her arm as she moved forward.

'For God's sake, Lia, lie down at least! Don't step on the edge.'

Seeing his alarm pulled her slightly out of the reverie that made her feel both avid and exhausted at the same time. She lay down on her belly and looked over the cliff. Down below, as her heart had known, were the Devil's Teeth. She watched the calm water swill around the visible peaks of rock.

'It was their place, the brothers. And he knew that if he did it here …'

Ed stopped, but Lia finished the sentence for him.

'He knew that if he did it here, onto the Devil's Teeth, there would be no hope of surviving. That's why Harry showed the Teeth to me from the boat. So that I would understand that.'

Lia buried her face in the bend of her arm and cried.

Six

There was something awesome in the thought of the solitary mortal standing by the open window and summoning in from the gloom outside the spirits of the nether world.

Arthur Conan Doyle, 'The Ghosts of Goresthorpe Grange', 1883

Ed didn't know what to do, so he pulled off his backpack and lay down beside her, putting his arm around her. Her sobs were muffled by her arm and the soft moss, but her body hitched with the violence of her emotion. He started to get scared that she wasn't going to stop but eventually she seemed to calm. At any rate her sobs reduced to hiccups and sniffs. He managed to get his free hand into the bag to pull out a few napkins. When he offered them, she sat up and faced away from him, wiping her face and blowing her nose.

Finally, she shifted back around towards him and sat with her legs folded under her. Her eyes were red but the pupils looked greener than usual, with flecks of gold and brown. Her cheek held the impression of the seam of her sleeve but otherwise her skin was clear and pale beneath her tan. She was beautiful and he felt almost afraid to talk to her.

She raised her chin in a show of pride.

'Sorry,' she said.

'It's fine.' He took her hand.

She entwined her fingers in his.

'It's better to know,' she said. 'Even just this much. I probably won't ever find out why.'

She gazed at him, as though searching his eyes for answers he didn't have.

She continued and he wasn't sure if she was talking to him or to herself. He held her hand and listened anyway.

'It might have been the separation, but he seemed OK. I'm not certain whose idea it even was. It might have been his. They never said.'

She plucked at the dark green grass. It didn't yield but squeaked as her fingers slid off the blades.

'Could it have been anything else?' Ed asked quietly.

She tried to pluck again and this time some shiny blades of grass gave in. She gazed at them traversing her palm.

Ed could feel a pulse in the hand he held, as though someone had tied a tourniquet on her arm. He tried to loosen his grip slightly but she held on fast.

'He liked his job. The city too, even though he often complained about it. He read a lot. Sometimes he liked to be on his own and sometimes he seemed to crave company. Jasmine, my mother, thought he was bipolar, always either up or down, but I think he just didn't know how to be.' She looked up at him. 'Maybe that was it. Maybe he just got tired of trying to figure himself out.'

Ed said nothing. He had no way of knowing whether what she said was close to the truth or not. She fell silent too. All he could do was sit there and hold her hand. He thought maybe that sometimes that's all anyone could do for anyone.

He looked at their hands together. He'd had a few adventures with summer girls, but they never involved handholding. When he thought about it, the last person to hold his hand had probably been his mother.

As though she sensed the change in his mood, she took her

hand gently away and tied her hair in a knot, tucking the loose strands behind her ears.

'I need to go home now,' she said. 'It's been a tough day.' Home? When had it become home? This place where her father had died?

He nodded and got to his feet, collecting the bag with the food they had somehow not eaten. He had hoped that it would be a nice day for her, but it was all too wrapped up in blood and tragedy.

'Will you let me know if you hear any news about Becky and the baby?' she said as they followed the path towards the pub.

He nodded.

She turned to go inside but paused.

'Thank you for showing me. I had to do it and … it was nice to have someone with me.'

'We did OK, I think,' Ed said.

She reached up and gave him a quick kiss on the lips before turning and disappearing into the pub.

He stood still, feeling the impression of her lips, feeling like the air would suddenly fall back with a thunderclap into the place where she had been. He had known her for about two minutes, but the idea came to him that if she were not there anymore he would feel the loss terribly. Strangely, this made him feel happy as well as confused.

He walked home, absentmindedly noting the thin cry of the buzzards. Only when he was approaching the farm did he realise that the shadows had grown long. He picked up his pace and ran the last few steps to the door.

He went in and turned toward the kitchen. Then something struck him in the back, causing a shock of pain to his kidney. He sprawled forward, skidding a few inches on his belly on the lino of the kitchen floor.

He rolled, feeling his back ache, and tried to stand. His

father shoved him back down with a dirty boot, laces trailing. He stood over him, almost smiling.

Ed had seen the look before.

Dan had an open can of beer in his hand. Ed had seen this before too. Punch with a fist, take a drink, punch again. Kidney pain or not, dirty boot to his chest or not, he knew he had to get off the floor to defend himself. He shoved the boot up and shoved himself backwards, and with the small distance scrambled to his feet.

Dan laughed. 'Where are you going to go, boy? Standing up won't help you.' With that, he whipped his hand forward, releasing the can of beer. It flew the short distance and struck Ed in the eyebrow. A trickle of blood and beer ran towards his eye, but he swiped them away fast. Fear went with them. Anger boiled up inside him and he felt the muscles around his mouth tighten, showing his teeth the way a dog might. Before the old man could move, Ed lunged at him and was rewarded by a thick fist meeting his ear. Pain rang through him, a bell tolling in the distance. He staggered, suddenly dizzy. He had time to deal out one or two punches before Dan overwhelmed him with his stupid, drunken rage at his son's tardiness and defiance. After a while, Ed didn't feel the blows anymore. He just felt the soft press of Lia's lips against his.

There was a long spell when Frank just wandered. He gradually became aware of the change in the light and frowned. There had been someone beside him but he had already forgotten who. Was there a baby? He couldn't remember. He still felt fantastic though. He patted his belly. It seemed flatter than it had been. Happiness flooded through him and he marched on, feeling tall and young. He had the whole world ahead of him and everything was really grand.

He paused often, looking down the slopes to the lacy trim of beach and rocks that circled the bottom of the cliffs but the view didn't satisfy him. He walked on, only to stop suddenly, gazing at nothing. Without knowing it, he had been looking for something. He felt hungry, in need of … what, he didn't know.

He spent a few minutes looking at the sky and the water. He could hear the sound of waves. Even in calm weather, the sea was never silent. He remembered days and nights on the boat, with the water lapping at her sides, bearing him up and onward, providing him and his family with food, and a living.

Rose didn't know what it meant to him, or to any one of the fishermen, to give up the boats. It was giving up being part of the sea and the sky. How could they know, the people who were anchored to the earth? They were the ones who were lost and they didn't even know it.

She was always there, the sea, sometimes whispering, sometimes roaring. On the wild nights he had heard her call his name. He never told anyone, but he knew the truth of it. The sea always called to him, either in desire or rage. Either way, the sea was as hungry for him as he had always been for her.

And that hunger was filling him now. He longed for the rush of salty liquid on his face. He wanted to bathe in it and breathe it in. His belly was empty and his mouth was dry and lifeless as the trilobite fossils in the cliffs below.

He had never lost his bearings, even in a storm. Many voices returned to him in his memory of the years.

Frank will know. He always knows the way.

He turned in a slow circle, letting the thing inside him feel its way to true north, the way it always had. He didn't realise that he had closed his eyes until he opened them and saw the Hall, solid and made of shadows all at once. His stomach grumbled and he set off, never taking his eyes off his destination.

It seemed to grow until it filled his vision. Before, it had been an ugly grey block. Now, he saw that it was full of beautiful life. Even at a distance, he could see lichen colouring the walls in patches of growth. The low winter sun was casting yellow light and shadow like a water colourist dabbing his brush, adding the final touches that made the scene come alive.

Stumbling over the broken wall, Frank stepped into the grounds of the Hall and started up the long driveway. The once perfect surface was riddled with dying weeds. He stopped where the driveway swept in two directions, in front of the house and behind to where the horses and carriages were once kept. He didn't feel right about going to the front.

Instead, he took the back way, but veered off before it could lead him to the coach house. His feet unerringly found an old path down to the private beach. It had been cut out of the earth, made for ladies to descend safely to the sand, unlike the steep and rugged paths around the rest of the island.

The beach was the best on the island. The people who had built here had chosen the right location on many counts. It had an unbroken view of the open sea and sky and different aspects of the house benefited from both the rising and setting sun, as well as the long summer day of light, and the silver of the moon. The beach was made of pale soft sand and curved in a graceful bay where a swimmer would feel sheltered from deeper water.

Of course, no one came here anymore. There was no one left to enjoy the long days and half-light nights. He knew that there had been wild parties in the house that had often spilled onto the beach. He could almost see the long dresses making swirling shapes in the sand and hear the drifting music from the quartet brought in to perform for the night. He experienced a sudden rush of desire to have been here then, when the Hall was the centre of life on the island. Back then the greenhouses had produced food and flowers that wouldn't otherwise grow here. The walled gardens and kitchens had kept many islanders in work. The very sea itself had been alive with a flotilla of boats, fishing.

He walked to the edge of the water and scanned the horizon. Of course, that was all in the summer. Winter here brought darkness and fear. The perfect position of the house in summer exposed it to the worst that the winter could offer. Most of the windows had to be boarded up and the glass taken out of the greenhouses. The side of the house turned towards the sea was cleaner than the rest, so constantly blasted was it by salty, sandy gales.

Whenever the family finally left the Hall, it must have been winter, because the windows were boarded up and the remains of the greenhouses were not sprinkled with shards of their own glass.

Many times, he and all of the islanders had heard the summer people exclaim over the beauty of the island, the wild flowers, the profusion of life in the meadows and cliff sides. Mostly they just smiled and nodded. The true answer they kept to themselves. *It is lovely. For a few months of the year.*

When the occasional person, an artist, a writer, people who worked from home, declared that they wanted to buy or build on the island, locals gently but firmly suggested that they visit during the winter first before committing to a purchase. There was usually a reason found to make them change their mind in any case. This was, outside of the summer, a private place, with its own ways and its own secrets.

Frank suddenly felt tired. So tired that he could no longer stand. He fell back one step, saving himself from falling in the water, but unable to stay upright for another second. He lay on the cold sand and looked at the sky. All the vitality he had felt all day was slipping away. He could feel it in his bones and joints, which began to ache. He hadn't realised how much they ached, like beads of glass grinding against his nerves, until it had been gone and then returned to him. His mouth felt like cotton wool, his tongue thick and flaccid.

He lay there, unable to get up, feeling his muscles weaken, his blood slow. It was harder to catch his breath. His chest felt like someone had balanced a weight on it. He stared at the sky. Birds flew in and out of his window of sight but they were blurred now, his eyes clouding over. He closed them.

He must have slept, or blacked out, because when he opened his eyes again the sky held the last traces of bruised yellow and the dog star was visible. He was still weak but felt better. He managed to get to his knees and then stand, shakily. The cool twilight felt good on his face. *I'm on the terminal line.* The terminal line, the marker that moved across the face of the earth from east to west, pushing light ahead of it, dragging darkness in its wake. He was standing in a precious and brief moment of time, when light was still a blessing, but the dark was inexorably coming, heedless of anyone's desire to hold it back. Frank heard the inner voice he had always heard since the time of the goat. It was distant now, but still within reach.

Anything can come with the dark. Watch for what comes from the sea. Make safe harbour before the storm.

These were the rules by which he had lived his life on the water. Where once he was the captain of his own vessel, master of his own destiny, rising unafraid to any challenge nature could throw at him, now he saw that his presence atop the waves had been a mere collection of bones and timbers, utterly vulnerable to the uncaring whims of the sea. He had survived until now, a tiny man in a vast and unknowable ocean. He had been lucky many times. Now, the voice and the compass inside him fell silent. There was no further thought of fighting or salvation. He had reached the edge of the world.

When he next heard a voice, he knew that it wasn't his and it wasn't offering him sanctuary from the storm.

It *was* the storm and there was no stopping it now.

Seven

Because if a woman's heart was free
a man might have hope.

Bram Stoker, *Dracula*, 1897

Jasmine sipped the wine. It was really very good. Ash always chose just right. This was their favourite restaurant. And somewhere she had never come with Will. The waiter arrived with their entrées.

'You're miles away, Jazz. Everything OK?' Ash said, when the waiter had gone.

She nodded and smiled.

He put down his cutlery. 'Is it Lia?'

'I'm just thinking about her, that's all. Everything is fine.'

She was constantly worried about her emotional daughter out on that island but it wasn't just Lia she was thinking about.

Will had only taken Jasmine to the island once, to meet his brother. They didn't like each other but they both played nice for the short visit. Will had brought her around the island, showing her everything with pride and love. Even wearing her lowest heels, her shoes were useless on the rough ground.

Lia was more like Will than her. Jasmine didn't care for

emotions very much. They were what led people into trouble. But on her first and only visit to the island, even she felt a strange stew of emotions coming from her new husband. After the novelty of being in a remote world so different to her own passed, she noticed that he seemed fizzy. Excited and nervous, almost afraid. He loved the island and was greeted with apparent pleasure by everyone they met. And yet, he acted like a man trying to enjoy a last meal before being brought to the gallows. He couldn't sleep, he was sweaty, and either manic or surly. Of course, at the time of their whirlwind romance and marriage, she hadn't realised that his heightened state was just an exaggeration of his normal manic depression. He refused to seek help or a diagnosis, but he was never as bad as he had been on the island with her.

He had such a good heart and he could be so funny, but his mood swings were impossible to predict and increasingly impossible to live with. He was never violent but he was a tall, strong man with a temper and she was sometimes afraid. Ash was more ... manageable. Was it her fault that, in contrast to her difficult husband, Ash seemed calm and sophisticated? Not sophisticated, she admonished herself. Ash was civilised. Now, more than ever, she suspected that Will wasn't, not really. There was too much of the wild islander in him. Even though he had happily left his life and his family to share her life in New York, he had carried the island with him, and never quite settled, even though there were many parts of city life that he had enjoyed.

And now her daughter, who was too like Will, was on that cursed island. Far away from her in more than miles.

She picked at her delicious food and realised that Ash was still watching her. She mentally shook herself and touched his hand.

'I'm sorry. I'm here now, honestly. How's your food?'

He smiled at her, appearing reassured and happy to move

on. 'Wonderful. This wine complements it perfectly.'

She returned the smile, thinking how easy it must be to be him. She couldn't imagine it. Maybe she was a little more like Will and Lia than she had realised and maybe that wasn't so bad.

Eight

I looked upon the sea, it was to be my grave.

Mary Shelley, *Frankenstein*, 1818

Next morning, Lia woke up slowly, with the sounds of the kitchen below sinking into her half-dreaming state. She opened her eyes and couldn't think where she was. Someone had left the window partly open and a chill breeze was moving the curtain. It brought the smell of the sea and with it a rush of memories from the day before. Her eyes were sore and her throat raw. Oh God, she had cried first in front of Ed, then later when she saw Harry, too like his brother. She hadn't cried like that since … well, she hadn't ever cried like that at all. Yesterday, the fright of Becky's emergency and all the blood, and then seeing the place where her father had gone to his death, had finally broken whatever dam she had built inside and her grief had come pouring out.

She knew she had to ring Jasmine now. They had been hard on each other, not knowing the right way to grieve, or even how to start. The distance between her dad being alive and being in a closed coffin had made it all unreal. She thought now that she and her mother had both felt abandoned. They expected to see him again and that moment never came, leaving everything unfinished. The coffin was closed and Harry had done the identification in Ireland. Jasmine had insisted on burying her husband in the plot they had bought together in New York. Even the ceremony had seemed empty of meaning.

Who even knew if it was her dad who was in that wooden box buried in the cold ground of a city cemetery with room for one more coffin beside it? Of course it was, but she had no proof of it. She was expected to believe that the man she had known all of her life was under the headstone. All of his kindness, his occasional nerves and desire to retreat to his study to read instead of going to glittering parties with his glamorous wife; all of his vitality when he was happy, playing with her in the park; his lovely piano-playing and awful efforts to learn the harmonica; his flashes of manic humour when he pranked her mother; all of it just irretrievably gone, which seemed impossible. Stupid. A waste.

Lia felt anger flare through her, but it lasted no more than a second. She had to be honest with herself. He was complicated and made up of both light and darkness. She supposed most people were but her dad had never achieved a balance. Instead, he had shared a teeter-totter, a see-saw, with an imaginary other, who sometimes let him ride high and sometimes pushed him down.

Lia knew that she was right. She had been right to come here. The hole in her chest was still gaping and raw, but she believed for the first time that it would heal. Slowly maybe, but inexorably. So, she took a deep breath and threw the covers back.

After a shower, she dared to look at herself. Her eyes were bloodshot and her face puffy and blotchy. Definitely a day for a bit of camouflage. When she was ready, she went downstairs.

She followed the sounds into the kitchen.

'Just in time,' Harry said. 'Here, eat this.'

He put a plate on the scrubbed table. Lovely buttery scrambled eggs on toast. He poured a mug of mahogany tea for each of them and sat down to drink his own.

Now, she thought, *he'll say things.*

But he didn't. He let her eat and he drank two cups of tea with lots of milk, all without saying a word. When she finished, he nodded.

'OK?' he said, his eyes on hers.

She nodded slowly.

'OK,' she said.

He nodded again and headed out to the pub, whistling through his teeth, which she had learned he did when he was busy.

She cleared away the dishes, wiped the table and stood in the middle of the kitchen, wondering what to do. It was too early to call New York. She wanted to say sorry to Ed for all that crying. First, she must find out about Becky and her baby – she had forgotten to ask Harry. She pulled on a jacket and passed through the bar looking for him. She heard him moving barrels in the side yard so she went that way.

'Harry, I'm going for a walk, but I wanted to ask you first about Becky. Has there been any news?'

'Oh, sorry, I should have said – she had the baby – a boy. Rose was with her. Matt didn't make it in time, but he wasn't too late. He's over there now. The baby is fine. Becky isn't great, but she'll be OK. Frank is the one everyone is worried about now.'

'Frank?'

'Rose's husband. Remember I told you he gave up the boat?'

Lia nodded, suddenly hearing Becky's voice again. *Dad.* It had sounded like she was saying *Dad* over and over.

'What happened to him?' she asked.

'No one can find him. The boys went out last night and searched for him. I stayed on here in case you … needed anything in the night. But they didn't find him.' He sighed heavily. 'Like I said, there's always something. Anyway, they're still looking for him. I'm going out in a while myself to search, in the boat.'

'Is there anything I can do?'

'Say a prayer if you're that way inclined. I'm hoping we missed him and he went on the first ferry this morning.' He checked his watch. 'Although we'd surely have heard by now. Anyway, you did everything you needed to do yesterday. If you and Ed hadn't come upon Becky when she was in trouble, who knows what would have happened?'

He took out his wallet and peeled off a note.

'Look, Ed's a good lad. Why don't you take him to the café for lunch? You won't be the only ones there, even at this time of the year. There are lots of retired people who don't bother cooking during the day. Not very exciting but the grub is great. Have the chocolate fudge cake.' He thought for a second and gave her another note. 'If she has a full one, bring it home. I love that stuff.'

She grinned at him. 'OK, Sweet Tooth. I'll see you later. Thanks for the money.'

He winked and went back to his work.

Lia went around the back, circling the pub until she was in sight of her robin friend on the sign.

It was still early, and she knew that Ed would have farm work, but maybe he wouldn't mind if she tagged along with him. Maybe she could even help.

Feeling better, lighter, than she had in a while, she set off on the road. The day was colder, the sky a slate grey. She realised that she could smell rain in the air and marvelled at it. She loved the parks in the city, but here she was somehow closer to the earth, the sea and sky. She could feel a difference in the air pressure too, especially when she got closer to the Hall. She was glad to veer off and follow the narrow lane to the farmhouse. The lane, lined with stunted trees, felt a few degrees colder and more shadowed. It gave her a bad feeling.

The farm was quiet. Maybe he had already fed all the animals, and they were munching peacefully. Yet she was almost afraid to approach the door of the house. Like her sense of rain, she knew there was something wrong. Hurrying now, she crossed the yard and knocked on the front door. There was no sound of movement in the house. She tried peering through the window, but net curtains effectively shut her out. She found her way around the side of the house to a door that looked like it was more well-used. There was a mud-scraper outside. She had never seen one before but its purpose was clear, as it was caked in dry crusty muck.

She knocked. The door was on the latch and slightly open. Slowly, she pushed it wider.

'*Ed? Hello?*'

Nothing.

If his father was in, surely he would have responded by now?

She stepped inside and looked around. It was clean but untidy, a bit like Harry's except without Rose's input.

Moving deeper into the room, her heart beating hard, she saw a laptop with a cracked lid on the floor, along with a scatter of glossy printer paper and a broken cup. On the other side of the room was Ed's camera, smashed to bits. Her hand flew to her mouth. Someone had thrown it. Someone had knocked everything off the table and smashed the camera.

She went to pick it up, but her foot slid. She looked down. Drops of rusty brown … something. *Not something, Lia. You know what it is.*

'Blood,' she whispered.

'Only a small bit.'

Lia let out a small scream at the sound of the voice, which didn't sound like Ed's.

But it was Ed. He was leaning against an interior door, not casually, but for support. His voice was thick because his bottom lip was cut, and his cheek was puffy. On that side, his eye was black too. Blood had crusted on the eyebrow above.

She rushed to his side.

'Careful, don't squeeze me.'

She gave him a gentle hug which he returned one-armed, burying his face in her hair.

She drew back and took his hand in both of hers.

'Who did this?'

He made a face and winced at the pain.

'Don't worry about it – it's nothing,' he said.

'Don't say that.'

He hesitated. 'OK. Sorry.'

'And everything is ruined. Your camera.'

He looked around her and she saw his face change.

'*Bastard,*' he said under his breath. He went red, then pale.

Lia saw him literally sway on his feet. She tucked herself under his arm and took him out of the room. He felt resistant at first but then let her lead him.

'In there,' he said.

She took him into a small sitting room and helped him to sit down on the sofa. She opened the curtains and sat beside him.

'Was it your dad?'

'Yeah. Always is.'

She took his hand again. The knuckles were scraped and bruised.

'You hit him back?'

'Yeah. He's heavy though. And mean when he's drunk. I'm out of practice. He hasn't done that since ... since Mam was alive. I guess he's back to his old ways.'

He looked at her.

'Not impressing you much, am I? You needn't stay. I'll be grand.'

'Shut up, Ed,' she said, making herself smile, despite the rage and fear for him which were competing for dominance in her heart.

'OK,' he said, trying to smile back through his split lip.

Lia sat quietly, thinking. Ed made a sound like he was falling asleep. She held his hand, watching his face. He dozed for ten or fifteen minutes before waking up again.

'Sorry. Had a restless night.'

'What are you going to do, Ed?'

'I don't know. Stay. Go. I don't know. It's not the first time. Not the worst either. Nothing's broken. I've taken a few painkillers. They're kicking in now. I feel better.'

'Where is he?'

'What time is it?' he said.

'About ten.'

'He's probably in the Rest, having his first pint. The animals aren't bawling so he must have fed them at least.'

'Do you want me to check?' Lia said.

'No, thanks. I'll do it. And then I think I might make myself scarce for a couple of days until he settles down.' His brows drew together. 'Oh God, my camera.'

'I know, I'm sorry.'

'I've got the pictures on a USB but it'll take me forever to get another camera.'

'It meant a lot to you,' she said.

'Yeah. I mean ... it's not just a hobby. I was trying to do something. Trying to be a photographer, I suppose.'

'You will be,' she said.

'I don't know. I can't see how at the minute.'

'Because if it's what you want, you'll find a way. It just

looks bad today. Believe me, I know how bad things can look.'

He nodded. 'Well, we'd better get out of here in case he decides to come back early from the pub. Like that's going to happen when he's on a tear.'

Ed got stiffly to his feet, but Lia could see that he was moving better than when she had first seen him. He wouldn't let her go upstairs with him to gather a few things, going red when she offered. She debated about tidying up but decided Ed's dad had made the mess so he could clean it himself. She did wipe up the nearly dry blood though.

'Hey.'

Ed had a sports bag over his shoulder. He bent down with difficulty and touched one finger to his broken camera. Lia knew nothing about cameras but she could see it was beyond repair. He put the bag down and managed to get the memory card out of the camera. He stood up stiffly and tucked the card into his wallet.

'The laptop might be OK,' Lia said. 'Maybe it's only the lid.'

'Hopefully. I'll bring it anyway. Would you mind putting it in its case?'

She did as he asked and hung it across her body.

Ready to go, Ed paused at the back door and looked back.

'My mother was here, always.'

'She probably wouldn't want you to stay here for her. Not if he's going to hurt you.'

Ed didn't reply. He just turned and left the house.

Lia pulled the door closed behind her, leaving it on the latch as she had found it. Together, they made sure that the animals had enough food, water and bedding before walking back towards the village.

'You can stay in the pub – Harry has lots of room,' Lia said when they reached the Robin's Rest.

'I can't pay for it. I'll ask Mrs. Glenn if I can sleep on her sofa for a couple of nights.'

'You will not. Stay here and I'll sort this out.' Lia used her sternest voice and, though she saw him smile at it, it worked.

She went inside. There were four men at the bar, talking quietly.

She beckoned urgently to Harry. He gave one of the men his change and came around the bar to her.

'What's up? I thought you wouldn't be back till later.'

She urged him outside.

Harry swore under his breath when he saw Ed's face.

'I thought he'd stopped all that after your mother?'

'He had. I guess he likes things the way they used to be. Is he inside?'

Harry shook his head. 'No, he came in and had two. Said he was going across and left.'

'Harry, can Ed stay here for a couple of days? I'll pay,' Lia said.

'He can, but no one will pay. Go on in, Ed, get settled. I'd better go back to the boys. You'll mind him, won't you, Lia? Get him something to eat.' He patted Ed on the shoulder and went inside.

Lia took Ed upstairs and got him settled. He didn't want food. He just lay down on top of the bed and fell asleep straight away. She closed the door quietly and went downstairs. God, what a couple of days!

She went outside and walked across the grass, following the path worn by feet, and sat down at the place her father had last stood. Remembering Ed's warning about not being too close to the edge, she lay on her belly, feeling the cold coming from the ground. She looked over.

The Devil's Teeth were more exposed, their tops poking out of the water.

Lia froze, burying her fingers in the spongy grass.

Dad. It's Dad.

He was on his back, facing the sky. The Devil's Teeth had pierced his body and held him still. His hands moved with the waves, and his head fell to one side, as though he were looking for her.

Harry and the other men came when they heard her screams.

It wasn't her dad, of course, but Harry could see why she would have thought it. Harry himself had gone cold all over when he saw the body impaled on the Devil's Teeth. The man looked like Will had done, except that his brother had been facing down, as though looking for something in the water.

'It's not your dad, Lia. It's not him. I think it's Frank.' He wrapped her in his arms, almost engulfing her against his chest. He wasn't sure she had taken it in, but then she took a deep breath and went still in his arms.

He held her away, seeing from her face that she had accepted the truth of it.

He took her back to the pub and left her in the snug while he ran up the stairs, woke Ed and told him what had happened. He wasn't surprised when Ed confessed he had shown her the place.

They went downstairs. Ed still had a bit of awkwardness about him, despite having to grow up too fast, but he was ready to take her into his shelter. Without Harry having to say anything, took her in his arms, then led her into the kitchen. Hot sweet tea was on the cards.

Harry arranged everything. The emergency services, local help with the retrieval of the body, the transport across to the mainland, the terrible phone call to the hospital to tell Rose that her husband was gone. He didn't mention the whiteness of the man's face, or how his body had shrivelled, looking like the husk of a fly that a spider had drained. Everyone would say that he had bled out on the rocks after jumping or falling. Except the islanders who would say nothing at all.

Harry could hardly believe it had happened. Everything had been under control. At least he had thought it was. No one had suffered like Frank for a long, long time. People had died, but that had been the end. Now the climate had changed. The storms no longer brought bounty to their shores to keep matters steady and manageable. Something would have to be done.

Harry kept uppermost in his mind at all times that when Will's time had come, it was natural. He had lost blood on the teeth of the devil but, gruesome though his injuries were, they were normal for the catastrophic event that had occurred. He had died a man and had gone to his grave and his immortal rest as one. Harry clung to that. If he spent sleepless nights considering the value of a death like that, then it was no one's business but his own. If the other men sometimes showed signs of bad nights, then that was theirs. Nothing needed to be spoken about. The work just needed to be done.

Frank was taken away from the island, but when they were finished with him on the mainland, they would send him back to be buried in the rocks and soil of his birthplace. With a brick in his mouth.

Nine

Dan didn't come into the pub that night either. He really had gone on a bender on the mainland, if he wasn't washing up on the rocks like Frank. But Harry knew this of old. For a long time, while Patty was sick and after she died, Dan had laid off the drink a little. When Harry cut him off, he sometimes tried to get a drink out of someone else, but he mostly just went home quietly enough.

Like all the islanders, Harry had seen both Patty and Ed with bruises or long sleeves on hot days. He and the others had often taken Dan aside and told him to lay off. In the end, he always returned to his ways, and Patty stayed no matter what. There was nothing else anyone could do, although Harry still regretted that he hadn't acted more drastically. The problem, of course, was that Dan was one of them. One of the old gang. So, as bad as it felt to Harry, they kept watch on him and his family, being tough with him periodically to keep him roughly on track, to keep him from killing his wife and son.

Once Ed grew into a strong young man, and Patty fell ill, there were no more bruises, just misery and waiting. Now, the two were out there alone on the farm, too close to the Hall. And Dan had gone back to his old ways, as he always did.

Harry looked up at the ceiling. Lia was up there, sleeping away the shock of finding Frank impaled on the rocks and thinking it was her dad. Ed was up there too, in another room, sleeping restlessly probably, still hurting from the beating his father had given him. Harry's bedroom was between the two. He wasn't her father, but he wasn't about to allow sneaking about at night when he was looking after her.

At first, he thought that a brief romance between them would do them both good. But if Ed was going to bring trouble to her, Harry couldn't allow that. He also couldn't allow harm to come to Ed. He was an islander.

It was late and he was tired. It had been a rough day. After giving Rose the news, he had wanted to lie on the old couch in the kitchen and sleep for the night. The world felt safer there, like it had when he and Will were ignorant children. But there were things to be done, decisions to be made. And kids to be watched.

He cleared most of his customers out of the bar and locked up behind them. The others were waiting for him when he came back. He pulled them all a pint and allowed himself one. They moved closer together at the bar and Harry leaned on it, thinking of the importance of continuity. He found himself regretting that he had no children on the island to keep up traditions, play their part.

As though he had heard Harry's thoughts, Andrew put down his pint, wiped the creamy head off his thick moustache and said, 'There's a Crowe child here now, Harry.'

'Don't you think I know that?' he said.

'You're acting as if you don't,' Brendan said, mumbling slightly.

'She's not mine and she's only been here a few days. She's not staying.'

The others shared a glance and no one said anything.

A surge of futile rage burned Harry's throat. He knew what they weren't saying: *She'll stay alright. She's one of the family.*

'And what about Dan?' Andy said.

'He's gone too far,' Harry said. 'We should have done something before this. Ed isn't a child anymore.'

'Well, then maybe he should handle his own problems like a man,' Andrew said. He had a way of speaking that stayed just the right side of respect for Harry, but his hatred was there in the twist of his lips as though he had just tasted something bitter.

Harry took a deep draught of his Guinness and looked at each weather-beaten face, all waiting for his answer. He nodded.

'I told his mother I'd keep an eye on him. When Dan turns up, we should go and have a chat with him. But I'll leave that up to you. I need to stay here and keep watch on the young people.'

There was some further talk about the weather and their plans, but the important matter was settled. They finished their drinks and left. Harry stood in the silent, darkened bar, not thinking, just holding on to the moment before the world changed again.

Through the window he saw a light flash out at the Hall, a single burst against the dark block that he couldn't see now but knew so well. He waited but it didn't happen again. Someone out hunting rabbits maybe. There were plenty who didn't know, who were happy to go out there at night, even if it made them feel a bit creepy. A big old empty house at night, of course it was creepy. The damn thing was scary during the day, never mind in the dark.

Harry hoped that whoever it was would get home safely

but he wasn't going out to make sure. He checked all the doors and windows before going up to bed. There was no sound from either of the kids' rooms. He didn't know if he should look in on them and hesitated in the hallway. He wished Will were there.

He rested his hand on Lia's door. She was an innocent, not even raised here. He went to his own room and got into bed, expecting to lie awake, thinking too much and watching for the reflection of a light on the cloudy sky outside the window.

After closing time, when people would have stopped moving around, Dan came out from behind the walls of the ruined church into the graveyard. The moon wasn't visible, but the clouds were pearly and he could make out enough not to fall over. He had a torch in his pocket but he didn't want to use it. With low cloud to bounce off, the light would be seen for miles. He knew the graveyard well enough without it.

He patted the shoulder of his wife's gravestone as he shuffled by. It gave him a pang of guilt which was quickly followed by anger and raw desire for a drink. There was half a bottle of whiskey at home in the press, but he didn't want to go home. Ed would be there looking at him with Patty's eyes, full of hatred. As a little boy he had loved his dad, Dan knew he had. Of course, he had to discipline him, no point in waiting for Patty to do that. She only mollycoddled the boy. If it had been left up to her, the boy would have grown up soft. He had a bit, with his pictures, but he was strong enough.

Dan put his hand to his belly. The way the boy had held that knife to his gut, that was good. He wasn't just his mother's son. He had even got in a few good thumps before Dan had knocked him down.

He'd be grand. It was only a few bangs, no more than he'd taken from his own father. It would toughen him up.

Besides, he had to get a woman and take over running the farm. Dan was sick of it. He was tired and couldn't a man just have a few drinks in peace without having to get up in the night to animals or women getting sick?

He put his hand out to the graveyard wall for support. He felt like the boy had put the knife in his belly after all. The nights when Patty couldn't settle for pain and getting sick, even though she had nothing in her stomach, had been hard. He knew he wasn't the best man in the world, he knew it. Still, he had stuck with her through those nights when the house smelled like sickness. *Don't kid yourself. It smelled like death*. She *smelled like death*. Even the animals seemed to know it. The old dog, since dead and buried himself, sometimes howled in the night, a lost sound that made goose bumps stand up on your arms. The cows were quiet. The fields themselves lay barren and flat, like the sea in a dead calm.

He had beaten the boy again. He hadn't even done anything wrong, except take his pictures. Patty had loved the pictures.

Tears fell freely, falling to the ground as he leaned on the wall. His thirst was terrible. He would have to face going home and getting the whiskey. He hadn't told the boy that there wasn't any money left. Patty had been good at all that. He had spent anything the farm brought in. They needed new animals and the land needed work. Ed liked the animals and the land, but Dan knew he didn't want to stay and farm. More tears fell.

Harry was lucky not having kids. At least he didn't have ones that wanted to leave him and their inheritance behind. It was a dark inheritance, but it was important. The young people didn't care. They all left in the end. Dan took a deep breath and wiped his nose with his sleeve. It was all over. Dead calm October and November coming in a few days.

Animals had to be fed no matter what.

He raised his head, like a dog sniffing the air.

'That's it,' he said. 'That's what I'll do.'

Andy had come to him after Patty died, wanting to take some of the animals off his hands. Andy was never happy with what he had and always wanted more. What he really wanted was Dan's land. Dan had told him to get out, but now Andy was there on the other side of the stone walls, his fields perfect and his cows fat and glossy. If he went to him right now, he'd take the animals. And the land. Dan would keep the house, but he didn't want the bloody land any more. The boy didn't want it either.

His head cleared a little. That was why he had hit Ed. He had come home to see the camera and the computer and they were so alien to the kitchen, to the farm, that he couldn't help himself. He smashed them and he smashed Ed too. He struck what he could reach because the boy didn't want to stay.

Well, he was going to take away any reason he had to stay. Let him go if he wanted. Andy would give him enough money to have a few drinks and a few spuds and take it easy for whatever length he had. He was surely not long for the grave now that Patty was gone, despite everything, and all the other women who had come before her.

He sniffed and straightened himself. It wasn't that late. Andy would still be up but Kitty would be in bed. It would be warm and quiet in Andy's house.

Dan found his way out to the road. The walk sobered him up some more and he felt quite steady by the time he reached Andy's front door.

He knocked quietly but Andy would hear the grass growing so he appeared fast, snatching the door open, his shoulders squared.

'It's just me. Andy, it's Dan.' He held his hands up.

'I thought you had gone across,' Andy said.

'No. No, I –'

'What do you want, Dan?'

Dan's legs wobbled and his insides rolled. Maybe this was a bad idea.

'Well?' Andy said.

'I ... Will you buy the farm and the animals? Not the house.'

Andy was still, then he smiled.

'Come in, Dan. I've got a few things for you to sign.'

Ten

Even if she be not harmed, her heart may fail her in so much and so many horrors; and hereafter she may suffer – both in waking, from her nerves, and in sleep, from her dreams.

Bram Stoker, *Dracula*, 1897

It was late but the hospital wasn't quiet. There was a chorus of coughs and groans, the rattle of metal being moved and dropped. It sounded to Matt as though someone was making noise on purpose. The nurses had been great though. Brilliant really. Someone was always pushing a cup of tea into his hand. They had taken pity on him and Rose, especially after Frank had been found.

Becky hadn't woken up properly yet. She had said a few words without opening her eyes. He thought she was calling for her father at one point. He would have to tell her when she did wake up that Frank was dead. He felt so numb that even this thought didn't shake him. The baby was fine. A gorgeous big boy. Becky was the one who had been in danger, but they had given her back the blood she had lost and they said they weren't worried.

But Matt was worried. She was so white, her skin like paper. He worried about Rose too. He looked at her sleeping face. She was pale and exhausted and he didn't know how she was coping with Frank's death.

He got up every now and then to stretch his legs, and to see the baby, but he didn't like leaving Becky even though her mother was there. It gave him a bad feeling, like the fog was drifting over him again.

They had decided months ago that if it was a boy they would name him Joseph after Matt's dad, but he reckoned that was likely to change now that Frank was gone. He would settle for Joseph as a middle name. Or any name. She could have any name she wanted. And anything she wanted. As long as she woke up and smiled at him once more.

It was time to move again. He stood up and stretched. His back cracked, a gunshot in the quiet space. No one stirred. The corridor was empty of people, but he could hear the murmur of conversation from the nurses' station. He went quietly past and no one paid him any attention.

The wards were in semi-darkness. It never really got dark, the same as it never really got quiet. In another few hours, trolleys would be rattling around with tea and toast and someone would start running a floor-polisher.

He walked to the nursery and stared in at them all. For once, every baby was asleep. He looked at his son. He had never been good at babies. Becky was always saying that babies looked just like so and so, but Matt had never been able to see it. Babies were all the same. Cute but, you know, babies. Except for Joseph. He caught himself – no, Becky would name him. For now he must be 'The Baby'.

The baby was his, unmistakeably. There wasn't one thing that made it so, it just was so. The nurses had exclaimed about it. Matt didn't know how to feel. He and Becky had made him, but they hadn't designed him. So he just smiled and nodded. All he knew was that the boy was his and Becky was his and he had not understood how much love that would make him feel. And how much terror.

He studied his son's sleeping face for another few minutes before going to the bathroom. He helped himself to a coffee from the nurses' station, as they had told him to do. He put lots of sugar in it and wished he had a drop of whiskey too. Rose's tea was easy. No sugar and enough milk to make it nearly white.

He went back into the room, careful not to spill the drinks, setting them down on the windowsill. He turned to check on Becky and she was looking at him.

He took her hand and couldn't speak past the lump in his throat.

'The baby?' she said, her voice raspy.

'He's fine. A fine boy. Oh, love, I was so afraid I'd lose you.'

'I think ... I think you almost did.' She smiled wanly and tightened her fingers around his.

Matt leaned over and kissed her as gently as he could. The hospital smell was predominant in the room but, being close, he could smell her. She always smelled like a sea breeze to him, fresh and necessary.

'Your mam's here,' he said, nodding towards Rose. 'She's pretty tired.'

Becky looked at her mother and sighed. Matt leaned close again, touching his cheek to hers, and when she spoke again the question was whispered like a secret.

'What happened to Dad?'

He drew slowly back and held both her hands.

'He's dead,' she said.

He nodded.

Her eyes filled and tears spilled over onto her cheeks, but her face didn't crumple. She was paper-white, but calm.

'How did you know?' he asked.

Her eyes glazed. She was looking through him to a memory.

'He was already dead when he touched the baby.'

Matt was finally asleep in the chair and Becky and Rose had been quietly talking. Matt's head had fallen to one side and his mouth was open. He didn't usually snore unless he'd been to the pub, but he was snoring now. He was exhausted. Becky was exhausted herself, so much so that her limbs felt heavy. With Rose helping, she moved her legs out over the edge of the bed, glad that they obeyed her instructions. Inching forward, feeling sore inside and out, she carefully stood and waited, Rose supporting her. The room swayed gently but settled back into its normal steady state, so she took a chance on moving. Immediately, the cannula in her arm pinched as she pulled against it. Rose let her go and grasped the IV pole. She nodded at Becky and lifted the pole as they moved forward in unison. Becky averted her gaze from the bag of blood. The bag was half empty and it was almost worse than when it was full, because drips and channels of blood ran down the creases in the emptying bag, like a stream splitting and rejoining the main course as it ran down the side of a cliff on the island.

Matt stopped breathing, then started again with a snort and a sigh. They waited until his breathing settled back into a rhythm before moving again. Once in the corridor, linking arms, with Rose rolling the IV, they headed slowly towards the lifts. The night-time wards were in twilight and the white light of the nurses' station ahead hurt Becky's eyes. The station was deserted and they plodded slowly by without incident.

There was one more private room before they were out onto the landing and the lifts. As they approached, the door opened and a child looked out. A girl, no more than ten, wearing a cheery oversize T-shirt draped to her knees. Her hair was gone and she was frighteningly thin. Her shinbones were like barely covered blades. Her skin was yellow and her head looked too heavy for her neck to hold.

Becky stopped and the three of them studied each other.

'Are you OK, lady?' the girl asked.

Becky felt tears sting and she nodded. 'I'm OK. Do you need a nurse?'

The girl shook her head. 'I just wanted ...' She stopped and made a helpless gesture.

Becky was trying to figure out how to give her a hug when Rose wrapped her arms around the girl. There were no tears or hitching breaths. There was just the birdlike girl, made of bones, and Rose, motherly as always. Becky put her free arm around the pair.

She wasn't sure which of them took more comfort from the hug, from the break from the night and the darkness, but it was brief, a tiny human moment, over too quickly.

The girl straightened and looked up at them, before silently turning and going back inside, closing the door softly. She left a smell behind her and Becky suddenly knew what it was. It was the smell of death and it was coming from the girl's breath and her skin, her life force yellowed and leaving her. Becky remembered it because she had last smelled it coming from her father on the bench. She shared a look with Rose and saw tears in her eyes.

A wave of weakness swept through her and she swayed against Rose, who threw an arm about her and supported her until it passed. Then they linked arms again and shuffled on.

They reached the lifts and made their way down into the depths of the hospital until they saw the sign they wanted. *Mortuary*.

The doors to the outside were open and there was a hearse out there, waiting for someone. The mortuary doors were open too and they could hear someone moving about somewhere close by. They went inside where the bright merciless lights shone on the great metal drawers and the clean examination tables.

An orderly approached them.

'You shouldn't be in here. Did you get lost? What ward are you on?'

Becky shook her head. 'We want to see my dad.'

'Sorry, can't do that. Come on, I'll take you back upstairs.'

He reached a hand out to take Becky's elbow, but she grabbed the hand instead.

'I nearly died having my baby. My father is in here in one of your horrible drawers. I'm not going to get to see him again and I won't go without screaming and pulling this out of my arm.' She rattled the IV pole. Her voice sounded husky and she suddenly had an image of how she must look. Her hair was always crazy after sleeping and she was wearing the giant nightgown that Matt had bought in a panic.

She saw that the orderly recognised that she was serious. There was something about him that was familiar. Some twist of his lips or the colour of his eyes.

Rose stepped forward and the orderly seemed to notice her properly for the first time. His expression changed.

'That's right, Tom Murphy, I know who you are and I've known your family long enough to know plenty about you. Now, just let us do what we need to do, and no one has to be any the wiser.'

He cast a glance over his shoulder and then up at the security camera, before moving Becky back a couple of steps, using her own grip on his hand. She grasped his fingers hard, finding the strength to squeeze. He was an islander. With the name, she suddenly saw who he was. Andrew's son, AJ's brother. He somehow looked different in the cold light of the mortuary.

As she looked at him, he seemed to waver.

'Don't change your mind,' she said. 'We have to do this.'

Without a word, he tore his hand loose and walked away without waiting for them to follow. He went to the back of the room and turned the lights down to their minimum. He went to a drawer and pulled it out, checking the toe-tag briefly.

Rose gripped Becky's hand hard and together they moved closer to the drawer in a world that had suddenly lost all sound and colour.

Frank was lying in perfect stillness, his eyes closed. Becky watched him carefully and eventually let out a breath she hadn't known she was holding.

Rose let go of her hand and leaned in closer to the body.

Tom came around by her father's feet and took Becky's elbow.

'Alright? Come on, let's get you back upstairs. You need a cuppa. Both of you. This is no good to anyone.'

Becky nodded. He was right. She did need tea, or anything hot with sugar in it. She felt hungry and sick at the same time. Her father wasn't like the bald little girl. His skin wasn't yellow and tired. He looked like he had done in pictures of them together when he was still fishing, when his hair was thinning but still there, when his eyes were a sharper blue. Those eyes were brilliant, sharp blue crystals.

And they were looking right at her.

Becky stared back into her father's eyes. A flood of relief washed through her. Her heart had known that there was something terribly wrong with him. Her unborn baby had known it. The knowledge had almost killed them both. Her nightmares had been full of it. For a brief moment, she was just glad that she wasn't mad.

'That's enough. I'll get in trouble. You have to leave.'

When she found her voice, it was a hoarse whisper.

'He's ... *look at him!*' she hissed.

The man looked at the body. His expression didn't change,

but Becky felt a tremor run through him as though there were wriggling snakes under his skin. His hand dropped from her elbow.

'I'm locking up. Either leave now or stay in here for the night.'

'His eyes are open. He's looking right at us.'

Tom shook his head and when Becky looked again her father's eyes were closed and he looked like a waxwork, lifeless and cold.

Rose made a small noise and Becky looked at her. Rose's eyes were blazing. A feverish red had mottled her cheeks.

'I knew it wasn't right,' she said. 'You did too, Becky. This – this thing is not your father, not my Frank.'

'C'mon, Mrs. Tierney, you're tired,' Tom said. 'You should both go back now.'

'Mam?'

Rose shook her head and Becky thought that she was going to refuse.

Instead, she looked again at the body and shuddered.

'Tom, I don't know what this is, but you do. All you bloody men do. Just tell me you'll take care of it. You'll finish this and – and let my Frank rest.'

He didn't answer and just looked down at his feet, miserable. There was nothing more to be said, so they let him lead them to the door.

Once outside, with the door closed, he turned to them.

'Go on to bed now. Try to get a bit of sleep.'

He looked at Becky, his eyes kinder than they had been.

'Go back to the island and look after your boy.'

They made their way to the lift doors and Becky pressed the button. When the doors opened, she glanced back and saw him staring into the mortuary, not moving.

The others came back from the van and stood beside Tom at the mortuary doors.

'They're gone?' one said.

Tom nodded. 'You'll have to take him. He's not dead.'

'They said that this would never happen again.'

Tom looked sharply at his cousin. 'Well, Mick, it bloody has and now we have to clean up the mess.'

Mick glanced at his brother. 'It's not *we* though, is it, Tom? It's me and John who have to do it. You're staying here.'

'Someone has to,' Tom said.

John, the stockier of the two, pushed Tom aside and shouldered open the doors of the mortuary.

'Whatever. We might as well get on with it. Mick, get the trolley.'

Being quick and careful, they worked together to load the van, and Tom stood in the bright cold corridor watching his cousins drive away with their cargo. He shuddered, glad he had the excuse of having to stay behind. He didn't envy the terrible duty that awaited the others.

They drove in silence for a while. Mick broke it first, clearing his throat. The sound was shocking. John twitched, his hands gripping the steering wheel as though welded to it.

'Sorry,' Mick said. He twisted in his seat to look in the back.

'Everything OK back there?'

'Yeah. Maybe it won't be too bad.'

John glanced at him. 'I wouldn't bet on it.'

That was enough to still any further conversation.

When they pulled in at the back of the funeral home, they got out of the van and went to the back doors.

'John?'

'Yeah?'

'What would happen if we just left it here and caught the next plane to America?'

John thought about it. 'Well, this fella wouldn't stay put

and he'd cause a fair amount of trouble.'

'But we'd be thousands of miles away.'

'True,' John said. 'We could go somewhere sunny, where the girls don't have to wear a lot of clothes.'

'Hawaii?'

John shook his head. 'No way. No more islands.'

Mick sighed and looked at his brother once more before pulling the back doors open.

John didn't want to show his brother how scared he was, but cold sweat had gathered in greasy beads on his forehead. The back of his short hair was wet. He and Mick had been told that no one had had to do this for a long time. That it would never happen again because they had everything 'under control'.

Sometimes they had to tidy up a corpse before sending it on. Mostly, there was nothing left to tidy and the bodies didn't reach them, but instead went to join the others underneath the blowholes on the island.

But they had made a blood promise that if this ever happened they would deal with it. It had sounded almost cool when they were eighteen and nineteen. Like an Xbox game. It was bloody different now, standing in the night-time funeral parlour back room, with plastic spread over the floor and with them wearing clear plastic coveralls and goggles.

Although he was a year older, Mick was waiting for him. John nodded, and a bead of sweat dropped from his forehead onto the body bag. He couldn't bear the sight of it. It ran down the mound made by Frank's shoulder. John fumbled at the zip but got it on his second try and opened it all the way down.

A smell arose from the bag. It was a dry smell, quite pleasant. John puffed his cheeks out. He didn't want it in his lungs. Mick pulled the bag edges apart, showing Frank's face.

He looked good. Fresh.

'They found him on the rocks?' Mick said.

'Yeah.'

'He looks pretty good then.'

Frank opened his eyes and they both yelled and jumped backwards.

'*Fuck!*' John said. '*Quick!*'

Mick grabbed the saw and looked at it blindly.

John pushed him away and took up the big knife. The blade was going into one of those blue eyes. He raised it above his head with both hands and paused. A warm feeling came over him and the strength ran out of his arms. Frank's eyes were so blue. He was just lying there, looking at him. John pitied him. He hadn't asked for any of this. Frank and Rose were just ordinary people living their lives and selling souvenirs to the tourists.

Frank's grandson had just been born. He hadn't even got to see him. It was such a shame. After all, Frank was an islander too. He put the knife down and Frank smiled at him. Such a nice kind smile.

Pain exploded in his cheek as Mick punched him and he staggered sideways.

The thing on the gurney hissed.

'*What the hell, Mick?*'

'*John, wake the fuck up! Don't look at him!*'

John blinked. His brother's punch had made him bite the inside of his cheek and he hastily swallowed the blood rather than spit it out. He gripped the knife and plunged it into Frank's chest. Frank belched, releasing a rusty-smelling bubble of spit and blood. Then, to John's horror, he laughed and showed his gums. His false teeth must have come out at some point. The gums weren't entirely bare though. White needles of bone had started to poke through, top and bottom. They were made for piercing, not tearing or grinding.

With his stomach roiling, he grabbed the axe and without hesitation brought it down on Frank's neck. He missed and his feeble blow glanced off a collarbone and bounced off. He looked in desperation to his brother, who was crying.

Mick picked up a second axe and struck, slicing Frank's throat and chin, causing a gout of blood to arc into the air. John jumped back but surged forward again. In a mixture of horror and desperation, he hacked at the throat until he severed the spinal cord.

Frank's hands came up and clamped on John's wrists, and the pressure was monstrous. Mick tried to pull the gripping fingers open and, once more, John met Frank's gaze. The blue of his eyes was fading, replaced by pale pupils that had stared out over a thousand seas. His hair greyed and his skin sagged. The deathly grip on John's wrists loosened and Frank's hands fell away. For a moment before life passed away from him, Frank's eyes blinked once and each shed one perfect teardrop, inside of which swirled a taint of blood. Then he was gone.

Panting, John turned to Mick and they clung to each other for a long time.

When they were able, they cleaned away the mess and stood together for the last duty. John was grateful when his brother took the brick from his hand.

Quietly, awkward from lack of practice, they said the Lord's Prayer.

Then Mick began to try to wedge the brick between the corpse's jaws. When it wouldn't go, John got the hammer and struck a blow. The sharp teeth (were they longer?) snapped into jagged edges.

The worst moment came when the lower jaw crunched and then snapped, and the brick plunged into the mouth.

Mick jerked his hand back with a cry.

The teeth had scraped the skin but not broken it. Mick laughed nervously and covered his mouth.

'C'mon, one more thing and we can go home,' John said.

They moved the body to the coffin and screwed the lid on tight, four screws in all, two either side, and then got the hell out of there.

Eleven

How good and thoughtful he is; the world seems full of good men – even if there are monsters in it."

Bram Stoker, *Dracula*, 1897

Ed got up early and found Harry already in the kitchen, having breakfast.

'Morning, Ed. You look terrible. That eye – all the colours of the rainbow, huh? Painkillers are on the dresser.'

'Thanks,' Ed said, taking two paracetamol from the foil. He swallowed the tablets with a mug of strong, milky tea.

'Help yourself to toast,' Harry said.

'No, thanks,' Ed said.

'Most important meal of the day, my mother always said.'

'True. Listen, Mr. Crowe – Harry. Thanks for letting me stay.'

Harry nodded and crunched toast.

'I'm going to the farm to feed the animals,' Ed said. 'I don't want Lia to come, in case …'

He looked at Harry, seeing understanding in his eyes, and kindness but no pity. He was glad of it.

'Right,' Harry said. 'Give me one minute.' He stood up and dumped his dishes on the counter. 'I'm coming with you. I can help with the animals and, sure, if your father is there, I can help with him too.'

'You don't need to.'

A strange expression crossed Harry's face. 'I do. Give me a minute.'

Ed said nothing more. He was grateful that Harry was coming. It wasn't just that he was a big man and knew Dan well. Ed just kept thinking about the potato knife. If his father came at him again, he wasn't sure what might happen.

'Come on then. I don't know my niece very well yet, but I'm betting she won't be told to stay behind if she catches us,' Harry said with a grin.

Ed smiled. 'I don't know her that well yet either, but I think you might be right.'

Ed was a good walker but, stiff and hurting, he had some trouble keeping up with Harry whose long strides covered the ground effortlessly. They stopped only once, to let Andy Carroll's truck go by, full and fragrant, with some cattle in the back.

Ed knew there was something wrong before he got near the house. The animals were too quiet. He hurried past Harry and started to run.

The shed was empty, gates standing wide. Straw and cow dung littered the yard. Ed rushed to the pig pen. The sow was gone as well. Someone had opened the chicken house and the fox had been. There was blood on the wood.

Harry stood beside him and looked at the empty roosts.

'What did he do?' Ed said.

'I was talking to Andy yesterday. He didn't say anything about going across with cattle,' Harry said.

Ed turned to look at him.

'He sold the animals to Andy? Why would he do that?'

'I don't know, Ed. I'm hoping it was only the animals.'

Ed felt like Harry had put his hand inside him and twisted everything in there. 'What do you mean?'

'I'm not sure. Look, let's go into the house. I thought he went across, but maybe he didn't.'

Feeling empty, Ed walked with Harry across the yard. The kitchen door was open. Ed stepped in as though into a stranger's house. The kitchen was still a mess. He went through into the sitting room. Dan was asleep on the couch with an empty bottle of whiskey on the carpet beside him. His mouth was hanging open and he had dribbled. His arm had slid off the couch and his loose fingers were touching stapled sheets of paper. Even from a few feet away, Ed could see his father's scrawled signature.

Ed started towards him, but Harry held him with a firm hand on his arm.

'Ed, if I were you I'd want to kill him. But that would be the last and worst thing he could do to ruin your life even more than he has already. I won't let him do it. We should have put a stop to it years ago. That's our fault, but I won't let him pull you down with him.'

Ed tried to yank his arm away, but Harry tightened his grip.

'Let me go,' Ed said through gritted teeth.

'I won't. I know I'm hurting your arm, but there are worse things.'

Ed tensed, ready for a fight.

Harry shook his arm sharply.

'Look, Ed, I'm no one's dad, but you need someone to be a dad now and it isn't him so it's got to be me. Get the hell outside and let me deal with this. It's for the best.'

'People always say that when they're doing horrible things,' Ed said.

Harry nodded. 'That's probably true.'

Ed waited for something else, some justification why he should obey but Harry didn't say anything, just waited calmly, with his fingers biting into Ed's arm.

'Fine,' Ed said.

'OK. Good lad. I'm going to let your arm go now, but I'm quick, so don't decide to go anywhere other than the door.'

Harry let his arm go and Ed felt it tingle as blood started to flow properly again. He stared into Harry's eyes, thinking. Harry waited him out and Ed knew he meant what he said. He looked over at his father. The rage had settled anyway. Now all he felt was disgust, and sadness for his mother. At least she wasn't here to be hurt by him anymore. He sighed, feeling exhausted, and without a backward look walked out of the house.

He kicked around the yard, trying not to look at the silent, empty pens. Facing away, he found himself looking at the Hall. Its blank expression showed only indifference. Or the wax-like coldness of a corpse's face. When Harry's hand dropped onto his shoulder, he bit his lip in the effort to keep from screaming.

Lia had slept late and after a trip to the bathroom had immediately phoned her mother in New York. As she expected, Jasmine's voice had been muffled by sleep, but Lia hadn't been able to wait longer. She had woken with the conviction that she had to speak to her mother straight away. They had each shed a few tears and apologised. For the first time in a year, Lia said 'I love you, Mom' before she hung up. It had been years since she had even called her mother anything but Jasmine, but it rose naturally to her lips now. Her voice hoarse with tears, her mom had told her that she loved her too.

After a shower she got dressed and went downstairs, bracing herself to face Harry and Ed after yesterday's traumas. But there was no sign of them, and Rose told her they had gone to check on the Wrays' farm.

Lia set about making a large fried breakfast, or brunch

rather – it was nearly lunchtime. She'd eaten hardly anything the day before, apart from the lovely breakfast Harry had made her in the morning.

She ate, thinking about the call to her mother. Still tearful, she found herself repeatedly dabbing her eyes with a sheet of kitchen roll. Her mascara was waterproof and hopefully would stay put. After brunch she ran back upstairs to freshen the tinted moisturiser she had applied to mask the shadows under her eyes. Glancing out the window before she went back down, she saw Harry and Ed coming, still a little distance away.

Harry was tall and imposing. Seeing them together, Lia realised that Ed was taller than she remembered somehow. He was thinner than Harry but his shoulders suggested that his lanky frame would fill out.

She checked her reflection in the mirror again, added some lip gloss and ran downstairs.

They came in the back door. She was taken aback at the sight of his battered face but then he looked at her and it felt like there was some electric connection between them. Harry said something she didn't hear. She nodded and before she could second-guess herself, took Ed's hand and led him through the still-open back door.

Ed's hand grasped her hand tightly.

'Where can we go?' she said.

'The beach beyond the village. C'mon.'

He started walking rapidly and purposefully as if whatever excitement had invaded her must have infected him, but beyond the village he slowed a little and she realised he must still be hurting from yesterday's injuries.

They reached the path leading down to the beach and climbed down.

Then Lia threw herself into his arms and without hesitation or nerves they were kissing. She couldn't have said who started it. Maybe they both did, filled with a stew of emotions from the last few days.

The kisses Lia had shared with her two short-lived boyfriends were a summer breeze compared to the storm now enveloping her. The electricity between them was a thunderstorm, a deep blue-black lit from within by forks of lightning. She barely knew where she was, but her arms were locked around his neck and his were wrapped around her waist, so wherever the storm brought them, they would cling to each other, flotsam, an island of their own, separated from the rest of the world.

Suddenly, Ed stopped and, taking her by the hand, strode across the sand towards the cliff face. She watched his face as they went. It was serious, almost stern. He led her into a shelter made of rock and she felt an easing of the cold wind off the sea. It was not a cave, but maybe the start of one.

Feeling both brave and natural, she leaned against the rock face behind her and waited.

'Lia,' he said hoarsely.

A shadow of sadness crossed his face, but he stepped closer and kissed her again as though he were hungry. After some unknowable time, they stopped by some unspoken understanding. Ed took off his jacket and spread it on the ground. They sat on it together, necessarily close. Ed put his arm around her and she leaned into his shoulder.

'Your lip is bleeding,' she said and kissed him gently, tasting the rusty tang of his blood.

He pulled out a tissue and pressed it against his lips as they watched the sea foaming against the base of the Chimneys and the wheeling gulls riding the air currents above them.

Ed sighed and she felt his chest rise and fall and marvelled at such a simple thing that had meant nothing yesterday. Today, it was a miracle. She wanted to take in every small movement he made, every flash of feeling to cross his emotive face.

'Dan ... I mean my dad ... he sold the animals and maybe the farm too. All my animals.'

She twisted to look at him.

'What? How?'

'Our neighbour Andrew got him to sign something last night. He's been trying to get him to sign for years. I suppose he had the paperwork ready. And Dad was drunk of course.'

'If he was drunk, would it void the sale?' Lia asked, kneeling up to face him.

Ed shrugged. 'I don't know. I don't really care about the land, or the house if it's gone. I want a different kind of life. It's just this last long while ... since before my mam died ... I've been looking after the animals.'

He looked into her eyes.

'They were the only friends I had. Everyone else went away to college or jobs off the island – most of them were from fishing families anyway.'

He paused and touched her hair, brushing it away from her face.

'It's hard here during the winter,' he said. 'Are you really staying?'

For an answer, Lia leaned forward and kissed the bruises on his face. Feeling like she was dreaming, both herself and not herself, she kissed the corner of his mouth avoiding the cut. His hands came up, one slipping under her hair to touch the back of her neck, the other unbelievably warm against her back.

They lay down and stayed there, lying against each other, kissing, with the sound of the seagulls and waves for music.

Twelve

There is no excellent beauty that hath not some strangeness in the proportion.

Francis Bacon, 'Of Beauty' in *Essays*, 1625

Dan opened his eyes and there was no difference. He blinked and dozed off again. Next time, there was a bit of moonlight in the sky and he was able to make out that he was in the sitting room on the couch. He couldn't move his feet and when he tried to move his arms, pain made him groan. Both hands were dead and he had to spend a long time wriggling his fingers to make feeling come back into them. Extreme pins and needles made tears come to his eyes. When the pain eased a bit, he tried to sort things out.

He was tied, hands and feet. His hands were tied in front which was some small mercy. Had they been under him, he would have been screaming by now. But whoever had tied them hadn't been too gentle. Plastic cable-ties cut into his skin. Probably his own ties. A commonplace tool that any farmer or fisherman had.

He was straining his neck trying to look at his bonds, so he made himself lie back and relax, in order to think. He was surprised at his own calm. He didn't even want a drink.

He was trussed up in his own sitting room. Listening carefully to the heartbeat of the house, he reckoned he was alone. There was a feeling about a house when it had other people in it.

And hadn't he driven Ed out? Images from the night before started to edge back in from the shadows. He remembered Andrew's kitchen, signing papers. He had given it all away, except the house itself. Andrew hadn't wanted it, or he might have lost that too. The money they agreed on was fair. Andrew wouldn't have anyone saying otherwise. But that didn't matter. The land was still lost. What good was money?

Dan groaned again. How would he tell Ed what he had done? He cried again and dozed again.

He awoke to the knowledge of who had done this to him. They must have been here while he was out cold. Panic started to eat at the edges of his earlier calm, a calm which the bottle of whiskey Andy had given him had helped maintain. They would be back, he knew.

They were, not his friends exactly, but important. A sob escaped Dan's cracked lips. He started to struggle and flop. He rolled off the couch, trying to take the fall with his shoulder. Once down, using the heavy old couch as support, he managed to get into a sitting position. If he could get to his feet, he might be able to hop to the kitchen and find a knife.

As he was winding himself up to make the first effort, he heard the back door open. Terror swept through him and he was distantly aware that warm whiskey-smelling pee was making a pool under him.

A tall figure stepped into the room, standing aside to let others enter.

'Hey, boys, how're ye doin'?' Dan said.

No one answered.

'Now there's no need for any of this,' he said. 'Everything is going to be grand. I'll go off the drink and I'll be as right as rain.'

He paused but still no one spoke.

'Honest, boys. I'll do anything. I'll … I'll go away even. Ed can have the house. I don't care about it. It's not been the same since Patty died anyway. I haven't been the same. You know that, you know I –'

'*Shhh*, Dan.' Andrew's voice held a trace of his sour humour.

This terrified Dan more than anything else.

'No, Andy, don't do it. Please. Please don't. Put me on the ferry in the morning. I'll go to my cousin in Dublin. I won't ever come back, not ever. Please.'

Andrew moved closer in the dark room and the others followed.

'Aw, Andy,' Dan said, hearing the tears in his voice, 'just put the light on, let me see your faces. Please. It's too dark. Let me talk to you.'

Andrew paused and seemed to look back. Someone flicked the light switch and although the bulb was dim and flickering, Dan had his wish and saw their faces.

He recognised the expression. He had worn it himself. Grim, sad and determined. He began to cry in earnest, great painful sobs that made snot run down his face.

'Where's Harry?' he sobbed.

'It was Harry who found you. He has left us to deal with you as we see fit.'

Dan kept up a stream of pleas, unable to stop himself. Hands grabbed him under the arms and hauled him upright. Instead of cutting the cable ties securing his feet, someone else, Brendan he thought, lifted his legs off the ground. Without a word, they carried him from the relative safety of the house into the night air. It was colder tonight than it had been, and he couldn't tell whether it was the air or horror that made his skin contract and shiver.

He didn't know what he was saying anymore, but he knew

where they were taking him and he started to struggle. Two of the others stepped in and helped hold him. He was tired and his wrists felt slick as his struggling caused the plastic ties to cut more cruelly into his skin – but he couldn't give up.

He heard the lock and chain fall away from the gate to the Hall and made one final, desperate effort to get away from the hard hands that held him. They almost dropped him and he began to beg for it.

'*Drop me, please! Throw me over the cliff! I'll go with Frank and ... and Will. Just please, please, don't!*'

They hoisted him more securely and walked on, the old gravel of the drive crunching under their feet in the darkness. Dan fell silent. Once they had crossed the threshold of the gate, the air felt different. The driveway was long, but not long enough.

The men stopped and Dan heard someone unlocking the big doors of the Hall.

In a whisper, Dan started to plead again.

'*No, boys, no, I'm one of you. Don't, please don't put me in there. I can't. I can't. I can't face it. Not this way, please.*'

But, as though they were not human, they carried him in and set him down on the tiles of the hall. There was a faint light falling from the top of the stairwell. The others hurried outside, leaving Andy standing over him.

'We had a problem because of the weather. And then we had a problem with you. We can't let you drive Ed away. This solves both problems. You can understand that, can't you?'

'Andy, there's another way, there must be. I'll fix it. I promise. Only don't leave me here. You can have the house as well. I'll sign more papers.'

'It's too late,' Andy said, glancing upwards.

'Oh God, please, knock me out. Kill me. Don't leave me. It'll be like Frank for me. It's different now, you know it is.'

Andy leaned down and Dan's chest filled with terrible hope that quickly fled, leaving him with nothing but mad terror.

'It's better if I don't cut you free, Dan. Running won't help.' He put a hand on Dan's arm. 'We'll take care of Ed. And keep the grave clean.'

Andy straightened and was about to leave before he remembered something. He smiled. 'Oh, and thanks for the farm. Just in time, eh?'

He turned and went outside, walking almost slowly.

Even with the faint light from above, the tiled hallway seemed darker when the big doors swung closed and left Dan alone. He shut his eyes. He didn't want to see. Instinctively, he remained completely still and silent, although he longed to scream. Maybe if he didn't move until dawn, he might …

A dry sound came from somewhere above him. It was the sound a bird made when it roosted in the roof timbers of the barn. A dry brush of dusty wings in a dark corner. Dan held his breath. The sound came again, followed by a movement of air and a thump on the tiles somewhere near him. Footsteps moved closer, each step matched by sharp clicks.

Talons. The clicks are because of the talons.

When it came, somehow Dan didn't scream. The sound was too big to get out. Instead, he went to whatever awaited him accompanied only by wet sounds and, somewhere distant, the cry of a gull, shocked out of sleep.

Dan became aware of light. He didn't want to open his eyes yet. He was snuggled somewhere toasty warm, sleepy warm. Someone had freed him from his bonds. He curled himself tighter, stretching his back before relaxing again. Where his skin was bare, he could feel softness, layers of it, nestling him. He drifted away into a kind of half sleep, half dream.

When he woke a second time, the warmth had changed. He no longer felt alone in softness. There was something else there. He was afraid to open his eyes, but he felt a brief sensation against his cheek, a butterfly touch. It occurred to him that the sensation might have been created by lips moving lightly across his skin.

The moment he thought it, the sensation came again, but this time it was a press of lips against his cheek, moving slowly to kiss the corner of his mouth, drifting over his chin and lower to his throat.

He suddenly found it hard to catch his breath. He longed to turn to whoever was pressing sweet kisses to his neck, soft lips against strong teeth, but he couldn't move. Although he had stretched earlier, now he couldn't move at all. He deliberately tried to move his fingers but they wouldn't obey his command. It was frightening but, as the kisses against his pulsing throat became more insistent, he gave himself up to both the fear and the desire. He was helpless to resist and he didn't want to.

Although he couldn't open his eyes, light must have been shining directly on his face, because he could see the veined red of his own eyelids. His breath seemed loud. He couldn't be sure it was his.

A flash of pain became all mixed up with pleasure and his eyes finally opened. The light was bright but not warm. Cobwebs or lace floated across his vision, clouding everything. He didn't have the words for it. Patty had been the one for reading.

He started to slip away again. His eyelids were heavy and he knew that he would lose the fight to stay awake and aware. There was white skin, long soft hair, a drift of something like feathers. He made one final effort against the pleasure and the drowsiness and opened his eyes wide. The sensations stopped and he saw intense, glittering eyes, incredibly beautiful. His body responded, as did his heart. It was like looking into an eclipse. If he kept staring, the image of brilliant light and profound darkness would blind him. He closed his eyes and gave himself up.

Thirteen

How blessed are some people, whose lives have no fears, no dreads; to whom sleep is a blessing that comes nightly, and brings nothing but sweet dreams.

Bram Stoker, *Dracula*, 1897

Lia leaned on the window and looked out into the fresh morning. Chill air pinched her cheeks. She felt a mixture of disbelief and happiness.

Although she had argued with Jasmine about going to college, she had known that she would probably go eventually, once she figured out exactly what she wanted to do. There had been a vague image of a boy whose face she couldn't make out in the back of her mind. She would meet him at college. He would be smart, probably aiming towards a career in law first and then politics. They would eventually marry and their lives would be easy, without an excess of emotion expressed in passion and rows as two opposites clashed out of frustrated love.

But now that she had met Ed, she was able to see that the misty vision of her future was just a pretty veil – that she was trying to get away from the relationship her parents had.

Ed was too tall, too odd, too deep and entirely uninterested in a normal career. They had talked for so long yesterday and been so honest that she felt she had known him for years. Unlike the imagined young man, he just wanted to take his photographs. He also wasn't sure if he could ever leave the island. He couldn't explain why to her and she could see that it wasn't just that he couldn't find the words. He didn't understand why himself. The island had a grip on his soul in some way.

After a long delicious time in the cave, they had walked up and down the beach, holding each other close, watching as the light faded from the sky, listening to the sound of the endless waves. There were silences between them that felt profound, broken by shared thoughts and memories, revealed histories and torments. He told her about his mother dying and what it had been like to look on her wax-like face after the life had passed out of her. He cried as she embraced him and the sound of his pain was swept away by the roll and hiss of waves coming towards them on the beach.

Eventually, they had to leave as the tide came in and climb back up the path with its occasional steps. Ed had taken her hand at every slippery spot and together they made it to the top without incident. Without a word, he had turned her into his arms and hugged her in a way that was not as exciting as his kisses but made her feel like they were melting together. Some part of his heart had knit with hers and later, when she was alone in her room, she began to understand why her parents had stayed together for so long. Despite their differences, they must have felt this same entwining. No matter how they pulled against each other, the bond of love was stronger and impossible to escape.

Except her father had escaped in his own way, onto the Devil's Teeth. What Lia was feeling had to be love. She had never experienced it before. It was a wild crashing of sensation, of touch and taste and hunger and a bit of insanity. Her favourite books had described love, but she hadn't expected the incredible force of it. A few days ago, she hadn't known Ed. Yesterday, her stomach was a bit flippy when she saw him, her appetite decreased when she thought of him. But someone had thrown a magic cloak over them as they lay on the cold sand and bonded them forever.

She watched boats in the distance. The sounds of the village reached her in a pleasant jingle-jangle of boats and gulls, carried on the sea breeze. She put her hands to her cheeks and felt heat. Her fingers were cold, but her face was burning. She didn't feel sick, although she could have caught a cold sitting out so long on the beach. She was burning but not from illness. This fever was born in the heart.

Her stomach suddenly dropped. What if Ed didn't feel the same this morning? What if he was sleeping soundly down the corridor, not dreaming about her? She checked her reflection in the mirror. Hot hectic patches of red made it look like she had overdone the blusher.

She quickly applied tinted moisturiser and a light brush of powder to hide behind. Unable to wait any longer, she tied up her boots and went out into the quiet corridor.

She stood listening for any sound of life and almost screamed when Ed's voice came from the stairwell.

'Morning.'

She saw her feelings shining in his honest face too and seemingly without movement they were in each other's arms. He pressed kisses into her neck, making her shiver. She clung to him and he lifted her briefly off her feet. The heat in her cheeks travelled all over her body until she felt that she was on fire. His breathing, close to her ear, was laboured. They hadn't even properly kissed yet. With obvious difficulty, he let her go, pushing her gently back against the wall, while he stepped back to his side of the corridor, putting a couple of feet of air between them.

'Hi,' she said, barely recognising her own voice.

He chuckled and the sound was infectious.

'So that's OK then,' he said. 'I was worried that you wouldn't …'

'What?' she asked.

'Wouldn't feel so keen on me this morning.' He made a rueful face.

'I … feel …' This time she stopped. She couldn't say the word yet. It was too big.

He nodded all the same. 'Me too.'

She fidgeted a bit and was almost brave enough to take the couple of steps back into his arms.

'Breakfast,' he said, possibly reading her indecision. 'Breakfast would be safer.' He grinned his crooked grin and held out his hand.

She took it, smiling. His hand was big and warm and the touch of his skin made her shiver again.

'We'll go out later but bring a coat – the weather is starting to turn,' he said, glancing out the window at the sky.

'Do you all know what the weather is going to do?'

'We get used to it, I suppose. It affects so much that we have to be ready.'

Harry greeted them, his eyes dropping to their joined hands.

'What's this?' he asked.

Lia felt heat rise to her cheeks, but Ed got there before she spoke.

'This is my girlfriend Lia.'

Her stomach fluttered at the word, and the pride in his voice.

'OK then,' Harry said. 'I think someone should make me a cup of tea. Some of us have been working half the day already.'

Lia laughed and both she and Ed set about making tea and toast. They brushed against each other as they did, and Lia suddenly found everything ridiculously funny. Her chest was full of champagne bubbles that wanted to escape. Ed waggled his dark eyebrows at her and she tried to return the gesture but her eyebrows weren't as expressive as his. He laughed good-naturedly at the faces she made trying to do it and she grinned at him, pleased.

With tea and toast inside her, Lia looked around at the table and her companions with a sense of happiness that she realised she had been missing for a long time.

Her eyes met Harry's. He was watching her, his face still, his eyes dark. Her champagne bubbles went flat at the look in those eyes. They were flat pools of unknown depth, hiding who knew what.

She glanced at Ed, more to take her eyes away from Harry than to attract his attention, but he was already watching her.

She looked back at Harry.

'Harry,' she said, 'what's wrong?'

Her uncle ran a hand over his face before leaning forward and resting an elbow on the table, looking from one to the other.

'Ed, your dad hasn't come back.'

Ed shrugged. 'I don't know where he would be, except some pub somewhere.'

'They'll be bringing Frank's body back later.' He looked at Ed. 'As the head of one of the old families, Dan should be here to help carry the coffin. If he's not here, it should be you.'

Lia frowned.

'I'm not the head though,' Ed said.

'Aren't you?' Harry asked. 'Think about it.'

Ed was about to say something, but Lia saw him hesitate. He went still as though listening. After a moment, he nodded slowly.

'You feel it, don't you?' Harry said.

Ed nodded again. To Lia's surprise, his eyes filled with

tears. He swiped them away with his sleeve before they could fall.

'Ed, what's wrong? Harry?'

'Nothing's wrong, Lia,' Harry said. 'It's an island thing. Nothing to worry about.'

'It doesn't look that way,' she replied, turning to Ed.

He took a deep breath and gave her a watery smile before asking Harry, 'What time will he be over?'

'Around one.'

'OK,' Ed said. 'Lia, could we go for a walk for a while?'

She nodded and got to her feet, leaving the used dishes on the table.

They fetched their coats in silence and went outside.

They set off along the cliff. The breeze was stiff and biting on Lia's face. She pulled a woolly hat from her coat pocket and pulled it down over her ears. Ed hadn't closed his jacket all the way up, but he didn't seem to be feeling the chill. He held her hand tightly but didn't speak – or couldn't.

Eventually, Lia couldn't stand it and asked, 'What happened, Ed? You realised something. Is it about your dad?'

'No. Sort of.' He shivered.

Lia stopped and pulled the zip of his jacket up, covering his chest. He wrapped his arms around her and rested his head on her shoulder, bending to do it. She rubbed his back, beginning to feel really frightened.

'Ed?'

She felt him sigh before he straightened up, taking her hands. The breeze was blowing his hair the wrong way, making him look oddly vulnerable.

'You know the way Harry said it was an island thing?'

She nodded.

'I never really thought about it before. Then, all at once, right there at the table, I felt ... different. It was like I suddenly knew that Dan was gone. Dad, I mean. There's no one else. I'm the last of my family.'

'But your dad will probably come back in a few days, won't he? Besides, you might have kids and they'll carry on the family name.' She blushed and felt annoyance at herself. She wasn't usually a blusher.

'It's more than that. I thought ...' He stopped again and looked around.

He let her hands go and turned around, his arms out.

'*Look at it!*' he said, raising his voice against the sharp breeze sheeting into their faces off the edge of the cliff, tasting of salt. '*It's beautiful and wicked and wild!*'

He pinwheeled, taking in a 360° view of the sea and the island.

'I always thought that I'd escape it. I had to wait until I was old enough, then Mam got sick, so I had to stay. Then, somehow, the old man made me stay. I was sorry for him, even when I hated him.'

He came back to her and put his arm around her waist.

'What happened in there was that Harry made me realise that I'm never going to escape. I don't think Dan will come back. I think he's dead. I got this feeling in my chest, like ... like someone just put a cement block on it.'

'Ed, no one can make you stay here if you don't want to. Look, come back to New York with me. You can take photographs of the city. There are lots of birds, I promise.'

He shook his head. 'You don't understand,' he said, not unkindly. 'It's not that anyone is going to make me stay. They don't have to. Like Harry said, it's an island thing.'

He gave her a sad smile and bent to kiss her. It tasted like goodbye.

Rose walked down the ramp of the ferry, vaguely aware that AJ was holding her elbow. She said thank you as he let her go and turned to go back up the ramp. This late in the year, she had been his only passenger and she was glad. She hadn't told anyone she was coming back and there was no one to meet her. The undertaker was bringing the coffin later and she was expected to arrive with it, in a car provided by the funeral home. She hadn't wanted that. She wanted to be back on the island before her dead husband was returned. She wanted just a few hours before it became the place where her husband was buried.

AJ had done her a favour coming over early with just her aboard. He was a softer man than his father. Andrew might be descended from one of the original families, but AJ had his mother's mainland blood in him. The ferry was the perfect job for him, travelling between both worlds.

She wiped her face with a tissue. Despite herself, tears rolled down her cheeks. She didn't even feel like she was crying. The tears just rolled from some interior reservoir like the sea, without command or obstruction.

The men on the island thought they controlled everything. Rose didn't know the full story but she knew enough, especially after seeing Frank. Maybe the other wives didn't but Rose had spent enough time in the bar, serving drink to men who thought they were whispering, to have picked up some words here and there. Unlike some, she also knew how to keep her mouth shut.

The baby changed everything. Rose hoped she would have time to mourn Frank properly but, right now, all that mattered was Becky and her infant son. In the long hours of waiting while her daughter was getting blood and recovering, Rose had had plenty of time to think.

She didn't have a plan so much as a mission. She was going to put an end to this before her family came back here, or they weren't coming back. In the middle of the night, she had made Becky tell her what had happened, even though she didn't want to.

There had been something wrong with Frank the night she had come home from visiting Becky. She had known it at the time and Becky had known it when she met him at the bench the next day. Neither of them believed that Frank was still the person they had known. She supposed the men would take care of things as they had in the past. They would all be there to take charge of the coffin. Brendan, Jim and Evan would already have dug the hole and Harry would have made the rest of the arrangements. All the family would have to do is stand there and watch the ground close over the coffin and that would be the end of Frank. But Rose knew in her blood that there was something more. There were no words for it, but the whisper of her island blood as it ran through her veins, pumped by a mother's heart, knew that there was danger beyond words. Someone or something had killed her husband and made him as he was now. And there was only one place on the island where that something could be.

Fourteen

Loneliness will sit over our roofs with brooding wings.

Bram Stoker, *Dracula*, 1897

Jasmine snapped awake, feeling someone shaking her. She sat up and put on the light, wide-eyed, confused. She was alone. Ash had wanted to stay over. He always did, but she wouldn't allow it. When they spent the night together, it was always at his apartment, never the house she had shared with Will. Yet when she woke, she expected to see someone. If not Ash, then who?

'*Will,*' she said aloud into the empty bedroom.

The sound seemed to echo through the room, out into the hall, down the stairs, around the kitchen, his study, the living room, searching through the empty silent house for someone who was not there and would never be there again.

'*Will,*' she said again, her voice feeling like a knot in her throat.

She had cried since her husband had died, had cried when he left and many times over their topsy-turvy marriage. These tears were different. They tore loose from whatever mooring she had constructed in her heart and swept over her, a tempest of agony and despair. She wept until the bed cover across her knees was wet, until her sobs had become gasps and her heartbeat sounded in her head, a relentless, painful thump.

Oh, if she could have him back, she would tell him ... what? What would she say? Sorry, yes. I love you, yes, but it wasn't enough. She had given up because he was too hard, and now there could be no forgiveness. Sorry was not enough to reverse the loss of a man such as him, to take back the hurt, the sharp words, even the passion of love that had hurt both of them.

And what was left now? She was alone in a house too big for one. Her husband was in the ground, her child three thousand miles away on a cold island with winter coming, and the man who wanted to be with her was probably sleeping, dreaming of charts and figures. Jasmine shook her head. Ash was a good man. He hadn't liked being the other man, but now that Will was gone he had settled into being a lovely boyfriend, sensible, kind, stable. It was unfair of her to imagine that his dreams were dull. He wasn't dull.

He just wasn't Will. Too late, Jasmine realised that her husband had been irreplaceable. Emotional, lost, quick to anger, restless, passionate and utterly, uniquely himself. She had been hiding a gaping hole in her heart and, now that she had found it, it seemed as though it would never heal. She stayed awake, rubbing salt in her wounds, thinking of all the good and bad times, looking through photographs, diaries, mementos, tormenting herself to finally discover the full pain and love that had been there all along, masquerading as polite grief, acceptable mourning and moving on. It had been a beast, hiding, and it was out now. God help her, it was out.

When dawn finally lifted the cloak of night, Jasmine took a long hot shower, scrubbing herself hard. She presented herself for inspection in front of the mirror that was usually kind to her. Red eyes, skin scrubbed almost raw, wet hair combed severely back from her face. She deserved to see herself just as she was. With all of her tricks and products removed, she looked like what she was. A lonely middle-aged woman trying to avoid her past while clinging to it like a shipwreck survivor.

She took a deep breath and sighed, making herself a little dizzy. Tying her hair back in a wet ponytail, she dressed in yoga pants, a T-shirt and one of Will's hoodies. Shoving her feet into sneakers, she grabbed her keys and ran from the house. Instead of getting a cab, she walked to Ash's apartment down town and was waiting for him on the street when he emerged from the building.

As always, he was impeccable in a dark suit, carrying his briefcase. She felt a pang of sorrow and pity when his face lit up at the sight of her. His expression changed to one of concern and, she saw, fear.

He walked slowly towards her.

'Ash, I'm sorry,' she started.

He shook his head and put an arm around her, awkwardly holding onto his briefcase.

'I've been hoping that you wouldn't decide this,' he said quietly before drawing away.

'I wasn't thinking about it before this morning,' she said.

'You were. You just haven't realised it. I was hoping that you would choose me, not him. Not Will.'

She was about to defend herself but she clamped her teeth together. He was right. She was choosing to love her dead husband over him. Maybe that would change with someone else in the future but, for now, he was right. She couldn't love him, be with him, when she was still in love with her troublesome husband.

Something had shaken her awake last night. It hadn't been a supernatural presence. It had been her own self, trying to shake sense into her. She still needed time to think things through, but she had blundered onto the truth through whatever dream she had been having.

'I'm sorry, Ash,' she said.

'It's OK. Well, it's not, but I understand. Maybe we'll meet again when you're ready.'

There was the tiniest hint of a question in his tone but she couldn't leave him dangling by that string when she had no idea what her future looked like. She shook her head, kissed his cheek and turned towards home.

'You look good without the make-up, Jazz,' he said. 'A little tired, but beautiful.'

She almost stopped. He was there offering love and comfort, just waiting to take her into his arms and worship her. But it wasn't fair to him. She would still always want her lanky, red-haired, complicated husband who had never worshipped her, but always loved her.

Fifteen

There are horrors beyond life's edge that we do not suspect,
and once in a while man's evil prying calls them
just within our range.

H.P. Lovecraft, 'The Thing on the Doorstep', 1937

Lia felt a sizzle of resentment rising in her like sap, all the way from her feet. Ed was brilliant and hot, though it made her blush again to think of it, but now he was gazing out to sea with a miserable, resigned look on his face. Words sputtered through her mind, but the sense of outrage that was bubbling closer to the surface was so big that it wouldn't let the words out. What the hell was wrong with everyone? Her father had preferred to throw himself onto the Devil's Teeth, leaving her and Jasmine behind, although she knew that he couldn't help what he had done. Now Ed was mildly accepting whatever fate he thought belonging to the island was thrusting on him. Normally she had plenty of words for an argument, especially with her mother, but this feeling was weird. Outside herself, she watched her hand come up and slap his arm as though she were slapping away a wasp. He looked at her in surprise and she turned away before he could see tears of annoyance in her eyes. She wasn't upset and she didn't want him to think that she was, or that these were weak tears. She felt like stamping her foot.

'Lia?'

She took a deep breath and turned around. When she spoke, it was through gritted teeth.

'We just found each other and maybe it's something good. We have both been through some bad crap and maybe we're starting to survive it. What is this wishy-washy *I-must-stay-here* noble garbage?'

Her voice had risen and, with it, his eyebrows. His honest, surprised face was suddenly funny to her and she laughed. He smiled uncertainly but, when she laughed harder, he joined her until they were leaning against each other trying to catch their breath.

'Ed,' Lia gasped, 'I might be hys-hysterical.' The word set her off again and the gales of their laughter joined the wind from the sea and swept away, carrying a touch of iridescence across the cold island.

After a while, they quietened and started to walk, slowly this time, holding hands.

Lia hiccupped. 'Maybe I'll try that again,' she said.

Ed waited, his eyes clear.

'I've been doing a lot of thinking,' she said, 'since Dad, you know, left, and even more since I got here. Everyone just ... reacts. My friends at school are all in college now, because it was the next thing to do. Dad ...' Lia swallowed before continuing, 'Dad came here and killed himself because it was the only thing he could think of to do. Jasmine went partying because that's what she knew how to do. Something happens and everyone reacts. I just want to ... I don't know, sit awhile, and think what I want to do. I'm all over the place at the minute, and now this!' She swung their hands. 'I want this,' she said when she saw his face. 'It's just so hard to describe. I don't just want to do the next thing that I have to do. I don't think you should either. Shouldn't we do the thing that makes us happy?'

'What is the thing?' he said.

She stopped dead and looked at him. 'I don't know yet. But I think maybe you do.'

'I know what I want to do. I always have. But it's not that easy.'

'Why? Why isn't it?'

He didn't have an answer. Instead, he dropped to his hunkers and gripped a sod of grass and ripped it from the ground, bringing a clod of dirt with it. He stood holding the cold earth.

'It's as if this has been holding me, forever. Holding Mam and Dad, and everyone on the island. It's horrible, but it's home. I have a responsibility.'

'To do what?' Lia asked.

But Ed just shook his head. 'I don't know.' He flung the clod of grass and soil towards the cliff and they watched it disappear into the cold silver air beyond the land's edge.

As though the clod had disturbed them, two seagulls swept over the cliff towards them, lifted by the updraft. They came close enough for Lia to be able to see their yellow eyes. One screamed as it passed, making her clap her hands over her ears.

Ed put his arms around her and tucked her into the warmth of his chest. Then he suddenly stumbled forward, almost falling over her.

'Ed?' Lia said.

'*What the hell?*' He put a hand to the back of his head and checked his palm. There was blood. 'A blasted seagull hit me.'

Before Lia could say anything, another gull flew over their heads, way too close. She grabbed Ed's hand and they turned towards the sea. Birds were climbing the updraft from the cliff in a stream of white and yellow. As Lia stared wide-eyed, they began to make their raucous calls. They were answered and overlapped by the sound of crows. Lia looked up and saw the dark birds circling above. It looked like they were waiting for the gulls to join them in their circle.

'Lia, that's not normal behaviour. I think we should get out of here.' Ed started to walk quickly back the way they had come, tugging Lia with him.

She threw a glance over her shoulder and pulled Ed to a stop.

'There's no time. We have to find cover.' She could barely hear her own voice, but it didn't matter. She saw the realisation in his face as he followed her gaze. A living cloud, like a storm, black edged with yellow, was roiling above them, filled with the screams and harsh cries of several species of bird.

'*Over here!*' Ed shouted. '*Run!*'

Still clinging to his hand, Lia ran. They crossed rough common pasture, making for a small hut. She couldn't look back, but she heard the sound of their wings, and as the first of them swept close over their heads she smelled the musty scent of their feathers. Ed let go of her hand to wrench the door of the hut open. He pushed her inside and struck a gull away, his blood scarlet on its white feathers.

Lia shoved herself as far back in the tiny hut as she could, rattling a shovel onto the ground and stumbling on an old bag of animal feed, which raised a cloud of mouldy dust. She coughed and buried her nose in her jacket, trying to take shallow breaths. Ed yanked her towards him and she found cold air streaming through gaps in the old timbers. There were thumps as the birds struck the sloping roof of the hut and the whole structure shook. Far from feeling safe, Lia was sure that the birds would crash through the rotting timber. Always a little claustrophobic, she began to feel sour panic rising to her throat. Ed said something, but she couldn't hear the words over the screams of the birds.

But she realised that a sound had joined the screams of the

seagulls and crows. A woman was out there, roaring against the terrible cacophony. She was getting closer and Ed turned to open the door, ready to pull her inside to relative safety. Instead, the woman slammed the door, shutting Lia and Ed back in the light-split darkness. Lia thought she heard words here and there, but mostly it was an inarticulate shriek of anger.

'*Lia!*' Ed shouted. '*Stay here, I'm going to get her! Close the door behind me!*'

He flung the door open again and ran out but stopped dead.

The woman had moved away from the hut and the birds had followed. Now, instead of attacking her, they were circling again, around and above her, black, white, touches of yellow and grey. One or two dived towards her and she swatted them away.

Suddenly the constantly moving circle of birds rose and, as though repelled from each other, split into species and groups, pairs and individuals. The crows flew, all together, inland. The gulls swept over the cliff's edge and out to sea.

Lia went to Ed and slipped her hand through his arm.

'It's Rose,' he said, his voice low.

'Why did the birds stop? So suddenly. Did you hear anything? Like a signal?'

He shook his head. 'I didn't, no. But, you're right, it was as if they were obeying a signal.'

When they were all gone, Rose seemed to sag. She was cut in several places, including a deep wound over her eyebrow. She swiped her sleeve over it and walked towards them.

'Rose?' Lia said. 'What was that?'

Rose shuddered. Ed reached out and took her arm. The woman looked about to collapse. Her face, soft and friendly a few days ago, was drawn and old. Her hair was tangled and there were chalky streaks of bird shit on her coat.

'I was going to the Hall when I saw the birds flock. I just wanted to lead them away from you, but something changed. It's like something called them off.'

Lia looked along the edge of the coast. The Hall loomed there as always. The morning had darkened.

'Why were you going to the Hall, Rose?' Ed asked, frowning.

'There's something … something going on … I don't know … something secret … but I think it's something to do with the Hall.'

'So you were going there … alone … to do what?' Ed shot an alarmed look at Lia.

'To find out …'

'I don't think going there is such a good idea, Rose,' Lia said gently.

Rose hesitated but then looked from one to the other of them. Her face softened when she looked at Lia and she nodded.

'You're right. It's not the time. Let's go back.'

Staying close together, they formed a threesome on the path back towards the pub. At some point, Lia tucked her arm into Rose's as well as Ed's and they walked to the Robin's Rest that way, linked and careful not to look behind them.

The sound of the door clicking firmly shut behind them was the nicest sound Lia had ever heard.

Harry came in, carrying a basket of logs for the fire he was making. He looked at Lia and dropped the basket onto the big hearth.

'What's happened?'

Even though they had only known each other a few days, Lia ran to her uncle and felt his strong arms go around her. Again, it was as if her father was there, holding her. She clung to him and his arms tightened around her.

'Rose, you're bleeding,' he said. 'What the hell is going on?'

151

'The birds gathered and attacked first Ed and Lia, then me. It's the island. Something about the island. You men know, you always have. I'm not blind. *Not anymore!*'

Lia felt the tension in Harry's body. He patted her back and moved away.

Rose flinched when he came close but allowed him to put an arm around her.

'Frank will be home soon, Rose. How about we get cleaned up and give him a good welcome, eh?'

At the sound of her husband's name, Rose's face turned even whiter, the streak of smeared red above her eyebrow in stark contrast to her pallor. She didn't cry, but let Harry lead her away into the kitchen.

'Ed,' Lia said, 'what's going on? What was that?'

Ed shook his head. 'The birds were acting crazy. Maybe there's a storm coming or something. They usually act funny and fly inland when the weather is going to change but I never saw them behave like that before.'

Lia blew out a breath. 'A storm? And the funeral is this afternoon?'

Ed nodded. 'Yeah, even in a storm. If people can stand up, it'll go ahead. Besides, it doesn't look ready to storm. Not yet.'

Together, they looked out at the white sky, dotted with flashes of white and dark, as the birds circled on the updrafts from the cliffs.

Lia stood at the dock wall and watched the ferry coming in. Harry and Ed were waiting at the tiny graveyard. Rose had gone back to her own house to shower and change clothes. A young priest in a long black soutane, with a square black biretta on his head, was first off the ferry, followed by the hearse, driven carefully by the undertaker's assistant. The undertaker sat in the passenger seat, face expressionless, top hat shining. A large black car, chauffeur-driven, followed. As it passed, Lia saw a big man in the back with Becky beside him. Becky looked out at Lia and frowned before recognition dawned. She nodded and Lia nodded back. She wondered if the baby was with them but couldn't see it.

There were no other cars, but plenty of people, falling in behind the slow procession. The cortege stopped outside Frank's house and Matt got out to take his mother-in-law's elbow and help her into the car beside Becky.

Lia was too far back to see any more. She trudged along slowly behind the other mourners. It felt like it was her father in the coffin waiting to go into the ground.

By the time she reached the graveyard, most of the mourners were inside among the gravestones. A small group waited by gate. She saw Harry and Ed standing by the hearse with some other men. Andrew, who had bought Ed's farm, and his friend Brendan were there, with another two she thought were called Evan and Jim. She joined the group of people by the gate.

Following the quiet instructions of the undertaker, the men slid the coffin out of the hearse and hoisted it to their shoulders. They moved slowly forward into the graveyard. The path from the road to the graveside was narrow and Lia's heart was in her mouth as she watched them manoeuvre around lichen-encrusted High Crosses.

The men lowered the coffin to the ground at the edge of the grave, positioning it on top of the two bands of yellow tape with which the coffin would be lowered into the grave.

Lia began to sense that the atmosphere was unusual. Grief she would have expected – or pity – or horror at the nature of Frank's death. This was more like tension. Rose stood staring at the coffin and her expression was unreadable and strange. It was almost as if she was waiting for something horrendous to happen.

Ed met Lia's eyes and she relaxed a little. She got as close to him as she could, and Harry gave her a little nod before looking back at the coffin.

Lia watched Harry's three-quarter profile from where she stood. He was more muscular than she had noticed when he was dressed casually. He was wearing an old-fashioned dark suit and Lia could see that his shoulders and chest were a lot bigger than her father's had been. It was easy to overlook because he was tall and long-limbed.

Suddenly Rose stepped forward. Lia gasped, having a vision of the woman throwing herself on her husband's coffin. Instead Rose confronted Harry, looking at him challengingly, her chin raised.

He returned her gaze calmly. Now the whole crowd was watching him, waiting for his reaction, but instead of looking exposed or embarrassed he appeared to be completely self-contained.

The graveyard was silent. Even the birds were still. The only sound was the constant shush and hiss of the waves against the bottom of the cliff beyond the graveyard wall.

Then Rose dropped her gaze and stepped back.

Sounding hesitant and uncomfortable, the priest began the ceremony. It was brief and the men lowered the coffin into the grave.

Lia looked at the islanders. It was the first time she had seen so many of them together. There were no children. She and Ed were the youngest there apart from Becky and her baby who was held in a chest-carrier by Matt. Becky stood in silence near her mother. She looked pale and ill. She hadn't made a sound or a move throughout the funeral, not even when her mother had confronted Harry.

Almost as soon as Lia thought about her, Becky looked up and met her eyes. It was the same look Lia had seen when the coastguard had taken her from the island. Stricken. Haunted.

Lia searched for the right word. *Dad,* she had said, over and over. *Dad.*

There was something hidden and secret here. Something fearful. Lia was suddenly convinced of it.

Lia glanced at Matt. The big man was watching Becky, Rose, the grave, the baby, trying to keep everyone in sight, protective and confused. Whatever was being hidden, he didn't know about it – but Becky did.

Dad. Dad. Dad.

Sixteen

*You must not be alone, for to be alone is
to be full of fears and alarms.*

Bram Stoker, *Dracula*, 1897

Father Benjamin O'Gorman had tea and talked to the
islanders who had gathered in the Robin's Rest, while he
waited for the undertaker to be ready to go. The undertaker,
however, then informed him that he was 'obliged to have a
few drinks' with the mourners before he left.

When he had finished his tea, Father O'Gorman slipped
out, knowing that no one would miss him.

He started to walk towards the village.

He wished he had never come here to this part of the
country. He was ashamed that he was still ringing his mother
every night out of loneliness and anxiety. He was just the
curate, thank God, but it was bad enough. Parishioners much
older than him came to him for advice about all sorts of
matters that were alien to him. He had never had a girlfriend,
or learned to drive, or even held a normal job. The parish
priest kept telling him that he had to toughen up. The old man
had spent many years in Africa and many more in a crime-
and-drug-ridden city and he had little tolerance for weakness

of any kind. Father O'Gorman, who still felt like Ben and not like Father anything, had enjoyed his studies very much, but was feeling that parish work might not be right for him. Perhaps he should enquire about a post in the seminary?

He took his missal out of the pocket of his soutane. The missal was worn and bent. When he felt anxious, it helped him to work it between his hands, rubbing the leather, ruffling the pages. He did that now as he walked, looking out at the bleak sea and the crumbling sea stacks standing between the island and safety.

He reached a bend in the road and stopped, trying to remember something. It was there, just out of reach. Quite maddening. He was sure it was important. He walked on. He hoped the undertaker would hurry along.

He found the ground under his feet quite springy. Looking down in surprise, he found that he was walking on the grass between the road and the edge of the cliff. He certainly did not want to go that way, especially as he was a little afraid of heights.

He turned around and headed back the way he had come. When he reached the pub, the lights had been put on and there was no sign of the undertaker, although the hearse was still there, shining and empty.

Father O'Gorman, who still thought of himself as Ben, slipped past the crowded pub, keeping out of the circle of light. Once away from the pub, he got back on the road and made better progress. Night hadn't fallen yet but the sky was a peculiar bruised blue like an oncoming storm.

He whistled a little to himself and felt better. The missal went back in his pocket and he began to walk with a little more confidence, not caring that the bottom of his soutane was wet from the grass and grimy from the road. He didn't go towards the graveyard. It was spooky there, another thing he couldn't admit to anyone. Ben didn't want to deal with spooky things. He didn't want to deal with the mess people made of their lives either.

His favourite thing in the whole world was sitting in a college library where the silence was like that in a church, but with books and papers all around him. He loved to gather the research and consider it for hours in the changing light until he had a good grasp of the material and could write his own paper. Doctrine, canon law, the history of the Church. Those were the matters that were precious to him.

He stopped, frowning. That was it. That was why he was so unhappy. He had a vocation, but this wasn't it. He wanted silence and scholarship. He should have joined a closed order where he could sink into old texts until it felt like he was made of paper and ink himself.

There was a big house ahead. Somehow, wrapped up in his thoughts he had gone too far, and he was walking away from the harbour, deeper into the island. It gave him the willies.

He turned sharply, about to hurry back, to pick up the skirts of his soutane and run if he had to. What time would the ferry go? Would they wait for him?

There was a girl standing in his way.

'Sorry,' he said. 'Excuse me.'

She just looked at him and didn't move. Girls made him nervous but this one was different. She looked sharp somehow. A word he had never said out loud came to him. *Predatory*. That's what she looked like. He tried to edge past her, but she turned with him and he couldn't seem to take his eyes off her. He wasn't attracted to girls. Some of the boys at school had said that he was gay, but it wasn't that. Those things just didn't matter to him. He never thought about s.e.x. at all, although it seemed to be all anyone else thought about or talked about in the confessional.

And yet, here was this girl. He felt an unfamiliar sensation in his stomach. A flutter not unlike fear, but not unpleasant.

It was her eyes, he thought. There was a look in her eyes he had never seen in a person before. Her silent study of him reminded him of something he had seen in a nature documentary. Silent, unblinking intensity. A deep consideration of him. He felt more exposed than he ever had during his training, during long bouts of confession in which he had struggled to think of sins. *Bad thoughts, cursing, pride.* In the end, he had made things up, sins they seemed to want to hear, to cleanse him of.

But this odd girl was cutting through to the heart of him. He felt a strange urge that he hadn't the strength to dismiss, because he had never had to learn that skill. Instead, he obeyed it. He flung his arms wide and looked up to the night sky, opening himself up, heart and soul, to whatever she wanted to do to him.

Seventeen

'Denn die Todten reiten Schnell.'
(For the dead ride fast)

Gottfried August Bürger, 'Lenore', 1774

After the funeral, Lia and Ed wandered back to the village. It was deserted. Even doors that usually stood open were firmly closed. A peculiar bruised light was creeping shadowy fingers over the houses.

Lia sat on the harbour wall, a place that was starting to feel like hers, and Ed sat beside her, almost touching her thigh, but not quite. She wished he would.

They had been silent on the walk to the harbour, the unpleasant atmosphere of the day still gripping them.

Finally, Ed sighed and some of the cold tension left him. He leaned closer and slung a companionable arm around her shoulders. Lia felt a little better.

'Are you OK?' he asked.

'I don't know,' Lia said, 'but I could really use a hug.'

He responded immediately, wrapping her into a warm embrace.

'I wanted one too, but I was nervous,' he said into her hair. She laughed lightly. 'Me too.'

He drew back and smiled at her. He took her hand in his and brought it to his chest. He was gazing past her, at the Chimneys, but he absentmindedly rubbed her hand with his thumb, held against his shirt. He had his jacket zip halfway down again.

They talked over the events of the day, agreeing that there had definitely been some peculiar undercurrents.

'Ed, what is going on? Remember what Rose said – about there being something hidden, something secret? I'm beginning to think she was right.'

Ed shook his head, but Lia thought she saw a cloud cross his face. It made her realise how dark it had become. With the realisation, a deep shiver ran through her.

'Ed,' she said, 'I think we should go home. It feels weird out here.'

She hopped off the wall and together they looked out to sea. The water and sky were a dark ominous grey. Behind them, the wide street that formed a sort of square was half in shadows, half in light, from the warm shards escaping improperly drawn curtains. Lia saw the blue flicker of a TV. She felt another shiver, this time of loneliness. She was suddenly aware of herself, standing with a boy she loved, but barely knew, in a remote village surrounded by steep cliffs and treacherous waters, thousands of miles from home with darkness falling way too early.

'Ed, I'm scared.'

'Come on, let's get back to the pub,' he said.

They started walking. Lia felt a building tension inside her, an almost irresistible urge to run.

'Ed,' she said, in a whisper.

'Yeah?'

'Is ... is there anyone behind us?'

His hand tightened on hers before he threw a sharp look over his shoulder, then walked faster.

The tension sharpened inside her. It hurt her chest to breathe.

'Ed?'

'Lia, don't look. Just keep walking.'

She knew at once that he shouldn't have said it. The urge to turn was impossible to resist. Before she did, however, she heard whoever *(whatever)* it was close the distance. The footsteps sounded like high heels, clicking on the flat old cobblestones of the village road. She turned, a scream rising to her throat. Ed pulled her sharply sideways, hurting her arm.

It swept over them, a hazy white like a clouded moon. Lia could smell it. It reminded her of snowy days in Central Park, a deadly cold that was lovely for those with warm clothes and places to go before the night fell.

A trail of lace and feathers moved across her face, making it hard to see and breathe. She clung to Ed's hand, briefly blind. Then his hand was gone and she was alone.

'*Ed!*' she screamed.

Then she could see again. Ed was there, staring at a girl dressed in a white gown. Lia had never seen anyone more beautiful. The girl was slender, with a perfect figure. Her face was lovely, her eyes golden. Whatever light there was seemed drawn to her, so that she was the only bright thing in a world of darkness. She tilted her head and looked first at Ed, then at Lia. Then she smiled and Lia saw that while she was still beautiful, she was also terrible.

Lia felt her bladder wanting to let go. All the little hairs on her body were stiff. A dog howled from someone's back garden and the sound was muffled, impossibly distant.

Ed put out his hand and groped for her. She grabbed him and stood close, even though it meant taking a step closer to the girl.

Again, the girl tilted her head, this time to look at their

162

joined hands. She held out her own hand, long white fingers tipped with sharp nails. Lia felt Ed move, as though to go to her. She yanked his arm, making him look at her.

A soft sound made her look back but the girl was gone. At once, the night was not as dark, as though she had released the light to return to its proper place. There was no sign left of her except for a single white feather which had fallen from her dress.

Lia caught movement from the corner of her eye.

Rose shut the door of her house and walked towards them. Together they waited for her to reach them.

Up close, Lia saw that her face was ravaged, tired and wet from crying.

'Rose?' Lia said. 'Are you OK? Where are you going?'

Rose's eyes flicked beyond Lia.

'Rose, you're not thinking of going to the Hall again, are you?' Lia asked urgently.

But Rose didn't seem to be listening. She nodded aimlessly and walked around Lia.

Lia shook her head. 'No, no, Rose, you can't go there. Let's go to the pub and get you a hot cup of tea or a hot whiskey. It's too cold out here, right, Ed?'

But Rose ignored her and walked on, slow but avid, a dark-eyed dove watching the hunting owl.

'*Mam!*'

Becky was hurrying towards them.

Rose turned around and terror animated her face.

'*Becky, get inside! Go back to the baby! It's not safe!*'

'Come with me, Mam, you shouldn't be out here either,' Becky said.

The fear in Rose's face was reflected in her daughter's. The two women stood, grasping each other's arms.

'We should all get inside,' said Lia. 'We saw someone ...' *Beautiful*, she had almost said. *Someone beautiful.*

Mother and daughter looked at her as though they hadn't seen her or Ed up to then.

'Lia is right,' Ed said. 'Let's go the Robin's Rest. Everyone is there.'

'You go, Becky,' Rose said. 'Where's Matt? Is he at home with the baby?'

'Yes, but I'm not going anywhere without you, Mam.'

Ed let go of Lia's hand. 'Becky – Mrs. Tierney – for God's sake, stop talking about it and *come with us!*'

Come with us ...

As his words died away, stillness fell over the night. Something was coming.

Lia heard the others gasp. She felt a wind ruffle her hair and looked up. She saw a flash of white in the dark, a passing moment, too fleeting to be identified, but the urge to flee and hide became too strong to resist. She ran.

Ed caught up with her, his long legs covering more ground. He grabbed her around the waist and swung her to one side. A strong force hit them and knocked them to the ground. Lia heard a scream.

Rose and Becky were standing under the last street light of the village, clutching each other. A movement too fast to see made Lia's eyes flicker. She blinked hard and saw the girl with the feathers and lace standing in the pool of light with the two women.

'*What are you?*' Becky's voice was almost a scream.

The girl moved towards her, her focus absolute.

Ed scrambled to his feet but before he could take more than a step forward, Rose shoved her daughter behind her and met the attack herself. For a moment, all Lia could see was flashing white, and a glimpse of Rose's furious face, red with anger and effort, ravaged by grief and horror, human in all its aspects, against the cold perfection of the girl. When all that flashing white was joined by a vivid splash of scarlet, all the breath left Lia's body as though she had been hit hard in the chest.

Becky's scream split the night. The unforgiving light, too strong to be emanating just from the lamp, showed every grim detail.

The girl was holding Rose's body over her arm, slight as she was. Rose was bent backwards and her despairing upside-down face seemed to be staring at Lia.

'*Lia, get to the pub!*'

The sound of Ed's voice was a shock.

Lia shook herself, feeling her stomach roll.

Ed ran towards the terrible tableau, shouting. The girl dropped Rose and turned. She was smiling.

Ed veered at the last moment and took off through the deserted village. Lia bit her lip to prevent herself from screaming after him. The girl was moving now, although not fast. Lia bolted for the lamppost where Becky was kneeling beside her mother. There was another flash of white and the girl was gone out of sight, following Ed's headlong flight.

'Becky, is she OK?'

Becky shook her head. She was holding her mother's hand.

'Rose?' Lia said.

The older woman's free hand was pressed to her neck, but blood had seeped through and settled in her knuckles and the dry patches on her skin. Her shoulder was soaked black with blood.

'Help me up,' she said, her voice small.

Between them, Lia and Becky got Rose to her feet and, one on each side of her, they started for the pub.

They had a long nervous period in the dark, but Lia knew that the girl had other interests. *Ed. Ed was out there with her. He could be hurt or ... or dead by now.* She told herself to shut up. She visualised the robin on the pub sign as if this would make it materialise faster.

At last they were walking under the robin and into the pub. They got themselves through the door and went right into the lounge. The noise stopped as everyone turned to look at them. Three women, covered in dirt and blood.

Then noise flooded back in. Harry was there, and Mrs. Glenn and lots of others. Lia felt strangely outside herself. She felt a bubble-like laughter inside and squashed it. It wouldn't just be laughter – again it would be hysteria. The others took Rose into the kitchen to deal with her injury.

Brendan was at the bar with Andrew and the two others she thought were called Evan and Jim. Those two always seemed to be together. They glanced at her as though she were the subject of conversation, which of course she no doubt was because she had burst in with an injured Rose. Yet she had the feeling that there was more to it than that. There was something odd about those two. She had noticed before how they deferred to Andrew. They seemed less like friends and more like comrades with a leader.

Lia felt as though her instincts were in charge, instead of her conscious mind. She hadn't cared one way or another about the group of friends, even at the funeral, but now she saw how they kept together and watched. After she passed them, she could feel the weight of their staring on her back. It made her feel strange. She had once been followed out of the subway by a man in a nice suit, who had a strange expression. He had watched her closely on the subway and showed no signs of moving until she got up for her stop. Then he followed her out onto the street, crossing when she crossed, stopping when she did. She had taken out her phone to ring her dad but, before she could, she spotted a police officer and hurried up to him. The businessman passed them by and hailed a taxi. Lia had stammered out a question about how to get to a street she knew well, and when she got directions that she didn't listen to, she walked fast to the corner and ran the rest of the way home. She didn't tell her parents.

Andrew's friends, or his men, or whatever they were, had that same expression on their faces. She couldn't identify it, but it made her feel bad, and scared and oddly sad.

In the kitchen, Mrs. Glenn was cooing over Rose, cleaning her up. Becky was hovering anxiously.

Harry grabbed Lia by the shoulders.

'Are you hurt?'

'No,' she said.

'Becky?' he asked.

Becky shook her head. 'I'm not hurt but someone please get Matt and the baby. They're at home.' She didn't take her eyes off her mother.

Then Mrs. Glenn moved slightly and Lia's stomach flipped. She was stitching Rose's neck with a needle and thread from the open sewing kit on the table.

'Lia,' Harry said, gesturing to her to move away, 'what the hell happened?'

'Something ... someone attacked us,' she whispered. 'Rose was protecting Becky. And, Harry, Ed led her away from us. He's still out there.'

'Come out into the hall,' Harry said and walked away, without looking to see if she was following. She glanced again at Becky and Mrs. Glenn tending to Rose before going after him.

Rose waited until Josie Glenn was finished stitching and sticking on a dressing from the pub's first-aid kit before she said anything. She hurt all over, from deep inside. That ... that thing had torn her neck and her shoulder, missing her jugular and her carotid artery. She'd be dead if it had had more time. Ed had distracted it.

But it had done something to her. Her wound burned and felt oddly like it was sizzling, still burning. She had been burnt by hogweed once and the blisters that rose and burst reminded her of this pain. A poison, but a burning one.

Josie put a mug of tea into her cold hands.

'Drink all that now. And swallow these down. You'll feel better in a minute,' Josie said.

Rose looked at the strange tablets. Whatever they were, they were definitely not paracetamol, but she took them with a gulp of tea. The hot sweet liquid actually did make her feel a tiny bit better. At least it was normal.

But then it came back to her again. She tried to focus on the kitchen, her daughter, Josie fussing about, tidying the table for something to do, but she couldn't forget the horror of the teeth tearing her flesh, like a seagull ripping at a big fish. She kept hearing the dreadful sound of a lump of her body being pulled away. It was almost worse than the pain. She thought about the pain for a moment. It seemed to be flying away from her. She could still see it, but it was distant now.

'You'll be able to sleep now, Mam,' Becky said.

Rose touched her daughter's cheek. She had been ready to die in her place and she wasn't so sure that she hadn't begun to, slowly but inexorably.

'Josie,' Rose said, 'you didn't see that thing.' It was hard to get her voice to work. 'The girl. But there was something wrong with Frank. Me and Becky saw him in the hospital. He was dead, but he wasn't.' She grabbed Josie's hand. 'I don't want to go like him. Promise you won't let me go that way. I can't bear it.'

'Shush now, Rose. You've had a terrible day. Let's just put it behind us and get you to a nice fresh bed, eh?'

'No, Josie,' Becky said. 'Listen to her. I saw that thing too. I saw it ... I saw it biting her.'

Josie took Becky's free hand in hers, linking the three of them together.

Rose's vision was blurry, and when Josie moved she saw coloured jet trails left behind, but she had to say more before she went out entirely. She gripped their hands. When she spoke, she sounded drunk.

'Josie, you know there's something bad here. The men know it and they hide it from us.'

Josie nodded, her face resigned. 'They think they're keeping their secrets,' she said. 'As if any man was ever able to keep a secret from his woman, even without telling. We didn't know exactly what it was before, but I guess we do now.'

Rose nodded, her head too heavy now. 'If it's got in me, you have to promise me to do something.'

'Mam,' Becky said, tears in her voice.

Rose squeezed her hand and looked at Josie, feeling that her head was like a sunflower on a thin stalk, gradually bending, ready to fall.

'How many more of those tablets do you have?'

Josie looked at her seriously and Rose knew she had got through to her, even though she now looked like a prism of colour made by crying.

'Enough,' Josie said. 'Enough.'

Rose nodded and saw nothing more.

Eighteen

Like one, that on a lonesome road
Doth walk in fear and dread,
And having once turned round walks on,
And turns no more his head;
Because he knows, a frightful fiend
Doth close behind him tread.

Samuel Taylor Coleridge, *The Rime of*
***the Ancient Mariner*, 1798**

It had been the only thing Ed could think of to do. She had hurt and maybe killed Rose, and it was only a matter of time before she turned to Becky, who had her new baby to take care of, and to Lia. He couldn't let anything happen to them. He suspected that he would never again feel about anyone the way he felt about Lia. For him, it was a once-in-a-lifetime thing, he knew. From the moment he had seen her when she asked him for directions, he had known. She was pretty and had gorgeous hair, but it wasn't that. It was like there was a magnet inside each of them. It was the same instinct that drew a mother bird back to her chick in a colony of thousands without error. They were bonded. He couldn't let anything happen to her.

So he had run at the beautiful creature holding Rose. He was shouting but he wasn't even aware of words. He ran at her, then swerved away. He had seen the way she looked at him. There was a curiosity in her eyes that made him think she would follow. The moment she did, he could feel her.

Judging by the way she had moved to grab Rose, there was no way he could outrun her. Whatever she was, she could seize him at will but somehow he knew she wouldn't straight away. He threw a wild look over his shoulder and saw Lia and Becky crouching beside Rose. Then the girl filled his vision.

He turned and ran. He had nowhere to go, no one to run to. He wished his mother was still alive. He missed a sanctuary which was now lost to him forever. He wished that he had escaped the island and was taking photographs of birds in the hot, wet forests of the Amazon. He wished Lia could be with him.

He wished and wished but time had frozen. All of the wishing and the Amazon birds had taken him only a short distance from danger with no hope of escape.

She struck him in the back, bringing him down on his face in the cold damp ground, thick with springy moss. She turned him like a boneless puppet and sat astride his hips. His arms were rubbery and weak and didn't want to obey him.

She cocked her head to one side, then the other, watching him. Her hair was flying in the wind sweeping over them, but it didn't tangle in her face. Instead, it floated above her as though they were beneath the surface of a rough sea. Like everything about her, it was white, a blazing white like the hottest fire, and yet she was cold. He could feel the cold of her wrapped around his hips. There was heat there too. He couldn't tell if it was his or hers, or both of theirs. She was ice, but there was fire inside her.

She moved on him, a small intimate shift that made him groan. She smiled then and leaned down over him. Her cold fingers touched his face and she kissed where her fingers had been. Her skin felt like the feathers of a dead gannet he had found on the beach. Soft, perfect, beautiful, lifeless. She kissed his mouth.

Sensations raced through him. His mind held nothing but

images of her, lithe, bare, like silk and lace, touching him everywhere. His body was likewise entranced, moving with her, helpless. She drew him into her and he went willingly.

She sat up, leaned on his chest and put her hand on his throat. Her long nails scratched gently over his skin. He felt a sharp little pain and then she was bending over him and her lips were on him. She was drawing something out of him, some vital thing, and he couldn't stop her. He didn't want to stop her. He lay on the damp ground and stared up at sharp points of light in the night sky, wheeling with the slow turn of the galaxy as though his life had taken on some trace of eternity and he could now understand past, future, distance, and time. It was glorious and terrible. She was going to take his strength from him and give him something other.

No. Down deep a voice spoke. *No,* it said. *Don't. Where is Lia? Where is my love? She is my life, my eternity. I won't give it, I won't.*

He felt her hesitate, and the exquisite pain faded. When it did, he suddenly thought of the chestnut of Lia's hair, glinting red in sunlight, warm and full. He thought of her sweet face, her voice, the taste of her fruity lip gloss, the feel of her body against his.

The beauty sat up and looked at him. He thought he saw a flicker of sadness cross her face, but it was quickly gone, replaced by her cold smile. She touched a finger to her lips and then to his throat. He swallowed and tears filled his eyes, turning her into a prismatic enigma. Then she was gone.

Ed walked into the pub and saw Lia talking to Harry in an agitated way. She stopped in shock when she saw him, then flew into his arms. He buried his face in her neck and hair, smelling the good, clean smell of her. She wanted to pull away to look at him, but he held her for another few seconds, feeling like he might float away if she let him go. But Lia was impatient and wriggled to be free.

'You're hurt. There's blood on your neck. Did she ... what happened?'

'I think it's OK. I just want a shower. Give me a few minutes?'

She nodded, but he could see she was cross with worry and impatience. He suppressed a smile and went upstairs.

In the shower, he let the hot water play on his neck and everywhere she had touched him. The skin on his throat was unmarked. He knew the blood was his, but the wound it had come from was healed. He closed his eyes and saw her touch her fingers to her lips and then to his throat. Somehow, she had torn him and then healed him. God, she was so beautiful, so cold. Even under the hot water, he could still feel the fierceness of her icy grip on him. And how good it had felt. He groaned in the privacy of the shower cubicle and scrubbed the heels of his hands into his eyes. He loved Lia. This other girl was a monster, but she had done something to him, or had almost done something, leaving it incomplete. He almost wished she had finished what she started because he was in limbo. He knew he was in love with Lia, but some part of him yearned for the other's cold. He ached for it. For her.

Hating himself, he scrubbed hard at his skin, trying to wash the feeling away. The tension only began to ease when he turned the shower to cold and let it hail painful needles into his body. By the time he got back downstairs, he felt like himself again. Almost.

Nineteen

All of the night was quite barred out except an owl's cry,
A most melancholy cry, shaken out long and clear
upon the hill,
No merry note, nor cause of merriment,
But one telling me plain what I escaped
And others could not, that night, as in I went.

Edward Thomas, 'The Owl', c.1915

Lia woke up, feeling as though she had been running all night. She had slipped into Ed's room and into his arms. After the series of shocks and a strange night spent sleeping beside another person, a boy, she didn't feel rested. Although they had lain together for company and comfort, the morning light brought different feelings.

She felt like she had a bird trapped in her chest. At some point, they both must have felt too hot. Ed's chest was bare and her own shirt was gone. She had on her bra and a cami-top. She was scared of whatever was out there, scared of being in bed with Ed, and her heart was banging so hard she felt sure he would hear it and wake up.

He was lying on his left side, closest to the window. His shoulders and back looked a lot stronger than they looked in his clothes. Normally, he looked a little lanky, but she had been right when she watched him walking with Harry. She thought then that he would fill out into a strong man, but his loose shirts had hidden how much of a man he already was.

Her skin burned at the thought that she was in bed, not with a boy, but with a man.

He stirred and turned over. His hair was comically sticking up but his face was serious. One moment he was asleep; the next he was kissing her. She kissed him back, each of them trying to pull the other closer. She felt mindless, gloriously lost in him. As gentle as he seemed during the time they had spent together, he was different now. He was almost fierce. She felt his desire match her own, or outmatch it. He was strong enough to move her and, before she could think, he was on top of her and their bodies were pressed together.

He kissed her neck, his breath on her skin making her shiver. He pressed his lips against her and nipped her. It sent a shot of excitement through her. Her body reacted and he made a rough noise deep in his throat. Then he rolled away and lay flat on his back.

'Have you … been with someone before?' he said, his voice funny.

'No. Have you?'

He nodded, not looking at her.

'Ed? What is it? You're making me feel weird.'

He turned to look at her then, taking her hand.

'It was pretty bad last night. I don't think either of us is thinking straight,' he said.

'Don't you want to be with me?'

'I do. I really do. But it's not the right time. I don't think so anyway.'

But she was ready, more than ready. She had said no to boys before and she knew that she had been right to. It was different with Ed. She wanted to be closer to him than she had ever been to anyone. The terror of the night made her want it all the more.

At some point in the night she had awoken to see him standing at the window as though waiting for someone. She hadn't been able to see his face, but something about the way he stood, the sigh he gave before coming back to bed, the cold of his skin against her, had dampened her desire then.

But now she wanted him. She loved him. He loved her. She felt ready in lots of ways. She trusted him, even though she had only known him for a few days. Something in him spoke to its counterpart in her. It was meant to be. And she thought that he was wrong. They would have to get up soon and figure out what the hell had happened. Who knew what the day would bring? Maybe they wouldn't even be here by the time night came again. She thought that they should seize these few moments. Plus the thought of being with him was thrilling and terrifying and right.

But there was that something in his eyes. She didn't doubt that they would be properly together, but he was holding back for a reason. Until that reason, whatever it happened to be, was gone, she would wait.

So, she kissed him quickly and pulled her shirt on.

'Come on then,' she said lightly. 'Let's get up before Harry comes in with a shotgun or something.'

He smiled but she slipped out before he could say anything, crossing the hall to her own room to shower and face herself in the mirror.

Twenty

Remember, my friend, that knowledge is stronger than memory, and we should not trust the weaker.

Bram Stoker, *Dracula*, 1897

Brendan looked down at the priest. He was ripped open. Brendan's stomach churned at the sight of his bare white ribs and bile rose to the back of his throat. He waited to see if he was going to be sick, but it settled down again.

He put two fingers in his mouth and whistled loudly. The rain was getting heavier and he could see the drops hopping off the man's bones, hitting his staring eyes. The rain was making the island misty, so he whistled again and after a few minutes saw Andrew coming towards him, striding as though he owned every bit of the land he was walking on. Brendan looked around. This had been Dan's land, so he supposed it actually was Andrew's now. He had got it, by hook or by crook.

Andrew stopped on the other side of the body, looking at it dispassionately.

Andrew was the closest thing to a friend that Brendan had on the island but, as he studied him, he knew that he wouldn't want to come up against him on any subject that mattered.

Andrew wasn't a big man, but there was something powerful about him. He walked with his legs spread, a colossus of a personality, though not a colossus of a man. Harry was a finer man by far, but Andrew was the kind of man that Brendan would always follow. He understood this about himself. Alone in his small house, he sometimes wished that he had made himself take a wife and had children. His was one of the old families, but he had no one to pass the name on to. The fact that he was attracted to men like Andrew didn't help, but at times in the lonely nights he longed for a warm body to hold on to, just for company.

Andrew looked up. 'You didn't find him,' he said.

Brendan almost spoke, before he realised what Andrew meant. He shook his head. 'No, I didn't find him.'

'Take his legs.'

Brendan did as he was told. Andrew caught the priest under the arms and together they carried him to the cliff. Brendan didn't like the view he had of the torn body. The longer he looked, the more convinced he was that he could make out individual organs in the ruined, red cavities. If he looked long enough, it might appear that the destroyed heart would begin to beat again. He had once read a story about a heart buried under the floor by a murderer, beating still, calling attention to the crime and driving the culprit mad. He didn't remember who wrote it, but it was such a horrible idea that it stayed with him. He often left music playing at night, so that he wouldn't imagine the sound of the heart in the dark.

But of course, he hadn't killed this man, this priest. He hadn't made him come out here in the night. Still, he had been a man and it didn't do Bernard any good to look at the remains of him. He knew that he would be leaving the music on tonight.

'On three,' Andrew said.

They swung the body between them, gaining momentum. Before they let him go, his guts swung out of his body, endless slippery loops of intestine. They let go and the crumpled figure flew out beyond the edge of the cliff, its innards flying behind like bloody pennants. It seemed to Brendan that the priest would fly forever, never dropping, but of course he did. He went down and they leaned carefully over to see where he had gone. The tide was in, covering the rocks, and the body was nowhere to be seen.

'We shouldn't have put Dan in the Hall,' Brendan said. 'What if she turns him, like she did with Frank? What if the priest comes back?'

'The priest won't, he's too much of a mess. She just had her fun with him,' Andrew said.

'And what about Dan?'

Andrew thought, his mouth twisted under his moustache. 'We might have to rethink that one until we get control of her again. Fuck sake, Dan never stops being a bloody nuisance.' He shook his head, sniffed and wiped his hands on a clump of grass. 'Right. I've got work to get on with. See you later.'

'Alright.'

Andrew regarded Brendan doubtfully. 'Are you OK?'

'Yeah.'

'Don't go doing anything stupid now.'

'I won't.'

Andrew marched off into the rain.

Brendan watched him go and then moved back to look over the edge of the cliff again.

The priest's body was down there, already taken by the waves, perhaps pulled into the network of caves that pocked this side of the island. It gave Brendan no comfort to know that the priest wasn't alone in the churning water. Perhaps the dead were knocking against each other in the dim light that reached inside the caves, bones mingled together by the evermoving sea.

He shuddered and cut back through the land towards his cottage. He should have taken a pup the last time Andrew's bitch had whelped. At least it would be warm and alive, happy to see him and something to hold on to at three in the morning when it seemed as though light would never come again.

He went inside and put the kettle on. When the tea was made, he sat at the small table and sipped from his old mug. He had work to do around the place but, not for the first time, he couldn't see the point of doing it. Instead, he looked out the slightly grubby window at the clouds. It was raining a little, but the clouds weren't ready to give their all yet. Brendan's eyes wandered over the kitchen. He did all of his living in here, such as it was. The parlour was unused. Sometimes, he didn't even bother going up the stairs to bed, but just stayed on the lumpy sofa in front of the fire. He didn't mind the lumps. They fitted him now after all the years.

The fire had gone out. Grey ashes had spilled onto the hearth and the old tin mug he sometimes used to stew his tea a bit stronger by shoving it into the burning coals had old milky tea in it, the surface scum marred by the butt of a rolled fag. The newspaper that covered the table was a few months old and covered in circular mug-marks.

He was ashamed of the way he lived. No one came here to see it, but he was once a different sort of person. He used to like nice clothes and looking well. Those days had gone. There was no one to care if his collar was grubby. There was no one at all. Not since Will had died. Will was not like him, but Brendan had loved him all the same. They had been friends and Will knew how he felt, but neither of them ever mentioned it. It was painful when Will left the island, and it was then that Brendan had started to let things slide, but when Will died Brendan gave up all pretence of keeping his life in order. So here he was, here they all were, still alive when so many others were dead.

Like a child then, he put his head on his arms at the table and let silent tears fall on the newsprint.

The lights. That was the key. The storm had become too strong. The captain said they had to make for harbour or the Lilith would founder. The high waves already had the decks awash. Corvo had tried to argue but gave up quickly. They had stopped once already to resupply the ship, but this felt wrong. However, there was nothing they could do against the power of the wind and the sea herself.

He clung to the rail, knowing that he was being foolish, that he should go below decks as the captain had instructed, shouting over the roar of the storm. Yet, he couldn't bear it. Down there, he felt as though he were in a crypt. For as long as he could withstand it, he would stay here in the wild, natural world. It was all about sensation. He could see nothing.

The dark was so intense that he couldn't see the water, although the owl figurehead on the ship's bow dipped perilously close to it after every mountainous wave. Having securely brought his dreadful cargo this far from Rome, it seemed as though the end of the journey might be nigh. Perhaps it would be for the best. If the sea took the ship, crew, cargo and all, to the bottom, it might herald the end of the nightmare. At the very least, it would end his nightmare.

But that wasn't what he had vowed. He had sworn to take the creature to those who would understand what she was. He was old now and had spent too long being her guard. New people who weren't yet fully in her thrall would have a better chance of keeping her, or killing her, whichever they could manage.

He saw the lights first. Struggling back to the captain,

he managed to draw his attention to the tiny flicker of hope. Some sort of harbour. Fighting the storm, they made for it.

Too late, the few lights they had left on deck showed the edge of a cliff. The Lilith grated alongside half hidden rocks and he heard her ribs open. Water must surely be flooding in, but she carried on, grinding through the treacherous water. He was knocked flat to the deck when she suddenly came aground. An animal shudder ran through her deck and he heard the screams of men below. He clambered to his feet, ignoring pain, and saw the false lights bobbing along the clifftop as the wreckers ran towards their prize.

The next giant wave came and lifted them bodily from the piercing rock, carried them forward and the ship, already coming apart, was smashed against the cliff. There was a brief ebb, before she was again lifted and flung against the steep wall. The screams of the men changed from pain and fear to terror. He knew then that the Strix was free. With the ship's innards broken, she had escaped her bonds and flown from his captivity.

For one terrible moment before the relief of death, he saw her at her most beautiful. She was nature itself, impervious to the storm, unafraid of the jagged rocks, enraged at her captivity. And alive. Beautifully, cruelly alive. Then the waves swept him from the remains of the ship to a clean death against the cliff of this unknown place. The others hadn't so lucky an escape. She had a thirst to satiate.

The lights. The false lights had to be positioned just right. For ships approaching off course in the storm, enough lights would look like a harbour. Any vessel would make for shelter from the wind and wild water. Some nights, the weather would turn so sharply that a boat could founder on the rocks without their help. Hidden rocks had taken lots of ships. Most of the ones brought in by the false lights would probably have foundered anyway. Probably. The goods and timbers were theirs if no one survived. It was easy enough to ensure that no one did. He checked the knife in his pocket.

This night was one of the worst he had seen. He was leaning into the wind, fighting to stay on his feet. The light above his head was swinging wildly. They wouldn't be able to stay long. Surely a sensible captain would stay far out to sea, too far to see their lights? But she had come. Had come to her doom on the Devil's Teeth. Even in the storm, he had been able to hear the terrible death throes as she was flung against the cliff, over and over again.

They saw that five of the bodies had been thrown up on a rocky ledge halfway down the cliff, something that invariably happened. Without consultation – it was routine – he and two of the others began to climb down the cliff, one by one, first using the knotted rope to climb over the outcrop. Then they climbed down the path they had cut out of the cliff-face to reach the ledge.

Some of the dead were wearing rings and earrings. He had to cut off some fingers and earlobes to get them, but blood washed off easily. They searched the broken bodies for purses of coin and found two well-filled ones. The rest of the treasure would have to wait until the storm passed or lulled. The shattered ship had now become trapped between the rocks and the cliff. From experience he knew that it would probably stay stuck there till the morrow, it and its cargo whatever that might be. Bodies and other goods would be in the nearby cave, along with the bones of past shipwrecks and crewmen.

They were climbing back up the path when they all heard the scream. Unearthly, it stopped them in their tracks. The man ahead of him was already hanging from the knotted rope to get over the outcrop. He froze and they all turned towards the wreck.

A girl was standing on a jagged rock, feet in the crashing waves. Somehow, she was standing still, her white gown whipping madly, her hair flying above her. He stared at her, not even sure how he could see her. She seemed to be made of light. Then she opened her mouth and that scream came again. That terrible shriek, born not of terror but of rage. It galvanised them all at once. There was no conscious thought, just blind animal panic. He shoved the man in front of him, who was already scrambling up the rope. He himself was being pushed from behind. They were caught in the worst place.

He started to climb, grabbing for the thick knots in the rope. The pushing behind him suddenly stopped but he didn't look back. Instead, he climbed faster, scraping his knuckles bloody against the wet rock, panic lending him careless strength and indifference to pain. The man ahead must have reached the top because he no longer struck against his boot as he reached for the next knot. He was almost there himself. So close.

Then he was grabbed from behind. He screamed, his voice sounding like that of a rabbit caught by a predator. He held onto the rope as he was lifted away from the rock, but it burned through his grasp, leaving a bloody gash on each palm. Then the rope was gone and there was only the wild darkness. He felt the wind catching his clothes and the moon, enemy to a man who earned his living by the destruction of others on the uncaring rocks of the island's rough coast, suddenly split the clouds. It showed enough to make him scream again. He was hundreds of feet in the air, wheeling on the fierce, freezing current swooping up the face of the cliff. Terror sharpened his focus and he could clearly see the rocks below, surrounded by broken timber and broken bodies. It *was only a matter of seconds before whatever had him would let go and he was dropped to his own crashing death.*

But it did not drop him into the sea. Instead, the sea was left behind and the ground on top of the cliff appeared. He could see plumes of foam erupting through the blowholes from the network of caves and cracks below. Then he was free-falling. Just before he hit the ground, a white shape flashed in front of him, buffeting him out of his fall, causing him to roll and tumble in relative safety. He scrambled to his feet, feeling pain in his back and hips that would tell later, if there was a later.

She was there: the girl with the white dress. She looked young, delicate, impossibly bright in the night, almost flashing like a wind-blown lantern as the moon slid in and out of clouds. She was the most beautiful and terrifying thing he had ever seen. He wanted to run, but he was the mouse. He had been seen by the owl and all he could do was await his fate and hope that it would be quick.

She stepped lightly aside and he saw the others on their feet, bloodied and bruised but alive. They moved close together, herding behaviour coming instinctively. She smiled. Someone was crying. It was only when he felt the tears on his face that he realised it was him.

He heard a shout and suddenly someone else was there. Someone glorious, bright and good. He wasn't involved in their pursuits and had often tried to stop them. Now, the sight of him was a kind of revelation. It felt like salvation was rushing towards them.

Then, still smiling, she took the best of them first and all hope of salvation was gone.

Brendan woke, terrified, the dream possessing him. His stomach churned and he barely made it to an already overflowing rubbish bin before getting sick. The act made him cry and made his throat burn. He gave in to it and fell back on the couch, sobbing. The rain grew heavier and a brief shower of hailstones struck the window, as though there was a beast out there, rapping to be let in.

Twenty-One

Little islands are all large prisons; one cannot look at the sea
without wishing for the wings of a swallow.

Sir Richard Francis Burton (1821-1890)

AJ waited on the ferry, watching his single passenger disembark and go hesitantly up the slipway to the village. He had been tempted to stop her, but it was none of his business, not any more.

He never set foot on the island anymore. He knew that the fact hadn't escaped his father, but it was the only thing that kept him sane.

A few nights after AJ had turned eighteen, his dad had come into his room and shaken him awake.

'AJ, get up,' he had said.

AJ had been so used to taking orders from his father that he had got up without a question. He thought one of the animals might be in trouble. Instead, when he had pulled on some clothes and boots, his father led him through the silent house and away from the farm.

His dad was acting weird and the stillness of the night made AJ himself silent. It felt like it would be a sin to break it. The whole thing had felt almost like a pilgrimage.

They walked the rough road towards the Hall. There was a moon sitting behind it, fat and full, and the sight of it shot an arrow of fear through AJ's heart. When they got closer, figures stepped out of the shadow of the house and AJ saw the shadowy figures of his father's friends. The usual gang.

'What's going on?' he said, looking at his dad.

The moon was bright enough to show his father's stony expression.

'You'll find out,' he said. 'Brendan, you have the key?'

Brendan said yes and then they walked into the shadow of the Hall.

AJ shivered. He liked the cold, bracing wind off the sea, with the smell of rain in it, but the shiver was like someone walking over his grave. He was about to retreat to the glassed-in quarterdeck when he saw his father walking his mother towards the ferry. When they got closer, he recognised the expression on his mother's face as two feelings fighting for dominance. Kitty looked delighted to be getting off the island but furious at being made to go by Andrew.

They boarded the ferry and his mother gave him a peck on the cheek before going inside to the heat. Andrew nodded at him and AJ was turning away when he felt his arm gripped by his father's hard fingers.

'I've let you go and play on boats for a long time, Andy. The time is coming for you to come back and play your part. Get your mother to her sister's and come back. Bring your brother. We need him here now rather than in the hospital.'

AJ didn't speak but waited until his father let go of his arm. He finally knew that when he took the ferry across this time, he would never pilot it again. This would be his last time past the Chimneys, if they even survived the oncoming storm. He would try to convince his mother to stay on the mainland and would need no convincing himself. He was through with his father's obsession and the madness of what he had seen on the night that they went to the Hall. He had mainland blood and, after years of being in between, he was choosing the land. In fact, once his mother was settled, he thought he might just catch the first flight to the place farthest away from this place and never, ever come back.

He watched Andrew walk back down the ramp, passing a few foot passengers carrying bags onboard. The people coming on were not talking and faces were grim. They knew the storm was coming. Several of them had dogs on leads and two women had cats in travel crates. One lady was carrying a small birdcage covered with a cloth. AJ waited for a few minutes after everyone was on in case there was any one else coming in a hurry, but he was itching to go, so he shut the gate and powered the ferry backwards out of the harbour. He spared one look at the Chimneys as the ferry chugged past, but the water was already getting choppy, so he wanted to concentrate. He caught a flash of white from the corner of his eye, but he chose to look away.

Bob Glenn watched the ferry leave. They should have been on it, but Josie refused to leave. Something about Rose being ill. Bob knew Rose had been through a lot and he did feel sorry for her, but she had her own family to look after her. Josie wouldn't listen, however, and Bob watched the last ferry go. The sky on the horizon was a deep blue-black. The storm was coming and God only knew what trouble it would bring.

Andrew watched the ferry out of sight. He knew that AJ wasn't coming back and wasn't bringing his brother either. There was a time he would have raged against them until they came to see his point of view, or at least do his bidding. But for the first time he was glad that they were gone off the island, all of them. He would never say that out loud, but it was true. He looked out at the approaching storm before turning for home. He had animals to feed before the world turned to wind and rain. As he passed the Robin's Rest, Evan and Jim came out and fell into step with him. He was glad. They weren't great company but they were better than nothing.

The baby had gone back to sleep after a feed and a change. Becky was moving around the kitchen, unable to settle. Matt watched her for a while, before catching her hand and taking her into his arms. Now that the baby bump was going, she felt little again, and he could hold her close. He kissed her cheek and felt her arms go around his shoulders.

'You've been very quiet,' he said, speaking softly. She had barely said a word since her mother had been hurt – or attacked as the women insisted. Whatever had happened had disturbed his Becky but it was time for her to talk about it. She was a talker and it wasn't right for her to bottle things up.

'Won't you tell me what happened, Becky?'

'You won't believe me,' she said.

'Of course I'll believe you. I love you, baby.'

She looked up at him. 'You're not from the island, Matt.'

'Not that again. I know I'm not but it's my home now and my family is here. Besides, what difference does it make to what happened last night?'

She shook her head helplessly. 'Everything. I wish you had gone across on the ferry and taken the baby with you.'

'Don't be silly. The baby must stay with you. And I'm not leaving you. We'll be fine. I'll go out and make sure the place is shipshape and ready for the storm. We have plenty of fuel and food. We'll just settle down here, the three of us and ride it out as we always do. This one won't be any different.'

He saw the doubt on her face. It made him feel bad, as

though she thought he wouldn't be able to protect them. He didn't tell her that he had a bad feeling in the pit of his stomach. He would have taken the baby across if she had agreed to go with them, but she wouldn't. She wouldn't leave her mother and her mother insisted on staying as well. At least he had succeeded in getting Rose to stay in their cottage with them. She was asleep in the spare bedroom still. The painkillers Mrs. Glenn had given her must have been strong. The woman had a supply of illicit stuff in the back of the shop, but at least she was careful with it. Without a doctor on the island, everyone turned a blind eye to the secret stash, because they had all had need of it in the past. She was a dab hand at stitching wounds too, as he knew from personal experience, carrying her implements in a normal sewing kit in the bottom of her huge handbag. He was glad that Rose was getting to sleep through a lot of her pain. The wound in her throat looked ugly, although not infected.

He gave Becky another kiss.

'Make the tea, there's a good woman. I'm going out to do manly stuff.' He flexed his muscles, earned from being on fishing boats from his teens. It always made her laugh, but this time she only had a ghost of a smile for him. It was better than nothing and would do for the moment. At least she had started talking. Later on, when they were cuddled up under a blanket on the sofa, she might feel ready to tell him more.

He smiled back. 'Love you, babe.'

'Love you too, Matt.'

He went outside, whistling a bit. Things weren't right but she was talking and loved him still, so it'd be OK. He had bought a few new DVDs for the portable player and the big generator would keep the lights on if the storm knocked the island out. He got finished quickly, stocking up on too much firewood and coal, just in case. Everything loose was in the garage and the windows were protected by storm shutters.

They were ready.

He turned for a last look, and saw a fishing boat way out, making for the main port across on the mainland. She was already diving into deep troughs and climbing steep waves on the other side. He said a quiet prayer for her and her crew that they would make landfall before the real storm hit. It was growing dark even though it was only around midday.

He checked his watch. The 31st of October. He had always loved the season as a child on the mainland. There, it was fun to dress up in a scary costume and go with a gang of his friends from house to house, collecting sweets and chocolate and nuts, to compare and swap afterwards, before heading home for family games and his mother's toffee apples. It wasn't such a big deal on the island. No one made a fuss about it. The pub didn't decorate with fake cobwebs and spiders, or skeletons or even pumpkins. It hadn't bothered him before that there weren't any children on the island to go trick or treating. Somehow, it hadn't bothered him before that there no children on the island. That girl, Harry's niece, was here now but between her and the baby, there was no one. He was away at sea a lot, but he and Becky had been so wrapped up in each other, sorting out the house and preparing for the baby, that he hadn't quite noticed. Becky hadn't wanted to live on the mainland and he loved the sea, so it didn't matter to him where they were. But, as he stood looking at the darkening afternoon, he couldn't have told a stranger why they were living here. Why anyone was living here.

A deep sense of unease made his skin goose-bump under his heavy sweater. The wind tugged at him. He had been alone on deck in cold seas, with nothing but the crystal sky and the dark ocean for company, and even then he hadn't felt as lonely as he suddenly did now.

The world was a boat-ride away, but with the storm it might as well have been on the moon. People would have left on the ferry. Those who stayed were about to become some of the most isolated people on the planet.

'No more,' he said, under his breath.

Now that the baby had arrived, he wanted to get off the island. It was beautiful here for a lot of the year, but this storm was bringing the winter and it was not for the vulnerable. He swore softly, wishing he had carried his wife and son onto the ferry, even kicking and screaming, with his mother-in-law over his shoulder. It was too late to get them onto a smaller boat now. Too late for a lot of things. He turned his back on the premature darkness and went back into the house that he suddenly didn't want anymore.

'I need help battening down the hatches for the storm,' said Harry. 'Ed?'

'No problem. Can we do the farm after if there's time? I know it's empty, but I don't want the windows blowing in.'

'Sure. If there's time.'

Lia watched their grim faces as they got ready for going out. The lights were on in the kitchen and no one was in the bar. She stood up.

'Hey, what about me? I want to help.'

Both men looked at her with practically the same expression. She felt a flash of anger. 'Or don't you think I can help because I'm a girl?'

'It's not that, Lia,' Harry said.

He and Ed shared a look.

'I'd rather if you didn't go out at all, Lia,' Ed said apologetically. 'That thing ... the girl could still be out there.'

'*You're* going out,' she said.

'Yeah, but ...' Ed said.

'But you're big strong men and I'm only a little woman that you have to protect?'

'Well ...' Ed was getting red.

193

She cocked one eyebrow at him.

Harry handed her a heavy jacket. 'No point in arguing, Ed. It's not dark yet anyway. Lia, collect up all the plant pots and leave them in the back hall. They'll be in France tomorrow if we don't bring them in.'

He walked out of the room and Ed, turning to go with him, made a rueful face at her. 'Sorry.'

She shooed him out and followed them out into the strange dark afternoon, her first Halloween in Ireland. No pumpkins or trick or treating, but a dark Celtic turning from summer into winter. *Samhain*. Her father had explained it to her. The time of the year when the veil between this world and the otherworld was at its thinnest. On this night, the beloved dead were to be welcomed into the home, and the evil were to be guarded against. That girl who had attacked Rose and followed Ed was beautiful, more beautiful than anything Lia had ever seen, but she had no doubts that she was also the most evil thing she had ever seen. She moved too fast, she had hurt Rose so badly, and she was so strange. Instead of being unnatural, Lia thought she was probably of nature, but nature red in tooth and claw. She was like nothing so much as a predatory bird, curious, sharp, vicious, uncaring.

The light was odd, a bruised blue and yellow around the pub. Out to sea, the sky was black. Lia shivered and quickly started moving plants indoors, as Ed and Harry secured the windows. She felt as though someone was watching her from behind. A seagull, heading for the middle of the island, screamed as it passed the pub and Lia almost dropped the plant she was holding. She was not sorry to be helping, but she was sorry that any of them were out here. She hurried through her task and helped the others. She felt like dancing on the spot with urgency, shouting at them to hurry up, *come on*. The spirit must have passed from her to them, because they did finish fast. Lia whirled around and headed for the back door, determined not to run and panic for no reason.

The girl was standing between them and the door. Her pale beauty was like moonlight on ice. She wasn't looking at Lia, but past her to Ed and Harry, with sharp avian interest. When she did turn her gaze on Lia, it wasn't friendly. Lia saw her start to move, and felt both Ed and Harry move as well, everyone with one goal. She turned to run and had a glimpse of white faces before she was grabbed and lifted. The girl's feet were talons buried in the thick coat that was saving her skin. The terror of being caught by a beast overrode the pain. Lia twisted, the instinct to escape stronger than the fear of falling. What she saw above her made her freeze before struggling harder. The talons simply curled and gripped her harder. This close, Lia saw that the girl was pale because her skin was delicate layers of tiny white feathers, each one perfect. Her arms extended into white wings that, this high off the ground, caught the light that the storm hadn't yet extinguished. The powerful beat of the wings swept them out over the sea and back in above the cliffs. Lia gave up struggling. Escape was impossible.

The creature took her over the village and out beyond the harbour into the oncoming storm. The first wave was hailstones, lashing her face. Before she closed her eyes, she saw the dark shapes of the Chimneys rising from the wild sea. A terrifying shriek filled the whole world, leaving her stunned. The talons unclenched and with a shake she was free, and falling.

Ed ran, following the creature as far as he could before she swept out over the sea. He heard the cry from somewhere out in the dark and it was like the owl, freezing its prey with terror. He stood on the edge of the cliff as hailstones reached him. She was gone. Both of them were gone. The water below was churning in the caves and he could hear the blowholes out on the far reaches of the island beginning to boom. He felt like the wind was going to take him and he almost wanted it to.

He ran back to the pub and halted again to stare out to sea, but he could see no flash of white.

When a hand touched his shoulder, he jumped and tipped forward. The hand jerked him backwards and he and the person tumbled onto the wet ground together.

The woman pushed herself up and shouted to make herself heard.

'*Where is my daughter? Where is Lia?*'

Twenty-Two

The sea had jeeringly kept his finite body up, but drowned
the infinite of his soul. Not drowned entirely, though.
Rather carried down alive to wondrous depths, where
strange shapes of the unwarped primal world glided to and
fro before his passive eyes.

Herman Melville, *Moby Dick or The Whale*, 1851

All of the watching they had done, waiting for the cover of a storm to lure a boat onto the Devil's Teeth, was pointless now. In all of the long years past, they had waited and caught food for the Strix, enough to keep her satiated and quiet. It had taken a long time to figure out how much would stop her from hunting for herself, but not enough to make her strong. Her gift in return was long life. Brendan looked at himself in the spotty mirror. The offer had seemed a good one, especially as it was that, or death, or worse than death. Now, after three hundred years of being alone with no companions but the small group of men who knew, Brendan realised that it was no bargain at all. It was better when Will was here, but after he was gone all of the hundreds of years weighed upon Brendan like the rocky soil of an island grave.

Oh, Andrew liked it well enough. He went through generations of wives and children, waiting for the day when death would finally come to them, so that he could create a new heir to help him continue the work of keeping the creature shut up in the Hall. It wasn't out of the goodness of his heart. That heart had always been black, before the Strix ever came to shore. He enjoyed the power. Brendan was closest to him, although they were definitely not friends. Brendan had liked Evan and Jim once but, over the many years, he saw them for what they were. Empty vessels. Long life suited them because they were not prone to brooding over the past or the future. They were like Andrew in one way, in that they enjoyed the life, but Andrew had depth where they had none. Andrew's depths were dark indeed, but couldn't be dismissed.

Brendan had a moment of shame. Surely they had dismissed the lives of too many? Had he learned nothing? Whatever they were, they were still here, his long-time companions. The island was emptying of other people.

The children didn't stay any more. Many of the sons fled, unable or unwilling to bear the burden imposed on them. The horror. For the daughters, who were spared that terrible knowledge, there were too many attractions on the mainland – including men to marry. The blood of the old families was growing thin. It was harder to find wives for the men who wanted them. Why would any woman want to live out here, especially in the winter? The storms were worse now than they had been when he was young, truly young.

But the storm had come late this year. The summer had lasted longer than it used to. Out here, where the weather was both adversary and blessing, it was easier to see the climate change over the centuries. When the storm hadn't come, they had, not for the first time, considered taking someone from the mainland, or a visitor, but they had waited too long.

She became hungry and didn't wait. The Strix. They didn't know what she was at first, but over the long years they learned. She came from the hills of ancient Rome and she needed blood to survive. She was beautiful when she was near to human in form, and beautiful when she chose to appear as the owl, white, perfect, murderous. He felt a kind of horrific love for her. They had kept her prisoner here, as she had kept them. They had sacrificed enemies to her. Those who had committed transgressions against them, or uncovered their secret, or like Dan had put them all in jeopardy. Ed, among all of the young ones, had stayed. Harry's niece had come home to the island. Their blood was strong and, if they could be linked, they would produce a new bloodline from two of the old families. Brendan could almost smell it off them. If they stayed here, they would live on. They could contain her and keep the world safe.

The ones who had brought her on the ship were trying to do the same. Wrecked on the Devil's Teeth, they had passed the burden on to the old families. The wreckers. Brendan thought it was nothing less than they deserved.

And now the Strix was beyond their control. He had heard her triumphant scream, the same scream he had first heard on the cliff path three hundred years ago. She was out there at her full strength and there was nothing any of them could do. Brendan looked around at the dirty kitchen. Nothing to care about him, not even a dog. He raised the cutthroat razor to his throat. Will's death had proved that they could die and he didn't want to see what was going to happen next. He had seen far too much already in a lonely life that had dipped and climbed between boredom and terror.

He touched the blade to his skin and made an exploratory nick. His blood ran in a tiny trickle down the column of his neck. The sight of it made him sick and he threw the razor on the countertop. It slid and fell into the sink, rattling against the dirty dishes.

That wasn't the right way. It was the sea he wanted. The right thing to do, finally, was to go into the water with the bones of the generations who had been devoured by the sea before. He left the house for the last time, leaving the door swinging open in the wind. It didn't matter anymore.

It was hard to walk against the rain but he knew the path well. He wanted to die where Will had died. Then he saw a group of people ahead so he dropped behind some low scrub, not caring that it scratched his face. The men were Ed and Harry, by the shape of them. There was a woman with them but it wasn't the American girl, the niece. He couldn't make her out. They were shouting something at each other. Brendan moved back along the cliff. After all, it didn't really matter where he jumped.

He got far enough away from them to a place where he thought he could clear the rocks and stood at the edge of the cliff. A wild feeling of exhilaration swept through him and he didn't hesitate. He spread his arms like a bird and flung himself into the wind. For a moment, he feared that it would blow him back onto the clifftop, but it hadn't gained its full strength yet and he plunged towards the waves below.

As had happened to him once before, his fall was suddenly interrupted by something striking him. It was *her*. This time instead of buffeting him to a softer fall, she dug her talons into him and carried him along the coast, so close to the water that his feet hit the sharp peaks of the Devil's Teeth.

She rolled him until he was facing her belly as she flew. He, who had never loved women, felt a surge of the thrall that the men all felt. He brought his hands up and buried them in her soft feathers. She was cold, but she lit a fire in him. His longing to finally die was replaced by a desire to never be parted from her again. She knew it and although her talons dug deeper, she bent to touch her face briefly to his. The touch was close to a kindness, as close as a creature such as she could get. And it turned out to be a goodbye. She circled around and dropped him. The wild water would embrace him and bring him to a final end on the rocky sea floor, where his staring eyes would turn white and his flesh would be consumed by the denizens of that realm.

His last sight was of her beautiful white form riding the storm back to the island, as cruel as any predator in nature. Not evil, but pure and instinctive. Fighting to survive. Then the heartless sea took him as it had so many others at his hands.

He thought he would drift to the bottom and have the sea above him when he took a breath and let the water in. Instead, he crashed into turbulent waves which swept him towards the cliffs. Though they were still far away, he knew that it wouldn't take long before he reached the first of the hidden rocks upon which so many ships had foundered.

He had seen the effects of those rocks on men as well as ships. He didn't want that fate for himself. He dived under the rolling waves and kicked down. The current threatened to take him up again, but he pushed through, swimming as deep as he could. But there was no peaceful moment of rest on the bottom. It felt like a giant had put a hand in the sea and was stirring it. He whirled and hit the bottom a few times before finding a piece of wreckage to cling to. Then before he could be swept away, he opened his mouth and breathed the sea in.

Water rushed down his throat, filling his lungs. The pain was a shock but he had heard that it passed to be replaced by a kind of euphoria. He waited, hurting but aware. Nothing changed. He wasn't sure how much time had passed but he wasn't dying. He was not only conscious but completely lucid. He could see better than when he had first grabbed the hunk of some lost ship's stern.

He saw something move in the dark water, coming towards him from the island. He wondered if it was her, the Strix, coming to take him fully into her world. Then he saw who it was. Glorious, bright and good. His red hair was a flash of colour in a monochrome world. It was impossible, but he knew well that impossible meant nothing here.

Will Crowe swam to him and they embraced. The waters still churned around them, but they were suddenly still, in a pocket of calm. Will smiled at him and Brendan found that the pain was gone.

I must be dead at last.

No, Brendan, not yet. Soon. I promise.

OK.

Lia is dying. The sea is taking her. Save her. Save one for all you didn't save.

How?

You'll see but you must hurry.

Will let him go and the current caught him, spinning and twisting him so that he didn't know which way was up. His lungs were on fire. He burst through the surface and water and bile poured out of his mouth. He sucked in cold air and coughed violently until he was sick again. Instead of being tossed about, he was being swept fast towards the Chimneys. A huge wave dumped him on a rocky ledge at the bottom of the western chimney. He stood up and scanned the wild surface. Nothing.

Taking a breath, he dived free of the sea stack and swam as powerfully as he could. He saw her then, spinning, being tossed by the careless waves. She looked dead, but Will had said if he hurried ...

He struck out towards her, trying to go with the current. He braced himself as the sea thrust them together, and he almost lost her. Her long hair saved her. He grabbed it and pulled her close and together they were taken up and driven hard towards the island. A perverse twist of the undertow pulled them away from the harbour and out towards the Devil's Teeth. Brendan tried to control the direction of their headlong plunge, but this close to the rocks the sea was intent on bringing them to a catastrophic end.

Look for the gap.

The voice was in the wind, the waves, inside him. He kicked out, struck the first of the Devil's Teeth with his feet and shoved them into the gap that only an islander would know. They shot through as though they were on a water slide, spun once, twice and, narrowly avoiding the cave, were thrown up on the rocks to the side of it.

The girl's lips were blue. Brendan thumped her several times in the chest, then turned her on her side. No reaction. He got up and hauled her into his arms, pulling instinctively on her chest from behind, hitching her until the water flew out of her mouth. She was still limp in his arms so he dropped her and started pumping her chest again. There was no dramatic coming to, but instead a single intake of breath. She shuddered and opened her eyes. She stared at the dark sky behind him and her next breath was released on a scream.

The Strix was coming. Brendan felt her in the cold terror knocking against the bones of his spine. He pulled the girl to her feet and they clung to each other, as the Strix swooped back over the cliff, dominating the wind, but passing them by. As soon as she was out of sight, Brendan let the girl go and started climbing. He heard her scream something, but the wind tore it away.

Everything hurt but the pain didn't override the terror of being left behind with that thing up there in the storm. Lia screamed after Brendan.

'Don't leave me!'

He kept climbing. He had somehow got her this far. With or without his help, she was going to survive. Ed was up there. Grabbing the rock face where he had, she found hand-holds and, praying, she clambered after him. Then they were on a precipitous path. She climbed, battered by the wind, sure she would be torn from the cliff face. Head down, clinging to tufts of vegetation, she bumped into him. She looked up. He had stopped and was holding the frayed end of a rope in one hand. He held out the rope, green with algae, and slippery. She took it but didn't trust her weight to it. He shouted something she couldn't hear. He leaned closer and shouted in her ear.

'It'll hold! Go! Quickly! The Strix is coming!'

She looked behind her. The waves were crashing, and farther out she could see the white shape of the girl wheeling against the black sky. The Strix. She slid her hand up the rope and found a knot. As she grabbed it, he boosted her upwards. She saw another knot and lunged for it. Then, feet against the rocky cliff face, she was climbing.

Even over the roar of the storm, she heard the girl scream, a furious shriek. The sound was growing closer and Lia climbed for her life, knowing that the talons would once more dig into her flesh and tear her from the cliff, dropping her to the rocks below, where her father had died, or keeping her for some other fate that she dared not imagine.

Brendan used the rock and one hand on the slippery rope to pull himself higher, squashing her against the cliff. Lia was surrounded by the cold wings, as the talons gripped the cliff face. Brendan's mouth was close to her ear and he screamed. She felt a warm splash against the side of her face, and then he was gone. Lia climbed, her skin crawling as she waited for the impact of the great wings, the teeth or the talons to sink into her and pluck her from the cliff like a bird takes a worm. She climbed until a hand grabbed her wrist and she was yanked free and up as though she weighed nothing.

Ed pulled her away from Harry and she clung to him. He held her tight. Other arms went around them both. She opened her eyes and Jasmine took her from Ed and held her, crying. Lia couldn't understand how or why her mother was there, but she didn't care. They hugged each other as they hadn't done in years.

Then the shriek cut the wind and suddenly everyone was running.

Twenty-Three

For life be, after all, only a waitin' for somethin' else than what we're doin'; and death be all that we can rightly depend on.

Bram Stoker, *Dracula*, 1897

Jasmine followed her husband's brother into his pub, all of them out of breath. She had known there was something terribly wrong, and that feeling had grown until she couldn't bear to stay in the city any longer. Throughout the journey, made expensive for the sake of speed, fear for her daughter had expanded so that she felt she couldn't breathe properly. The strange man on the ferry didn't help. She could smell the fear coming off him when he took her ticket. There were no other outbound passengers and he seemed about to say something to her but withdrew. Getting off the ferry alone, into an afternoon darkening with a developing storm felt uncanny. There was a sulphurous smell in the air, as though lightning had just crackled over the village.

She had been here just once before, when she and Will were newly married. The exposed island, with its few stunted, windblown trees, was dry and yellowed during that hot summer. She and Will had been so passionately in love that she had scarcely noticed the world for weeks, but the moment they set foot on the island, everything went wrong.

Her new brother-in-law didn't understand her. Thinking back, she later realised that she had been dressed head to toe in couture, wearing heels and a bit sniffy about the stark and simple lifestyle of her new family.

Harry had been overjoyed to see Will and the two had roughhoused as though they were still boys. With eyes only for Will, even then she had seen that Harry was the better-looking of the two, more impressive physically. None of that mattered. He seemed cold to her compared to Will's fire. Because he so obviously disapproved of her, she decided to disapprove of him.

Now, with the pub door slammed behind them, the unearthly scream of whatever was following them echoing in her ears and her bruised and bloodied daughter gripping her hand, Jasmine saw something very different in Harry. She had thought him cold, but there was fire inside him too, just under better control than Will had been able to manage. Like Will, he was strangely ageless. Neither of them had looked particularly young when she met them, but neither had life made changes to them. She had often bemoaned the fact that men aged better than women, when she had found the first greys in her hair and the first lines around her eyes. Despite his tanned skin, she thought Harry looked no different than he had twenty years ago when she came to the island as a nineteen-year-old bride. It must have been she who had changed because when he suddenly took her and Lia into his arms, she had a physical reaction to him. He was bigger than Will, bigger than Ash. Without heels, she reached only to his chest and she heard his heart beat for the brief moment that he held her. He smelled like Will. It was all she could do not to cling to him.

Lia saved her. 'Mom, what the hell are you doing here?'

Jasmine dug her nails into her palms. She felt like she was

running a fever. She focused on Lia, although every fibre of her body was still attuned to Harry.

'I couldn't stay away. I suddenly felt that something was terribly wrong. I went straight to the airport – there was a cancellation and I got a seat on the next flight to Shannon. I felt that was an omen that I was doing the right thing.'

'Oh Mom, I wish you hadn't come! I mean, I'm so glad to see you but it's dangerous here.'

'And that's why I'm supposed to be here with you.' She looked at Harry. 'So what was that – that thing we were running from? What's going on?'

No one answered.

'Are we safe here?' she asked.

Harry nodded slowly. 'I think so. For the moment. I'll stir up the fire in the lounge. Ed, would you lock all the doors and check the windows are closed? Lia, you look like you need a shower. Jasmine, maybe you could make tea and something to eat. That'll make everyone feel better. If you don't mind.'

Jasmine shot him a look but he didn't notice. Ash would have been crushed and apologetic if he implied that the women should do women's work, but either Harry didn't notice or he didn't care. After he had made up the fire, he joined them in the kitchen and started cutting slices off a cooked chicken. It occurred to her then that while Ash would never have said anything sexist, she had also never seen him do anything domestic. Of course, he had a cleaner and always ate out. As she spread rich yellow butter on slices of bread, she glanced at Harry's hands. They were big, long-fingered and veined. Man's hands. God, what was wrong with her? She was acting like a silly teenager.

Harry finished slicing chicken and glanced at her. Something passed between them, like a flame.

She put the sandwiches together and poured the water onto tea bags in a faded flowery teapot. And, all the while, her mind was spinning. There were so many memories of Will here. No one had explained who Ed was but she saw how he was with Lia. And there was Harry. She had been certain that she would never feel like this again. Could it be real, when Will felt so close?

She tried to tell herself not to be ridiculous, but he was like a magnet and she was drawn to glance in his direction. Lia came back from her shower, still bruised and stiff, but looking better. Together, not yet able to talk, they focused on setting out the food.

The others trooped in and everyone ate in silence.

Finally, when everyone was sipping the last of the tea, Jasmine spoke up.

'Someone start. Tell me what's going on.'

Lia started, but Ed joined in. Harry didn't say anything, just listened and watched her reactions.

The Jasmine she had been before Will died might have said that they were all suffering from some sort of group hysteria but, whatever her intellect might tell her, she had seen that winged creature and heard that unearthly scream.

She looked at Harry. 'Can she be killed?'

His eyes darkened. 'Killed? I don't know. Maybe contained. This, whatever this is, is new to me too.'

'Kill it with fire,' Lia said.

Everyone looked at her. She blushed.

'Well, that's what the entire internet would say.'

Harry stood up. 'No one is doing anything tonight. It's too dangerous out there. We'll make a plan in the morning. For now, I think we should stay put and stick together.'

Jasmine could see the wisdom of this. Something terrible had been out there. The sound of it was enough to chill her blood. Besides, the wind had built to a howl and rain was striking the windows. In the end, they pulled mattresses into the lounge and all settled down in front of the built-up fire.

Jasmine thought that no one would sleep, but stress and the heat of the fire worked on them until the room was quiet. It was almost comforting to be inside listening to the storm outside. It was like the storms that Will had described to her. She drifted into an unsettled sleep, filled with strange images and Harry's face, close to hers.

Evan stood in the door of the barn, listening to the cows chewing behind him. He loved the sound and the sweet scent of the silage and the animals themselves. His own farm was mostly tillage, providing winter feed for the island's animals.

'Alright?' Jim said.

Evan nodded. Jim leaned against the opposite side of the door and lit a fag. Together, they looked across the yard at the main house. Andrew had gone straight in and not bothered to help feed his own animals.

'So, what do you think about all this?' Jim said.

Evan glanced at the man who was his closest and oldest friend. Jim was the oldest of them. He had grey in his hair and his beard grew nearly white when he let it. It was just growing back after a period of being smooth-shaven, dusting his lip and chin with a touch of snow. His red nose showed the signs of his whiskey consumption.

Evan considered the question. Neither of them were talkers, but the oceans of time behind them had led them to a deep understanding. They both had wives and children at the moment, which was hard. It would have been better if they had been between families. Still, it was what it was.

After a while, during which Jim waited patiently, smoking, Evan answered.

'Sure, it's all coming to an end, I'd say – wouldn't you?'

'Aye,' Jim said.

There didn't seem to be anything else to say, so they watched the bursts of cold rain lash the cobbles of the yard.

When the wind and rain came properly, as it would very soon, it would be hard enough to hurt, to knock unstable fences, to break holes in sheds, to lift anything that wasn't nailed down. The sea was already much too dangerous to take a boat out, although they had considered it.

Andrew thought they were here because they were brainless followers of his. Clever as the others all thought they were, it had never occurred to them that he and Jim did whatever it took to get by. Being overlooked had often proved useful and it might again. It meant that they were here in the warmth of the animals instead of in the Hall with whatever Dan had become. That was another mistake Andrew and Harry had made. They didn't have a grip on things anymore. They all would have been better off if Dan had been thrown into the sea. The days when the Strix was happy draining a body for sustenance were apparently gone. Maybe she was lonely for others like herself.

They heard her shriek, somewhere out there.

'She's having fun tonight,' Jim said.

'Yeah. Tomorrow night will be different.'

'Aye.' Jim carefully crushed the butt of his cigarette in a puddle and lit another.

Thunder rolled in the distance.

'I think Brendan's gone,' Evan said.

'It's like when Will went. You can feel it.'

Jim was right. Evan could feel it. It felt like a missing limb. There but not there.

He turned to his old friend.

'I've had enough. I'm tired.'

'Me too,' Jim said.

After a pause, Evan put his hand out for a fag and Jim lit it for him.

'So what would happen if someone, not naming anyone now, if someone went up there tonight and set the place alight?' Evan said, drawing a circle in the dull light with the end of the cigarette.

'Hmm.' Jim blew a smoke-ring which was swept away by the wind.

'I mean,' Evan said, 'it would break the bond and certain people might just be able to get on with things the way they're meant to be.' He pulled on the cigarette. 'I'm fond of the lads,' he said, nodding in the direction of his house, where his wife and eldest son were waiting for him to come home. The other kids had gone across to be with their mainland wives and husbands. They were better off.

'Aye. Supposing a couple of lads did that, while herself is out having the craic. Before she settles in for the serious business.'

Evan nodded and dropped his cigarette beside Jim's first one, watching it sizzle. Jim put his down and ground all three with his boot heel.

'Will we head off so?'

'Aye,' Jim said.

Twenty-Four

Though sympathy alone can't alter facts,
it can help to make them more bearable.

Bram Stoker, *Dracula*, 1897

Rose woke up in the dark, feeling ill and thirsty. She could hear Becky and Matt talking quietly in their bedroom. Her neck was throbbing painfully but that wasn't the worst of it. There was something in her. It was like she had got a bit of the virus that Frank had been fully exposed to. She could feel it crawling through her veins, a creeping parasite exploring its new home. She wanted to cut into herself to get it out, but she knew that wouldn't work.

Frank had done something to Becky when he touched her bump. To her, or the baby. Becky had nearly died. There was no way that Rose was going to be a danger to Becky or the baby. She couldn't stay here with them.

The first part of the storm had come. It was now November. It felt cosy here, with the baby asleep in his room and big, solid Matt in the kitchen, but she knew that it was an illusion. That thing, that creature, was out there and nowhere was safe. And the men were somehow responsible.

She thought back over the many nights she had helped out

in the pub, when drink had loosened their tongues and made them believe they were whispering. There had been a word she didn't understand. She thought she hadn't heard it properly, but now it came to her clearly, like her blood was screaming the name of its invader. *Strix*. She didn't know what it was, but she knew its name. One part of her wanted to recoil from the word. That was the part that wanted to protect Becky and the baby. It was the part that had made her try to lead the birds away when they were attacking Ed and Lia. It was the part that forgave Matt when he broke her china because he was too big and built for the outdoors.

The other part was new. It sharpened and focused as though the word had called it. It wanted to be close to its maker, to serve and to worship. If she allowed that part to grow strong, she would lose herself and those she loved. And she knew it would become strong, because that part of her was alien, not really her at all. That part of her, spreading through her veins was the Strix. That wild creature was at once somewhere out there, and inside her.

She sat out on the edge of the bed, moving carefully, thinking about the Hall.

She had been going there before the Strix attacked her and Becky. She must go now and allow nothing to stop her.

There was probably nothing that she could do against such a fearsome enemy, but nothing was going to prevent her trying to protect her family. She was going to have to die anyway, before the creeping thing inside her turned her into a beast. Josie had enough tablets to do the job, all being normal. But she feared it would take something different to kill what had got into her.

She found a selection of her clothes in the wardrobe, brought here by Becky no doubt. She quietly dressed in jeans and jumper and pulled on an anorak that also hung there. If she was quick, she could slip down the hall and out the front door that was seldom used. She stood at the bedroom door which was ajar and listened.

'We can't stay here, Matt, house or no house,' Becky was saying. 'Not after what happened with that thing.'

The Strix, Rose thought.

'I don't know what that was, but you're right. I don't want to raise the baby here. It's not a good place. I didn't see it before, but I feel it now.'

'And we're bringing Mam,' Becky said.

'Of course. We're all going,' Matt said.

Rose's eyes stung. She was glad they were going, and wished she could go with them, and see her grandson grow up. She blew a silent kiss in their direction and slipped down the corridor, peeping in at the sleeping baby for a last look. She hoped they would decide on a name soon. The child needed a name.

From experience, she held tight to the front door as she opened it. The front of the house having no protection, the wind nearly ripped the door out of her hands. She ran out and pulled it shut behind her. She feared they wouldn't have missed the sudden howl of the wind, so she ran as fast as she could down the hill to the road, glad that Becky had brought her sneakers. Even with them, her knees hurt. It was a long time since she had run anywhere. She carried on through the pain, through the wind snatching at her breath.

If they had heard the wind, they would have gone to check the baby first. What would they do when they found she was gone? Becky wouldn't leave the baby and Matt wouldn't leave the two of them alone. Becky was a good daughter, but she had her own family now. She couldn't put her mother above the baby. She had already left him to follow her after the funeral and nearly got killed over it. Rose was glad that no one followed her this time, even though she had never felt so alone.

The storm was here, trying to knock her off her feet, but the way the sky looked she realised that there was worse to come. Out over the ocean, something was awake and beginning to roar.

She forged onwards against the wind, past the pub and on to the Hall whose sharp outline cut the sky. At last she was climbing over the broken wall, her progress raising a small flock of birds sheltering in it. They puffed up like a drift of brown leaves, before settling back down. She made her way through the wet grass and weeds towards the house.

It had been years since she had been over here, and she had never got as close to the house as this. She knew it must have been magnificent once, full of life and light, but right now it was a dreadful relic of better days. Even the sight of it always caused a shudder but, with the Strix inside her, she felt differently. If she had wanted to turn back now, she wasn't sure that she could.

The huge front door was locked. Andrew probably had a key. His and Dan's land bordered the Hall, once part of the great estate, when the farmers were only tenants on the land they had worked for generations. She moved around to the back of the house. Most of the windows were boarded up but, close to the old stables and coach house, she found one where the board was hanging loose, with the glass smashed in behind it. She pulled the board off, hunted around for a rock and used it to knock the remaining glass away, wincing at the noise she was making. She had to drag an old crate under the window to climb on, testing her weight gingerly. The last thing she needed was a fall, out here in the cold and wet. She would never be found. The end was coming for her, but she didn't want it like that. As much as she could, she would take some control over her own fate.

Ignoring the pain in her knees and back, at least as much as she could, she hoisted herself up and by force of will squeezed through the broken window and managed to get onto the floor inside. The house was all around her and at first she couldn't move away from the cold air coming through the window. But there was no point in delaying. It had to be done. A long shard of glass winked at her from the floor. She slipped it in her pocket.

She moved through the room carefully. The floor of any other abandoned house might have been covered with empty beer cans and other rubbish, but this one was free of debris. It looked as though the house had been left untouched since its last occupant left centuries ago.

She pulled open the damp swollen door of the room and found herself in a corridor. It led to the large front hall. There was no apparent light source, but a soft luminescence filled the space. The stairs was magnificent. It rose to a landing and continued both left and right from there.

Rose could see that it had once been beautiful. The wealthy family who had lived here had wanted for nothing. Although covered in dust and mould, she could make out the fabulous ladies and scenes in the many paintings that graced the walls.

There was nothing to hear except the wind echoing around the building and yet she felt them coming. She pressed herself into an alcove and watched, terrified and fascinated.

They came in twos, ladies and gentlemen, finely dressed, enjoying some unheard music. As she watched, the couples turned to face each other and began to dance. They were colourless and Rose couldn't make out their features. It looked as if their faces and bodies were veiled in cobwebs. As they moved, small contrails of it followed them. They didn't seem to be aware of Rose. After some indeterminable time, they faded from sight and Rose was about to move from her alcove when the silent procession began again, this time from a different part of the hall. Again, the couples started to dance, filmed in whatever was veiling their features.

Rose moved out into the hall. None of the dancers reacted to her. Her bladder was suddenly full and she was afraid that she might wet herself. Nonetheless, she pressed on and when she had to slip through the dancers she did so, somehow confident they wouldn't see or feel her. When she brushed against them, it felt like dewfall, soft and otherworldly. She was left with a sensation of sadness instead of fear. When she looked back, the dancers were gone.

Rose started up the stairs. It seemed to go on forever. Rose was in a nightmare world, where the corridor never ended and the stairs climbed higher and higher. She bit her lip hard and took one more step to the first landing and turned left, climbing with the aid of the bannister. At the top, she stopped to catch her breath. The black-and-white tiles below were very far away.

'*Rose.*'

The voice was unmistakeable. She had taken enough orders for pints from him over the years. He was in shadow, but she knew.

'Hello, Dan. We thought you were gone across for good.'

He chuckled and the sound made her skin crawl. The invader in her blood responded.

'That's funny. I did go across after a manner of speaking,' he said.

Rose nodded.

'Seems like you're heading that way yourself, woman.'

'Let me see you, Dan.'

He had been waiting for her to ask. He stepped out of the shadows and she saw what she had ahead of her. The voice was the only part of him that was familiar. In every other way, he looked more like that girl. He was beautiful, as he had certainly never been in life. His face was white, and the unearthly light caught the tips of the tiny feathers that overlapped on his face. The transformation was not complete, but even since he stepped out she could see that it was continuing, filling in the bare patches of skin still left on his body. One part of her knew that it was hideous, but it was like the paintings that Becky showed her in her art books. They were mix-ups that Rose couldn't understand but there was something strangely magical about them. Dan was a monster and all she wanted to do was be close to him.

'Come on then, come to me.'

Rose almost went. She had taken the first step when she heard a cry like a bird or a child. It pierced her.

Becky. Oh, she had been so small. Premature. They let them go home but they thought she mightn't live. Rose had tucked her to her breast and kept her there next to her heart. Frank had made her a sling. She slept in a chair with the child and carried her around all day, praying silently. It had been summer at least, so she had spent a lot of time sitting on the bench looking out at the Chimneys. Funny that it was at that very bench that Frank himself had almost caused the loss of Becky's own child.

And she had thrived. The doctors were amazed and, Rose thought, a bit put out that they were wrong. To them, at the time, there was no reason why a mother's love could save a child's life. But that had often been true and Rose had no doubt that it would be true again. After all, it was why she was here. To save her daughter and her daughter's son. She wished they had named him before the storm had come.

'Rose, come to me. You're so close.'

She walked towards him, but her mind was her own again. She could feel the pull of him, like the moon pulls the tide but, for this one moment at least, she was herself.

He extended his arms towards her and his face sharpened and became rapacious. She slipped the shard of glass from her pocket and went into his embrace.

He hadn't fully changed. When the shard went into his

heart, he screamed and blood gushed over her hand. He clamped his arms around her, crushing her face against the blood and feathers. She couldn't breathe and the blood kept flooding but she could feel his arms loosening. If she could just hold on long enough, she would be free.

And then she tasted the blood.

They had siphoned petrol out of Andrew's car and filled a jerry can. When they were ready, they had set off towards the Hall. The wind had picked up and they had to lean into it. Although it was impossible, Evan felt more like himself than he had since it all began.

With the Hall looming over them, he stopped and rubbed his knee. Jim watched, then raised his bushy eyebrows.

'*I hurt it the night she came, remember?*' He had to shout against the wind, which was trying to get into his lungs.

Jim frowned. '*Aye, but it hasn't hurt all this time,*' he yelled.

'*No!*'

They moved on, accepting the change. The pain in Evan's knee was fresh and he felt a trickle of warm blood run down his shin and into his sock. He didn't say anything.

They gathered sticks and rubbish and set the kindling at the door of the house. Neither of them wanted to go inside, even though that would have ensured the job. They poured petrol over the mound they had made and stood back. Jim lit a cigarette with difficulty, turning away from the wind. When he had got it going, he flicked it onto the pile. They stood back, but it didn't catch straight away. Evan was about to put his boot to the wood to shift the cigarette when it suddenly caught.

The wind helped. The blaze rose quickly and Jim pointed to the bottom of the door which was blackening. They waited until a flame flickered on the door itself before turning away.

At the bottom of the driveway they stopped, even though the storm was lashing their faces. They watched while the fire grew, racing up the front of the house.

Evan's knee throbbed and he saw Jim rubbing at the arthritis in his knuckles. It was working. It might mean death for them, but it would be welcome after so long.

Then they saw a woman running from the side of the house. She stopped when she saw the fire and seemed entranced by it. Evan looked at his old friend. Jim shook his head. She would be far from the first innocent they had left to die by their hand. Yet, Evan had wanted to be finally free of all his past deeds and their dreadful consequences. Would it help to wash his sins away if he saved this one woman? He reached for Jim's hand for a handshake, but the older man refused the shake. Instead, he shrugged his shoulders and trotted up the drive towards the woman. Evan, surprised, started after him, despite the pain in his knee.

They skirted the fire, going through what had been a garden, and coming out behind the woman, seeing what she saw.

The fire was blazing higher than the roof of the Hall, but it was a tower of flame, not touching the building. There was a burn on the door where they had seen the first flame, but otherwise the house was not damaged. Evan stared at it and, with terrible regret, felt the pain leave his knee.

The woman turned to look at them. It was Rose, but Evan only barely recognised her. She was covered in blood, looking as though someone had slit a pig's throat with her standing underneath. She smiled at them and her teeth were impossibly white against the dark blood on her face.

But it was not just the blood. They could see that she was transformed.

Jim looked at Evan, and he looked back. For the first time in their long friendship, Evan groped for Jim's hand and was glad when his friend took it. Together they faced the creature that had been Rose. As she came for them, they ran to meet her, driving her back with them until they fell together into the flames. For a moment, Evan thrilled to the feel of it wrapping him up. It was curiously like the deadly cold of falling into a winter sea. Then it burned off his clothes and his hair and he opened his mouth to scream. The eager fire rushed down his throat and consumed the part of the beast that had lived inside him since the night of the storm in 1695, the night when they had brought her here and she had paid for her freedom with centuries of life for them all. And still, like men before them, they had held her as their captive, as she had held them. They fed her, and she fed them. Without one, the other couldn't exist.

When the fire had taken his eyes and his last thoughts were of nothing but pain, he heard the terrible scream once more, this time emerging from Rose as the fire forced the beast from her veins and she returned to a brief mortal existence, full of pain. Together, he, Rose and Jim became part of the fire. The heat burned them to ashes, and sank back into itself, a smouldering mess extinguished by the rain. The Hall lived on with only the shadow of the fire visible upon its face.

Andrew watched the fire and, when it was done, he went around to the back of the Hall and quietly let himself in.

Twenty-Five

*There is a reason that all things are as they are, and did you
see with my eyes and know with my knowledge,
you would perhaps better understand.*

Bram Stoker, *Dracula*, 1897

Something hit the window and shocked Jasmine awake. Ed
and Lia were snuggled close together on Ed's mattress.
Jasmine propped herself on her elbow and looked around.
The fire had bedded down and was low and red. Harry was
standing by the window. She got up quietly and went to stand
beside him. He glanced at her.

'Is everything OK?' she asked.

He nodded. 'Rough night.' He put his arm around her and
she leaned into him. It seemed the most natural thing in the
world.

'Are you scared?' she whispered.

It took him some time to answer and, although his
presence was reassuring, his answer was not.

'All things must come to an end. It's something I've learned
over and over again, but I guess I just keep forgetting. This
feels like an end.'

She slid her arm around his waist and they stood like that,
watching lightning flash behind a big house on the horizon.

He turned her to him.

'Maybe it could be a beginning too.'

He bent and kissed her cheek before letting her go. She went back to her mattress and watched as he banked up the fire and lay down on his own makeshift bed. He threw his arm across his eyes and went quickly to sleep. In the low red light of the fire, the resemblance to her husband was startling, unsettling. She looked over at Lia. She had turned on her back and she too had an arm over her eyes.

Unable to sleep, Jasmine slipped away from the others and quietly moved a chair to the window to watch the lightning. This time there was a peculiar light out there. A red glow. She looked back into the room and realised that it hadn't just been the light of their own fire. Something was burning out there, perhaps struck by lightning. She watched it, hypnotised by the way the fire flickered in the wind. It would blow out, or it would spread. She had done some fundraising for injured fire-fighters and had heard their stories about how fire could seem to have a life of its own.

She could dimly see her own reflection in the glass. She was wearing a white T-shirt and leggings, thanks to Ed, who had grabbed her bag as they ran. The pale image was superimposed over the red glow in the distance. She changed her focus to the reflection instead of the fire and found that the image was regarding her. She recoiled. The image was not hers. There was a girl standing out there, just within the reach of the meagre light from the room. She was a gorgeous girl, but Jasmine didn't rush to the door to bring her in from the storm. The storm was having no impact on her, except to play with her long hair. She looked at Jasmine with her head on one side and then moved, too fast for Jasmine's eyes to see. She blinked and found herself face to face with the girl, with only the glass between them. The girl was standing close to the window, her features distorted by the rivers of rain on the surface. Jasmine had never seen anything like her.

She cried out and then others were moving. She couldn't take her eyes off the girl. Lia put her arm around her in the same way Harry had earlier. Ed was standing beside Lia. The girl was watching him intently.

Harry was last. He walked past them and went close to the glass. The girl turned towards him and Harry did a curious thing. He raised one hand as though to touch her face, and she responded by tilting her head towards his hand. Although there could be no contact, the gesture was given and received, and a blink later the girl was gone. Harry stayed looking out the window, then turned to face them.

'The Hall is on fire.'

There was nothing they could do. Jasmine could see that Harry was agitated, but he had no way of fighting a fire, even if it had been safe to go out in the storm with that girl out there. The lovely girl with the birdlike gaze was dangerous. As with Harry though, she had felt a magnetic pull towards her. In the end, it didn't matter, because the fire burned itself out, or yielded to the storm. Either way, in flashes of lightning, the big house could still be seen, standing on the horizon.

Becky was sitting in the kitchen in the soft glow of a candle. Matt shuffled in, wearing thick socks. The stove had died down and the house had started to cool. He threw dry sticks into the stove and opened the vents. It was still hot inside and the sticks caught as he stood there.

'Electricity is gone,' Becky said.

'The generator is running though.'

'I know. I just didn't want to put the lights on,' she said.

He filled a kettle for tea and put it on the gas hob.

'Can't sleep?'

She shook her head. 'I still think we should have gone after Mam.'

'I looked as much as I could, baby, without leaving you.'

She nodded.

'The baby is a good sleeper, isn't he?' Matt said.

'I fed him and he went right back.'

'Sorry I slept through it,' he said, taking her hand.

'That's OK. I –'

She didn't get to finish her sentence. With the wind and rain clattering against the windows, the house wasn't completely silent, but both of them jumped when they heard the noise. Something had thumped onto the roof.

'A branch maybe,' Matt said, although he was holding her hand as tightly as she was holding his.

When a window at the front of the house smashed inward, she screamed. They both jumped to their feet, Matt heading for the window, Becky for the baby's room. The baby was too quiet. Cold ran through her and she slapped at the light switches as she ran. Although it was a small house, she was in a nightmare where the corridor to the baby's room was infinite. His door was open wider than she had left it. Becky's childhood music box was playing its whirling waltz. It should have been closed on the dresser.

She struck the light switch with her palm and ran to the cot, her foot hitting the music box where it lay open on the floor. The cot was empty. She turned and saw what she had run right past in her panic. The baby was awake but silent. His eyes, unable to focus yet, were wide open. Becky put her hands to her belly. She had felt his fear before, while he was still inside her. Now, she could see it.

The girl, the creature, whatever she was, had the baby. She was cradling him in one pale arm, holding him close to her body. She was alien to the cosy room. White, sharp, somehow perfect. Becky looked down. What appeared to be a flimsy lace dress was long feathers. Her feet were concealed beneath, but as she swayed with the baby, Becky saw that they were bare and ended in talons. They stood in a tableau, with the music-box waltz winding slowly down.

Later, Becky understood that she was deaf from the sound of her heartbeat in all her pulse points, pounding in her ears. Later, she remembered that her vision had narrowed, blackening at the edges as though she was blinkered. Later, she saw all the things she could have done, or tried. In the moment, she was overcome by adrenalin and rage. She launched herself across the small room, her hands out to snatch the child from the arms of the creature.

Her bottomless horror and fury almost succeeded. She came within a hair's breadth of seizing her baby. Instead, the girl brought up her free hand and struck Becky to one side. She hit the wall and her teeth snapped shut on her tongue. The iron taste of blood filled her mouth and she spat. The girl's lips pulled back from her teeth.

Then Matt was there, snatching the baby from the creature's grasp. Shooting a desperate look at Becky he turned and ran, the baby's silence and terror breaking into screams.

Becky scrambled up, crying out at the pain between her legs as some of her stitches tore free. She ran at the girl, then swerved, her soft socks skating her past into the hall. It was a hopeless move, destined to fail. She had seen before how fast the other could move. She felt a sharp pain in her scalp, so real was the image in her mind of the girl's hands grabbing her hair and yanking her back into the room. But, instead, she felt the wind of the girl passing over her in pursuit of Matt and the baby.

Francis. That was his name. They had decided months before that if it was a boy they would call him after her father. A girl was to be named for Matt's mother.

Now, she knew that what her father had become was not his fault. It had been this devilish creature, this *bitch* who had taken him from them. Not just him. Since her mother had left the house as the first waves of the storm had made landfall, she had known that she too was lost.

She got up, feeling like the floor was molasses. She ran to the kitchen. The door was hanging from one hinge. Someone had shoved the table so hard that the corner of it had knocked a hole in the plaster of the wall. Matt was lying on the ground, not moving. Becky stepped over him and ran into the night. The wind should have made it impossible to hear anything. But what she was listening to was the absence of sound from her child. That monster had him up there in the dark clouds, in the heart of the storm.

Matt came to, feeling a monstrous throb of pain in his skull. She had thrown the table at him and snatched the baby from his arms as he fell. He must have hit his head. All he wanted to do was shut his eyes until the pain subsided, but a rush of cold air snapped him into full awareness.

The baby!

The front door was open.

'Becky!'

He got to his feet and the room wavered and spun around him. After a moment, the dizziness passed, and he lumbered to the door. Becky was running down the hill in her pyjamas.

Outside, the world was dark and howling. A broken branch struck his shoulder and he raised an arm to protect his face from flying debris. Then he saw Becky spinning, looking skyward.

He ran to her and wrapped his arms around her. She struggled but he held tight.

'*She's got my baby! She's got my baby!*'

'*We'll get him back!*' He was roaring the words to make himself heard.

Becky tried to break free again. '*Let me go!*' she screamed.

'No!' He held her tight. 'We need help! We need the others! Come back to the house, love.'

Becky stared at him, furious and desperate.

'I need to get my bow,' he said, 'and you have to get some clothes and shoes on!'

A shriek pierced the storm and they both turned their faces up to the rain.

That monster was up there somewhere with their baby. Becky shook in his arms, rage rising through her like sap.

'*Hurry!*' She screamed the word at him and together they ran for the house.

Twenty-Six

The last I saw of Count Dracula was his kissing his hand to me, with a red light of triumph in his eyes, and with a smile that Judas in hell might be proud of.

Bram Stoker, *Dracula*, 1897

Jasmine couldn't sleep. Dawn couldn't be far away. She got up and opened a small window to let some air in and immediately heard the crash of the waves followed by a terrible booming noise. She shut the window against it. If anyone had still been sleeping, they weren't any longer.

'It's the blowholes,' Ed said, from where he lay, his eyes still closed.

Lia sat up.

Ed sat up beside her, yawning.

'They're holes in the rock that go down to caves and when the sea goes in, it shoots up and makes a booming noise,' Lia said.

'Oh. Your father told me about them, but I didn't expect the noise to be so ...'

'Boomy?' Lia said.

Jasmine laughed. 'Yes, boomy.'

With everyone awake early, tea seemed to be called for and they sat in front of the replenished fire and Jasmine noted how they all, including herself, looked to Harry for leadership.

'The storm has eased, but there's worse to come. I think we should try running a boat across with whoever wants to go.

'Is it safe to go out?' Jasmine said.

Harry cast a haunted look at the window. 'It'll be light soon. I think it'll be OK. It won't be a smooth crossing though. I'll go down to the village to see what boats are in.'

'It's still nighttime,' Jasmine said, frowning.

Harry stood up, too restless to finish his mug of tea. 'It's not really dark anymore. Look, it's starting to go grey. Stay inside, just in case. I won't be long. You won't be able to take much so put together what you can't do without.'

He turned to go but paused.

'Be ready. I might be in a hurry when I get back.' With that, he shrugged on his coat and went out, leaning into the wind.

Ed tied his bootlaces. 'I've got to get to the farm to check the house.'

'I'll come with you,' Lia said.

Jasmine stood up. 'Lia, you are not going out there.'

'Mom, we'll be quick. I promise.'

Jasmine took her hand. 'I can't lose you.'

'You won't. I'll be with Ed. And Harry is right. It's getting brighter.'

Lia gave her hand a squeeze, as though Jasmine were the child. Then she and Ed pulled on jackets, their faces lit up with the excitement of getting out into the wind, together, despite the horrors of the night. It was easy for them to cast aside nightmares when morning came. Still, Jasmine saw them check the wild sky before they left the shelter of the pub.

When they were all gone, the pub seemed to fade twenty years into the past. There was very little to show that time had moved along at all. Suddenly, her thoughts were not of Harry and these strange new feelings. She could clearly see memory's echo of her young self, with her new husband, his hair as fiery as his temper, as hot as his passion. She shook herself and sorted through her bag for a few cosmetics, her hairbrush and her credit card, then sat uneasily in front of the fire, waiting for someone to come back to her.

It was great to be out in the wind. The storm had flung a few things around, but it all had the look of a poltergeist storm, more mischievous than malevolent. Harry thought that there was a bigger storm to come and Ed agreed. Still, being out together in the whirling, salty air, with the wind snatching their breath and making them laugh, was suddenly the best place to be. It felt to Lia like she was being as alive as anyone could be.

They sobered up when they reached the driveway of the farm. It was too close to the Hall.

Together, they turned off the power and closed shutters, sealing the place up as tight as they could to help the house ride out whatever the winter brought.

Outside again, Ed moved anything that could be lifted and dropped, tying gates more firmly shut so that they wouldn't be broken from their hinges. When he was satisfied with everything, he rested his hand briefly on the outside wall of the farmhouse. The gesture was goodbye. Lia gave him a moment, turning to look across the yard at the barn.

Something moved, attracting her attention. She frowned. She knew next to nothing about birds but this bird, sitting on a tree growing against the yard wall, looked distinctly out of place. She watched it, hoping it would still be there when Ed was ready to go.

It didn't move much, just shifting slightly with the occasional gust of wind in the sheltered yard. It was a soft grey, almost white, and the wind was playing with the feathers on its chest.

Ed took her hand and she squeezed his fingers.

'Look,' she said, nodding in the direction of the bird.

Ed frowned.

'Do you see it?' Lia said.

'Yeah, but I shouldn't be seeing it.'

'Why not?' Lia said. 'Is it rare?'

'Typical Strigidae, genus Megascops. European Screech Owl. Nocturnal.'

'Nocturnal?' Lia said. 'What's it doing out now then?'

'Don't know. It's not right. Maybe it's sick.'

He walked slowly across the yard at an oblique angle. When he got closer to the owl, he stopped and looked carefully up at it. Lia saw his hand move towards the camera that no longer hung around his neck. He checked the movement and stared up for a long time and the bird appeared to stare back at him. When Ed came back to her, he looked odd.

'Does it look sick?' Lia asked.

He shook his head. 'Looks good. Beautiful actually. Really beautiful. Come on, let's get out of here.'

They set off down the drive again. Lia screamed when she heard a shriek behind her. The owl was flying, almost touching their heads as it swooped over, climbing with the wind into one of the stunted trees that were dotted here and there along the farm wall.

'What's it doing?' Lia asked.

'I don't know!' His voice was abrupt, almost unfriendly.

They walked on as fast as they could, leaning into the wind that howled up from the cliff edge.

Lia didn't look back but was convinced the owl was following them, battling the conditions to keep them in sight. Finally, in sight of the pub, she couldn't stand it any longer and whirled around. Nothing. When she turned back, she saw Harry outside the pub. He raised a hand, beckoning urgently, then went inside. Ed took Lia's hand and they hurried on.

At the door, Ed gave her a quick kiss on the cheek.

'Sorry I snapped at you back there. I didn't mean to. The bird was freaking me out.'

'Me too. It stopped following us though.'

'No, it didn't.'

'Yes, just before we saw Harry, I looked for it and it had gone.'

'Lia, it stayed with us the entire time. I was watching it,' Ed said.

They stared at each other and a shiver ran through Lia.

'That's so creepy.'

Ed looked behind him and then ushered her inside. 'It's still right there. Plain as day.'

'Oh my God, that's messed up.'

The others looked up at them. Harry was back and Matt and Becky had arrived. Becky was white. She had been crying but Lia had never seen anyone who looked so filled with fury.

'What's happened?' Lia asked. 'Is Rose OK?'

'Rose left late yesterday afternoon. We haven't seen her,' Matt said. He was holding Becky's hand, their fingers white-knuckled. He was carrying a weapon Lia had never seen before, but that she recognised as a crossbow.

'That thing, that creature took my baby,' Becky said. 'I'm going to kill her.'

'A Strix – that's what Brendan called it,' Lia said.

'Whatever the bloody thing is called, we're going to the Hall,' Matt said. 'We need all the help we can get, but if you're leaving, we'll still go.'

'We can't leave,' Harry said. 'I checked the harbour. It's pretty rough, but it wouldn't matter if it was like glass. Someone set the boats adrift. Some are wrecked and the rest are missing. We're not going anywhere.'

'*We,*' Becky said with emphasis, her voice deepened and hoarse, 'are going to find my baby.' She stood up, pulling her hand free, and looked at her husband. 'I know what you're all thinking. Even you, Matt. You're thinking that my baby, my son, is dead. That she took him and did something to him.' She glared around at them, daring any of them to contradict her. '*I know he's alive*. I would feel it if he wasn't. He's alive and I'm going to find him. You can come to help, or you can go to hell.'

She pulled her coat around her and pushed past Lia, pulling the door back and leaving it wide open. Matt grabbed his weapon, crossed the floor in a couple of strides and ran after his wife.

Jasmine hurried towards the door and Lia joined her. Harry and Ed followed. She saw Ed looking at something in the sky that she couldn't see and her skin crawled. Either only Ed could see the bird watching them, or Ed had gone crazy. After the last couple of days, either could be true. She grabbed her mother's arm and was glad to feel her return the squeeze.

'Mom, what are we doing?'

Jasmine shook her head. 'All I know is that I can't let that girl go to face the monster that took her baby without help. I would do the same as her, and I hope someone would help me.'

'Are there other people on the island, Harry?' Lia asked. 'Did you find anyone?'

Harry answered. 'The people who run the little shop are there, but they're not moving. There's a couple of other families, but they wouldn't answer the door.'

A gust tried to lift them off their feet. Jasmine and Lia screamed but managed to stay upright. The sea was slate-grey, topped with rushing white crests. The scudding clouds of earlier had gathered and darkened. As Lia watched, lightning forked at the heart of the cloud mass and, as though the electricity had torn the sky, heavy rain started to fall again. It felt like night was falling, despite the time.

Their little cortege tightened up until they were walking in a bunch. Lia didn't know if this was a good or bad idea with lightning flashing all around them, but no one wanted to walk alone. The worst was when they were huddled together, hurrying up the driveway to the Hall. It was the last place in the world that Lia wanted to rush towards, but they had to get under some sort of cover.

It was hard to see through the dark veil of rain, but it was impossible to miss the huge patch of burned ground where there had been a fire. There was an untouched strip of weedy gravel between the burnt ground and the house, as though there had been some sort of firewall. It cut a straight line across the front of the building. Only the front door of the house had been scorched.

Although the door was huge and thick, Matt gave it two almighty kicks and drove it inward. The lock didn't give way, but the door took the frame with it, falling inside the house.

Terror ripped through Lia as she stepped over the threshold into the Hall, gripping Ed's hand until he suddenly let go. Becky set off across black-and-white tiles towards the magnificent staircase. Lia looked around for Ed and Jasmine but saw only Matt outside the door. He was shouting but she couldn't hear him. She turned back to call Becky, who had stopped walking. Something clattered onto the floor behind Lia but before she could look to see what it was, she saw that Becky was surrounded with what looked like floating cobwebs. With a few more steps, Lia felt it herself. Cold. Awful cold. Her heart stuttered in her chest and it was all she could do to keep moving. She thought she heard music, and then she was out of it. And completely alone.

One minute, Ed could feel Lia's hand in his, expressing fear in the tightness of her grip, the next she was gone. Ed stood on the black-and-white tiles and looked around. Where there had been dampness and age, there was now a pristine hall, glowing in the light of oil lamps. Where there had been only the small group of people who had entered the building with him, there were now people everywhere. He backed onto the bottom step of the staircase, bumping into someone. He turned quickly, Lia's name on his lips. The woman gave him a contemptuous look that turned to interest. She was wearing the sort of ball gown that Ed didn't have the word for. Her hair was piled on her head and her skin was powdered pale. She swished past him to join her companion, a tall man with a neatly trimmed beard. Ed blinked hard and his vision doubled. The colourful people wavered as though they were underwater, or he was.

Then music started and everyone turned to look at the stairs behind Ed. He looked too and his stomach flipped. It was her.

She was the most beautiful creature he had ever seen. She was a girl really, but something noble about her expression and the way she carried herself made her ageless. She moved slowly down the stairs, ignoring the gasps and spontaneous applause from the assembled crowd who had become her captive audience. Instead, she looked only at Ed. He was frozen to the spot as she swayed towards him.

She stopped at the bottom and tilted her head for a kiss. He pressed his lips against her cheek. He could feel his blood rushing around his body. She smiled at him, her eyes golden, her skin shining. Taking his hand, she led him into the crowd, which parted for them. Together, they walked through the hall and into the ballroom. The others fell into procession with them.

The ballroom was impossibly large. Ed couldn't see the end of it and when he looked back he could no longer see where they had entered the room. There was no time to react. Still in charge, she led him into a dance that he couldn't have known and yet did. Dizzy and with his eyes sometimes becoming unfocused, he danced with her.

She swept him around until they were in the curve of a bay window. They sat on the window seat and Ed looked out at the path to the beach, lit by footmen standing with lanterns.

Her hand touched his cheek, bringing his attention back to her. He brought the hand to his lips and pressed a kiss upon the palm. When he opened his eyes, his vision blurred again. Her hair, which had been fair enough to be called white, was now falling in messy chestnut waves past her shoulders. She was still pale, but her lips were red. He shook his head, saw vivid green eyes and jumped to his feet. She stood, again pale, her eyes golden once more.

Not Lia, he thought. *Beautiful, but not Lia.*

She leaned into him, trapping him against the panelled curve of the window alcove. He groaned because he knew that if she wanted him, there was little he could do to stop her, and little he would want to do.

He would be hers, forever, if she wanted it. Some secret place inside him, hidden deep down, would love another, but it wouldn't matter.

Her lips touched the skin of his throat and he turned his head to allow her freer access. Unlike before, when she had sliced his skin with her long nails, this time he felt the cool press of sharp teeth. It was unbearably exciting.

'*Get away from her!*' came a strong a male voice.

She paused. The word *don't* came to Ed's lips, but no sound came out. She drew back, leaving him bereft.

Andrew. The endless ballroom was empty except for Andrew.

'*She is mine,*' Andrew said between his teeth. His face was dark red. 'I've been with her from the beginning and no one is going to take her from me. We're going to do whatever we want, forever. You are just an interloper. You don't matter. This island is mine.'

He walked closer and took her slender hand.

'We belong together,' he said, his voice soft.

She looked down at her hand, then back at Andrew, head cocked to one side. Then she turned her head to look at Ed, her expression hungry and sharp.

The attack was slow enough to see, but too fast to stop. She leapt, sank her teeth into flesh, and ripped Andrew's throat so deeply that his head lolled onto his shoulder, only barely attached. He stood for a horrible moment, with blood sheeting down his body and pooling at his feet. Then he folded, his feet skidding on his own blood. When his head hit the floor, it briefly closed the terrible wound in his neck like a mouth, before it gaped open again exposing the curve of the neck bone.

Ed leaned over and vomited, his eyes streaming. With his throat and nose burning, he leaned against the wall.

She was still there, still beautiful, even the blood on her mouth beautiful, but now he could see more clearly that she was sharp, silent and strange. As he had done before, he called Lia to mind, remembering how they had pressed so close against each other, how she had been ready to be with him, how the memory of his terror and arousal from his experience with the girl had made him stop. He didn't want anyone on his mind but Lia when the moment came for them.

As before, filling his mind and heart with Lia gave the creature pause.

This time, she didn't look sad, she looked angry, and he became afraid for Lia. But he had misjudged the situation. She flung him to the floor and crouched over him. Without hesitating, she bent to his throat and sank her teeth into his jugular vein.

Ed screamed into the dark, empty house and couldn't tell himself if it was a scream of pain and horror, or one of awful pleasure.

Jasmine had tried to follow Lia into the house, but the wind caught her like an invisible hand. It lifted her and took her breath away. She had flashing impressions of being flung through dark clouds with piercing forks of lightning all around her. Then, as though she had reached the calm eye of the storm, she was suddenly released into a vacuum. She dropped, screaming, and crashed through the surface of the rough sea. Water rushed into her mouth and darkness surrounded her.

When she regained consciousness, she felt quite calm, though she must surely have been drowning. She felt no pain, or desire for air, and wondered if she were really awake.

I'm underwater. It can't be real. Not happening. I'll close my eyes and when I open them Lia and the others will be here and everything will be normal.

Someone spoke but she heard it not with her ears but in her mind.

Jazz, open your eyes. Don't be afraid. Be strong. Save our little girl.

Will? Is that you?

Open your eyes.

She did. Will wasn't there but the bodies were. Some were relatively fresh and intact, but others were just bones with some rags attached. The worst were the ones in between. Something had been at them, tearing lumps of rotting flesh away, leaving exposed bone. She could see ropes of grey intestines bloated with gas and ordure, floating above corpses. Her stomach jolted, and bile tried to rise up her throat. With it came the agonising need for air. She pushed herself upwards, her head pounding. She sucked in air desperately, coughing and spitting. There were bodies on the surface of the water too and one moved.

It was tangled with a mass of other corpses but it clawed its way free, its bones green with algae. A feathery frond was growing from an eye socket. Jasmine screamed, half sinking.

She clamped her lips shut, not wanting to swallow any of the filthy water.

The other bodies shifted and squirmed. She tried to back up but found herself against a rock wall. She kicked frantically, terrified that she would be grabbed from underneath. There was a stone ledge against which the water surged at the back of what she now saw was a cave, so she swam for it. The ledge was wide. Clambering up on it didn't help, because a glance back showed her that the water was churning with more than the incoming sea. Bodies and bones were protruding above the surface and all the empty eye sockets were focused on her. There was nowhere to go. She shut her eyes again.

Sorry, Will, my darling. There's nothing I can do. I'm trapped here.

There was no answer but the sound of the sea. She heard the click of the first bony hands reaching onto the ledge, but then the sound was drowned out. The eye of the storm must have passed. The wind and sea began to whirl and roar. Together, they sounded like a furious animal charging her. She opened her eyes and saw the base of an enormous wave racing towards the cave mouth. There was nowhere to retreat. She took a huge breath and braced herself.

Let it take you, baby. Go with it.

Will?

The sea rushed into the cave, pushing dead bodies before it in hideous ranks. It washed much higher than the ledge and Jasmine found herself in churning water with corpses swirling around her. She was as helpless against the force of the water as they were. Together, she and the dead were lifted and thrust upwards, knocked hard against the sides of what seemed to be a vertical tunnel. She covered her face to protect it from the broken bones flying around her.

She was suddenly free of the tunnel, carried into the air on a platform of water. Lightning flashed and the water dropped away, throwing her onto soft spongy grass. She lay in the rain, cut, bruised and winded, listening to the boom of the blowholes breathing in and exhaling the cold ocean. Bones clattered around her. Winded or not, when she saw a disembodied arm twitching beside her, she got to her feet and ran.

Lia crossed the black-and-white tiled floor, her foot kicking something that slid away. She pushed double doors open, revealing a ballroom. Immediately, she felt stuffy warmth on her face and heard music and chattering people. The room was empty. She backed away, her heart thundering. The house was haunted by more than the Strix. It was one thing to come in here with her mother and Becky, and three big strong men, and quite another to be wandering around on her own, after everyone disappeared, and hearing the sound of a party that wasn't there. Then the music faded and she heard Ed's voice. She ran to a bay window which looked out over the dark sea. Whirling, she tried to look everywhere at once. She had heard him. He must be here. After all, he wasn't a ghost. And neither was she.

What if you are? What if you're dead and that's why you're alone and hearing echoes of things.

She shook her head and realised that there was blood on the floor. It was different to the drops of blood she had seen in Ed's kitchen after his father had attacked him, but it was unmistakeably blood. It flooded onto the floor from an invisible source and began to pool. Lia backed away. The blood continued to move and grow on the surface of the floor, until it formed a shape that Lia knew from crime TV shows. Forensic people drew chalk outlines around dead bodies. This was blood, but it took the same shape, flowing around an unseen obstacle, creating a deep red outline, in which Lia could see the yellow flicker of oil lamps. A moment later, she heard a scream, that of a man crying out in terror. There was no reason for her to know, but she knew anyway. It was Ed and he was in terrible, terrible danger. Ignoring the blood, she searched the area, more with her hands and her heart than her eyes. She couldn't find him although she thought that he was close. Sobbing with fear, she ran back to the tiled hall and called his name.

'*Ed!*'

'*Lia!*'

She was answered, but not by Ed. It was Harry's voice from somewhere above her.

'*Harry!*' Lia ran, taking the stairs two at a time. When she reached the landing, she called again, and this time she heard a baby gurgle. She rushed forward. Becky's baby was here, alive.

Again, the sound didn't lead to anyone. There were people in the house, her people, but she couldn't reach them. She turned back to the stairs and gasped. Instead of being covered in dust, it gleamed, polished and shining in the light cast by many lamps. She ran back down to the hallway and this time saw a family walking from what looked like a sitting room into the dining room. They were dressed in old-fashioned clothes and were plainly father and mother, twin boys and a tall, attractive girl with her hair scooped into a thick roll on the back of her head. Lia saw them being greeted by a butler and seated around a long table.

She was invisible to them. They talked and ate while she watched. Feeling trapped and despairing, she went to the long windows and looked out over the driveway. She leaned her forehead against the cold glass pane and tried to think.

It was not just the Strix. The Hall itself was haunted. By ghosts, by the past, she didn't know exactly. If it was the Hall, then maybe all she had to do was go back out the door she had come in.

Walking quickly, she went to the big front door and pulled

it open. The wind and rain took her breath away as she stepped outside.

The sea was rumbling close by and a path was lit leading down to what was probably the Hall's private beach. Not knowing what else to do, and not wanting to leave entirely, in case the others could somehow find her, she set off down the path.

Becky was in darkness. Utter stygian black. She put her palm against her nose but couldn't see a thing. She stood completely still. She had walked across the black-and-white tiles towards the stairs, with the others around her. Then all of life had winked out. She put her arms out and made a slow half-circle with them. There was no one else within reach. She had a funny feeling that she shouldn't call out. She had read a saying once, something about how if you were in a room with a tiger, it was better to have the light on.

The tiger could be staring at her, its eyes better adapted to the darkness than hers. Weren't there stories of tigers stealing children from villages? She knew it wasn't a tiger, but from the moment she thought of it, she was certain that a hunter was there with her. She could feel its eyes burning into her.

Then she heard a sound that she knew with every fibre of her being. A little gurgle.

Francis. He's here somewhere.

Her muscles tensed and she almost took a step forward into the unknown.

Careful. For Francis' sake, go carefully. Think.

She closed her eyes and touched her eyelids. Maybe it wasn't the room that was without light. Maybe it was her. Was she blind? It didn't seem possible that there wasn't the slightest hint of light or shade. Never mind, that would have to be considered later. Right now, she had to make her way in the direction of the tiny noise Francis had made.

She hunkered down, moving slowly. At the very least, there

was solid ground under her feet. Feeling around her, she felt safe enough to kneel and shuffle forward, feeling ahead all the time. The surface was cold and she was crossing straight lines, so she was probably still in the hall of black-and-white tiles. This thought gave her the confidence to move more quickly.

Her sliding hands struck something solid. She explored and realised that she was at the bottom of the stairs. She found the rail and stood, keeping her hand on the banister, and listened. After a minute, she heard him again, this time a little above her. He was moving. She guessed the Strix was still carrying him, climbing the stairs, watching Becky coming after her son, shuffling and blind.

Giving up caution, she ran up the stairs, using the banister as a guide. Although very old, the staircase was perfectly made and each step was even and the same height. Still, she caught her toe near the top and just saved herself, swinging around and hurting her shoulder in her effort to hold on to the rail.

She waited again, thinking. The Strix was watching her, mocking her and always keeping out of reach. There was no way she would be able to save him like this. What would her mother have done?

Becky swallowed a sob. She hadn't admitted to herself before then that her mother was dead. She had needed to hold herself together in order to find the baby and that was no different now. Rose had always been the one that Becky could turn to, so she did so again.

Help me, Mam. I have to get him back. Please help me.

At once she smelled her mother's perfume. Rose had never been big into fashion or beauty, but she did like her old-fashioned *L'aimant* perfume. The scent of it now was an answer. She put out her hand and felt it being gently taken. The essence of her mother filled her, replacing her own senses. She felt Rose's sorrow and love. The combined weight of her mother's pain along with her own was too much to bear.

Dear. Look up, dear. I'm here. I'm helping you see.

Becky did look up. It was no longer fully dark. She could see outlines of the house around her, edged in blue, like the phosphorescence emitted by marsh gases.

Careful.

Yes, careful, she thought. *Don't let her know that you can see a little.*

Becky took an unsteady step forward and turned the corner to the second tier of steps. Being careful not to focus on any one spot for too long, she saw the Strix at the top of the stairs, with Baby Francis still held in one arm. Her little boy was goggling at the girl holding him. He didn't look frightened. He was too young to be able to focus but something had fascinated him.

As Becky slowly mounted the stairs, she saw the Strix touch a taloned finger to the baby's cheek. Francis closed his eyes and a bubble formed between his lips.

Becky reached the top step and started to walk cautiously forward but at a slight angle away from where the Strix stood. She checked the floor ahead with her foot each time, allowing herself to drift gradually towards the Strix. She had no hope of getting the baby – she had seen how fast the Strix could move – but she didn't care. She didn't know how, but her mother would help her, as she had thrown herself into the path of danger before when the Strix had attacked. All Becky could do was trust that her little boy was not meant to be taken from her. She believed in the bond between herself and her mother, and herself and her new baby. Someone was going to have to die and if it had to be her instead of Francis, that was fine.

Without thinking or planning anything more, she turned to face the Strix and lunged at her. The Strix was much stronger than her, but with the added strength of Rose filling her, Becky clamped her hands around the throat of the creature who had stolen her child. The baby let out an outraged shriek as he was caught between their bodies.

Becky gripped hard, digging her fingers into flesh. She was gratified to hear a guttural noise escape the Strix's lips, but she showed no signs of weakening.

Mam, Dad, help me! I can't do it on my own!

She felt hands cover hers. The skin was calloused and rough from years of work at sea. Strong hands and fingers. Thick wrists. Becky knew that even with their help she couldn't kill the beast, but it didn't matter. They were together, for one brief final moment. She pulled her hands out from under her dad's and heard the creature gasp as his stronger hands closed on her slender neck. The Strix's hands flew up to grapple with his and she dropped the baby. Becky's arms were waiting to catch him. Instantly she turned to descend the stairs then glanced back and, with the last of her mother's sight, saw a hazy image of her dad struggling with the monster, holding her down, his face contorted with effort.

Becky rushed down the stairs. Francis was bawling now and it thrilled her to hear it. It was real and alive, as he was. She skidded across the tiles, seen now in shades of grey, and ran from the house. Matt, soaked to the skin and pacing furiously, grabbed her. They hugged the baby between them and kissed, both of them wet with rain and tears.

But they weren't safe. The shade of her dad wouldn't be able to hold the creature for long. Matt tucked the baby inside his coat and they ran for their lives.

Reaching the beach, Lia stood under a rocky outcrop and looked out over the water, shivering, shielding her eyes from wind gusts full of needle-sharp grains.

There was a ship out there, being cast up and thrust down into the turbulent sea. She couldn't see, but she heard it grinding against rocks and smashing against the cliff. The thin screams of the passengers and crew reached her over the howl of wind and water.

Lights came and men came. The lanterns were seldom still and showed her glimpses of the broken ship, dead bodies, men on a ledge above the sea pulling things from corpses, bending over dying people. They finally finished and started back up the rocks, following a path she recognised as the path she had followed with Brendan. Then she heard the Strix scream and shortly after that, the remaining lanterns lit up the flashing image of huge white wings. Lia fled back up the path towards the house. This was the past she was seeing. The men of the island had stolen the lives and valuables of everyone on the ship, but had brought ashore a creature from another place, one that should never have been here.

When she got to the driveway, she saw the Strix, talons outstretched, crash through the long dining-room window.

Lia ran into the hall and heard the screams. The dining room was once again old and damp and there was nothing to see. Still, she could hear awful screams and moans. Finally, there was a heavy silence.

Then a hard clicking sound. Taloned feet walking towards her.

Someone grabbed her from behind, lifting her by the waist and swinging her out of the dining-room door. Whoever it was pulled her back against the wall. She didn't scream. The person was warm and alive. The sound of the talons faded and Lia turned around.

'Harry,' she whispered. 'Thank God. What the hell is going on?'

'I don't know. Everything is all mixed up,' he said.

He sounded strange. Less in control than usual.

'You're the first one I've seen since we came in,' she said. 'I was alone. Have you seen the others?'

He shook his head, but he was looking over her head. She got a creepy feeling and moved to stand with her back to the wall beside him. He fumbled for her hand and his fingers were icy cold.

'What is it?' she whispered.

'Look,' he said. 'Outside.'

Lia wished she could shut her eyes and not look, but she couldn't help it. The darkness outside the open front door was moving. She squinted her eyes and suddenly everything came into focus and she saw clearly what Harry could see.

Hordes of the dead, all waiting. Most of them were just bones, but some still had fleshy parts. As if seeing them had raised a barrier, they began to shove their way in the door. Bones rattled across the tiles and, in the shove, several fell and smashed into individual parts. Fibias, tibias and a dice-like scatter of finger-and-toe bones.

Lia moved closer to Harry and was glad that he was holding her hand.

'The sea sent them back,' Harry said.

'What?' she whispered.

'They're the drowned, the murdered.'

'So many?' she said.

He didn't take his eyes off them.

They were a terrible sight, but strangely Lia wasn't afraid of them. They were helpless, lost. The sea had returned them but they weren't an army. She felt a deep sorrow for them. Some still had long hair attached to their skulls. One small one, plainly a child, had the shredded remains of a blue ribbon in her hair. Others wore necklaces, whose pendants rattled inside their hollow chests. They were restless and unburied.

And suddenly among them, she saw faces she knew. These were also numbered among the dead, but their demise had not been at the hands of wreckers, luring their ships to the treacherous shore, to the Devil's Teeth. She saw Rose, lips moving as though she were silently praying. Brendan came into view, and Lia thought he smiled at her before his eyes focused on something she couldn't see. It was a haphazard parade of the island's dead. Evan, Jim, Frank. Andrew. Harry's hand tightened on hers when he saw them. He was hurting her, but his hand went loose before she could say anything.

Lia looked again and felt all the strength run out of her legs. Her face felt cold and stiff. Her dad was with the dead but, unlike them, he was standing still, and staring at her. He started towards her and Harry, and the others let him through.

Lia, my darling girl. I've missed you.

Tears filled Lia's eyes and the image of her father blurred.

Hello, brother.

Hello, Will.

The night was clear and calm, with a doldrums feel. It was an ordinary night, not quite summer, not quite fall. Lia was no longer in the Hall. She was standing at the end the foot-worn path from the Robin's Rest to the edge of the cliff, the dry ground spongy under her feet. A half-moon lent its light and the sky was orange on the horizon.

Two figures were walking along the path in single file. Their voices carried on the still air. Harry and her father. They passed without seeing her and sat at the cliff edge, dangling their legs over.

'Been coming out here a while without you now, Will,' Harry said. 'It's good to have you back.'

'I told you, it's only for a little while, Harry. I'm going back to New York, to my family.'

'Your family is here. Always has been, always will be.'

'You're my family, but the others are not. Why don't you come with me? Sell the Robin and come to New York with me. Get to know Jasmine and Lia.'

Harry shook his head. 'You must be mad. You know what

happens if we break the bond. You're already looking older than me.'

'What good is it to you, Harry? You've had hundreds of years. All of us have, but has any one of us ever been happy? Andrew and a couple of the others have been through wives and families, but the children always leave and the wives always die. Look down there.' He pointed to the Devil's Teeth below. 'The bones of the wives are down there with the bones of those you all shipwrecked.'

'There couldn't be a record of successive wives – you know that. As for the shipwrecks, what we did you knew about.'

'Yes, and tried to stop you,' Will said.

There was silence for a while before Harry spoke again.

'You're going back to Jasmine after she's been unfaithful to you?'

'I drove her to it, because I couldn't settle. I was torn between here and there. Between my brother and my wife. She loves me still. It can be fixed.'

'We have been brothers a long time,' Harry said. 'If you go, you will die.'

'Yes,' Will said. 'But not for a few years. I'll have my time with Jasmine and Lia.'

'They're worth that to you?' Harry said.

'They're worth more than I could ever tell them.'

Harry sighed and stood up. He held his hand out and Will stood and took it.

'Your family here loves you too. I love you.'

Will shook his head. 'No, brother. It's been too long. You crave more life than any man has a right to and all you love is her.' He gestured with his free hand towards the Hall, invisible in the dark, but felt in the bones. 'She took death from us but her gift bore a terrible price. You choose to stay and exist, and I choose to leave, to live and die a mortal man.'

Lia had loved and trusted Harry almost from the moment

she had arrived on the island. She had known him for a mere fraction of his long existence compared to his brother, her father. Yet in that moment she knew not to trust him and she screamed to her father to watch out, but he couldn't hear her. She tried to run to him but she couldn't move. This was a window to the past and no more.

Harry let go of his brother's hand and opened his arms. The two men hugged.

'Goodbye, brother,' Harry said.

He broke the hug, put his hands on his Will's chest and shoved.

Lia screamed again. Will, the more slender of the brothers, flew backwards, his arms pinwheeling. He thrust out a hand for help but there was no hand to meet his. He fell out of sight over the cliff and Harry stood still, his head down. Then he turned and went back along the path to the Robin's Rest.

With his departure, Lia was able to move. She threw herself down on her belly as she had done once before and looked down. It was too dark to see much, but there was enough of a moon to show a man caught on the Devil's Teeth, with gentle waves washing around him.

She cried, the pain like a physical lump in her chest, trying to stop her breath. The truth overwhelmed her. Then a glimmer of comfort dawned – her father had not jumped to his death after all – the 'witnesses' had lied. With this thought, she felt the window to the past close.

When she opened her eyes, she was back in the Hall again. There was no one there with her except Harry. He was standing with his back to her, his broad shoulders low, his head bowed. She tried to move quietly along the wall, but he turned. His eyes were red-rimmed as though he had been crying. But they were full of knowledge. His features seemed more pointed, more cruel. His generous mouth had tightened into a thin line.

She broke into a run, trying to dodge past him. He grabbed

her arm and spun her off her feet. When he let her go, she fell and slid along the tiles. Before she could get up, he was on her, holding her down with his body, pinning her wrists to the floor.

'You're not going anywhere. You are one of us, or you will be soon. Ed is already one of us. You can be with him forever. He's a full-blood islander and you're half. You'll make children that will stay.' He cocked his head to one side, bird-like. 'She's coming.'

His weight was suddenly knocked away. Lia scrambled to her feet.

It was Ed. He and Harry were rolling together on the ground. Ed was strong, but Harry was so much stronger. Lia looked around but there was nothing she could use as a weapon. Harry now had Ed pinned to the ground. Lia flung herself onto his back and went for his eyes with her nails. He roared and bucked but she clung on. He was forced to let Ed go but, instead of standing up, he rolled away and crushed her beneath him, knocking the air out of her lungs. Ed struggled up and pulled Harry off her, but Harry rolled again and pinned Ed down.

Lia, looking up and trying to breathe, saw her before the men did.

She didn't look much like Ed, but she had the same intense expression that he wore when he was concentrating. She was less solid, less *there* than Will had been, but she had enough strength to pull Harry away from her son.

'*Mam!*' Ed called but she was gone.

Harry fell backwards but sprang quickly to his feet.

Lia tried to grab Ed's hand but he pulled it away. He was different. Some part of him had wanted to protect her from Harry, but whatever the Strix had done to him had changed him. His eyes had a sheen of gold about them now. Ed was gone. Harry had killed her father. She should have wanted to run and get away from all of the horror, but the little girl who wanted to run away was no longer inside her. What she felt instead was rage.

Twenty-Seven

Later on he will understand how some men so loved her,
that they did dare much for her sake.

Bram Stoker, *Dracula*, 1897

Harry checked himself. He had no quarrel with Ed or Lia.
The future depended on them and he must make them his
allies.

Will had been wrong to leave. He hadn't really been one of
them, but the Strix had bestowed the same gift on him as she
had on them all. Their reward for setting her free from her
confinement on the ship. Will had always pulled against them.
Going away and only visiting infrequently made the bond
weaker. Going away forever and throwing the gift back in her
face was just wrong.

Still, the memory of his hands on Will's chest and the
sensation of pushing his brother away from him, out over the
cliff edge and down to the Devil's Teeth, would never leave
him. Sometimes, he sat and looked at his hands, wishing to
erase the sensation of the push. He dreamed of hugging Will,
and in the dreams they said goodbye and Will went back to
America. These dreams were worse than nightmares. After a
nightmare, he woke to discover that the monsters weren't

real. After the dream of his brother, Harry always awoke to discover that the horror was real, the monsters were real, and he was one of them.

Those moments were few. Most of the time, he could feel the Strix moving inside him, sliding along the corridors of veins and arteries in his blood, and could feel himself moving inside her. Nothing else mattered. Just taking care of her, keeping things square on the island, and living on and on.

Harry had grown to despise those of the old families who thought they loved mortal women. It led them to choose women from the mainland. The blood was being diluted. Harry could feel that they were gone. All of them. Andrew, Brendan, Jim and Evan. Will. He was the only one left, but Ed was a full-blood islander and Lia was half blood. They would make a strong line, more deeply connected than any had been for a long time. Harry would make sure that they stayed. Ed had already been visited by the Strix. Harry could feel the link between them growing. He might take Jasmine for himself. The Hall had let her in but never the likes of Matt. Mothers and babies shared blood. Lia must have passed a little of the old family blood to Jasmine. She was a beautiful woman and would be a good partner for a few years until she joined the others in the sea below.

Ah, he could feel the Strix approach. He turned away from Ed and Lia and stood at the bottom of the stairs, the place where they had thrown so many half dead people for her meal. She appeared at the top and slowly descended. When she reached the bottom she leaned in to him for a kiss. It was a kiss that went on for a long time. He basked in her touch and her attention. It was only towards the end of the kiss that he began to feel that something was wrong. He often felt weak when he was with her, depending on whether he was feeding her or she was feeding him but this was different.

He found it harder to keep his arms around her slender

body. It became such an effort to hold them up that he stopped trying and stood there while she kissed him. He was dizzy and cold and for a moment he tried to struggle but his limbs wouldn't obey him. If she had let him go, he would have fallen.

He opened his eyes and saw that she was watching him, her golden eyes intent.

He knew then that she was saying goodbye in the only way she knew how. Death was the only thing that could part them and she had decided to bring Death to him. She had chosen someone new. Rage and jealousy made him able to struggle a little but her strength was much greater than his. The bond between them hadn't yet broken and, as she continued to kiss his life away, he knew that she had chosen Ed as her new companion. Would he have the same gift of long life, or would he change and become like her? Sharp, beautiful, fierce. Was it Lia who would have to stay and feed them?

He was struck by the image of Lia, forever sixteen, finding her own way to bring prey in return for life. Now that his connection with the Strix was coming to an end, his love for her was no longer his driving force. Pain and sorrow filled him and tears rolled down his cheeks.

There was so much to regret. He and his friends had wrecked ships and stolen gold and jewels and lives before the Strix came. Will had been the good one. He didn't deserve everything that happened to him. Together, they had watched their parents grow old and die. They had themselves married, only to watch wives and children live and die, like the mayfly, a whole life in the blink of an eye. Now that the centuries were coming to an end, he couldn't quite remember why he had killed his brother. Disloyalty to the Strix and to his old companions didn't seem a good enough reason. The connection to the Strix and the others upon whom she had bestowed her gift was suddenly tenuous.

There were so many dead. So many strangers, so many loved ones. He knew he had not been a good man but he no longer understood how to pray, or to ask for forgiveness. It was too late anyway. There was no more time left.

He felt like sleeping. There was some pain, but it was distant. She was no longer kissing him but inhaling something of his. His joints ached and his eyes grew dim. He understood. She was taking back the gift she had given him and his body was growing old, too quickly and all at once.

Darkness began to fill in his vision from the sides and he watched her lovely face through a shrinking window.

I'm dying. I'm finally dying. It's all over at last. At last.

His heart stopped beating. She pressed her cheek to his and he felt the sensation in one last second of mortality before he slipped out of this world and into the next.

The storm was getting worse. Jasmine had to fight for every step on her way back to the Hall. Whatever power had thrown her out was not going to stop her getting back to her daughter. Halfway there on the narrow road, she suddenly realised that the feelings for Harry that had flooded her were gone. He was once more her husband's brother who she didn't really like or trust. There had to be something wrong with a man who would stay on this awful lump of rock.

She forged on, sopping wet, half blind in the rain. The gusts were so strong that several times she felt herself being lifted as though a giant hand had scooped her up. She stepped off the road and walked along by the stone wall that edged the fields. It was no good as shelter, but it was something solid to lean on when the gusts came.

After a while, she started to feel disconnected to her body. The physical effort of walking through the storm in the darkness, often falling, had sent her mind into a strange state of near-euphoria. The world shrank to putting one foot in front of the other, but she felt like she was flying above herself. She had never before wanted to kill any creature, but she wanted nothing now except to save her daughter and to kill whatever monster lived in that horrible house.

Will had saved her from the cave and from the bony, grasping fingers of the dead. He seemed very close to her now, although she couldn't hear him or see him. She sent out thoughts like swallows to him. Love, sorrow, regret. Love was the swallow who kept returning home, despite storms and serpents, despite deserts and oceans. She had let stupid things get in the way. His temper and restlessness, her own snobby ideas of what life should be like, what *he* should be like, when all he had ever been was himself.

If only they could go back to the beginning and erase all the mistakes. If only.

She almost missed the locked gates of the Hall in the dark and had to backtrack to the broken section of wall. She crunched her way up the long driveway to the house and walked in. The strange diffuse light that hadn't been visible from outside showed her the scene clearly.

Lia was standing near Ed. Her clothes were torn and her hair was loose and tangled. There was something wrong with Ed. He turned to look at Jasmine and she saw how cold his eyes were. The rich stormy blue had been replaced by pale gold. He reminded her of a bird of prey she had seen at the zoo.

She had been refusing to look at the stairs and what was happening there. Lia hadn't seen her yet but was staring instead at the horrible scene. Jasmine forced herself to look, the tendons in her neck feeling stiff and brittle as she turned her head.

Harry, looking too much like Will, was in the arms of a woman, a creature. The creature who had stood outside the window of the pub. The Strix. She looked like Lucifer himself, a white angel, beautiful and too proud. She had her mouth pressed against Harry's lips, but it didn't look like a kiss.

Then it was over. The creature dropped Harry to the ground and his body lay there, somehow diminished, crumpled and utterly lifeless. The Strix turned to face Jasmine. What had appeared to be a filmy white dress opened into a huge pair of wings, as white as a swan's, but there was nothing serene about her face. Instead, she looked sharply curious, hungry and predatory. Jasmine had a moment to imagine that her mind would break if the Strix came for her, before her body yielded. She had walked in the streets of New York all of her life and had seen and experienced danger from other human beings. This was all nothing compared to the way this creature's cold regard made her feel. She was helpless, a morsel of prey caught out in the open by the hunting owl.

Then the Strix turned to Lia and Ed.

Helpless fear fled from Jasmine's body, replaced by white-hot fury. She started across the wide hall, her foot kicking something hard on the floor, making it skid in front of her.

The Strix put out a hand and Ed went to her and took the hand. She folded her wings closed and they proceeded up the stairs, elegant and powerful.

Lia made a guttural noise and started across the hall.

'*Lia, no!*'

Lia didn't hear her.

'*Lia!*' Jasmine screamed, running towards her.

This time Lia stopped, startled, and turned. Jasmine opened her arms to her, but Lia ran for the stairs.

Jasmine, exhausted though she was, but glad of all the work she had done in the gym, bent to pick up the object she had kicked, and followed her daughter.

He could hear his heart beating fast. There was something

wrong with his blood too. He could feel it inside him and it felt like her. He had lost his ability to see colour but the world was in sharp focus. Even in the dark, he had no trouble seeing, taking in every scrap of light and using it. Under his clothes, his body was changing. He felt so strong and free, except that he was connected to the beauty that was leading him up the stairs. A brief flash of the past had led him to help the girl, but whatever that had been, it was gone.

They reached the top of the stairs and went down a long corridor with a high arched window at the end. There was a tiny hint of light in the sky. Not yet the end of the storm, but the promise of it. He wasn't afraid of it, but it made him want to sleep. The night was his and the day no longer interested him.

They turned into a room near the window and she, his beauty, his love, took him in her arms.

Lia was running in treacle. It was the nightmare. She wouldn't reach Ed in time, if indeed there was any time left. Jasmine was behind her but, fit though her mother was, she was exhausted. Lia, even though she still felt she was so slow, held back by the house itself, was halfway down the corridor before her mother was halfway up the stairs. There must have been something wrong with the Hall before the Strix had come. Or the Strix had released the wrongness. Alone out on the edge of an isolated island, it had soaked up the evil of the early settlers, those who had killed for profit. Centuries of victims being fed to her had kept the Hall in the darkness. In her head, Lia could hear her parents shouting at her to get out, to leave Ed, to run before she was taken or killed. She ignored the voices and stopped outside the door near the window.

She pushed the door open, suddenly apprehensive, and stepped into the room.

Heat. Ammonia. Rustling. Darkness. Lia, aware that she presented a perfect target in the doorway, moved, pressing her back to the wall, waiting for her eyes to adjust. The room was big, and full of old couches. It had been some sort of sitting room or lounge in its past life. It was dominated by a huge inglenook fireplace, reminding Lia that generations of families had lived here, riding out the winter, or being caught by storms before they could get to safer lodgings on the mainland.

The fireplace resembled nothing so much as a hollow in a tree. The Strix was in it, her wings fluffed out. She hissed at Lia.

Ed moved from the corner and stood in front of the Strix.

'Oh, Ed,' Lia pleaded. 'What's happened to you? Don't you know me?'

He didn't answer. Lia went to him. He let her take his hands in hers but his expression didn't change. She drew him away from the Strix, closer to the door, before he resisted.

'*I love you*,' Lia said.

A tiny frown appeared between his dark brows.

She said it again. '*I love you*, Ed. You love me too. Try to remember.'

She put her arms around him and kissed him. His lips were cold but after a moment, he began to kiss her back. His arms came up around her and he held her tightly to him.

When the kiss ended, he half-turned towards the Strix, confused.

She rose up and stepped out of the hollow.

Lia heard a strange noise and her attention was drawn to movement behind the Strix who stretched her wings and hunched, hissing.

Lia looked past her, trying to decipher the shapes and movement she saw. Then the Strix moved slightly and Lia felt the breath leave her body.

Ed also moved, putting himself again between Lia and the Strix protectively.

But Lia had already seen.

She had young. They were clustered together in the fireplace, fearful and making small sounds of distress. They weren't like the Strix, or like anything Lia had ever seen. They wore soft grey feathers, but had sweet human faces, missing the sharpness of their mother. Their wings were short, not yet ready for flight.

'Ed,' Lia said, 'I don't want to hurt them. Just please come with me.'

Ed frowned again and walked over to the window, turning his back on both Lia and the Strix.

'*Lia, look out!*' Jasmine's voice was frantic and furious.

Lia turned in time to see the crossbow in her mother's hands, ready to fire. If she screamed the word '*No!*' aloud, it was drowned by the shriek of the Strix as the metal bolt flew through the air and pierced her white breast. The young screamed then, terrified. Lia instinctively ran towards them, but they hissed at her, extending their stubby wings. Their mother fell against the side of the fireplace.

Ed crossed the room in a few fast strides and took the Strix in his arms. She was once again a slender girl, easily held, gazing up at him. The bolt stuck out of her, and the feathers on her breast were turning red.

Everyone went still and silent, no one knowing what to do.

Then the Strix stood up.

Corvo woke. Something had changed. The night was fierce and the Strix was free. But the Lilith *was intact. He stood at the bow, as the captain, invisible in the dark, guided the ship away from the rocks. The sea rose, carrying the vessel with it. Instead of crashing back from the wave into a trough, the ship was lifted higher and higher. With the wind against her, she still flew along the crest until a great house came into sight, with the first grey light of dawn catching windows like a shine in a cold eye.*

Ah, Corvo thought. It is time.

There was no sound and no hesitation. The Strix moved fast and took Lia to the ground. As her head plunged towards Lia's throat, Lia flung her arm up and caught the bite with her wrist. The Strix moved back and looked into Lia's eyes.

Then, in the Strix's eyes, Lia saw Rome from a high vantage point, followed by darkness with no escape. Then a ship and the sea. Then Harry and the others gathered together. Then her young. Then Ed. *She's showing me her life and what matters to her.*

Lia felt a surge of pity for the Strix who had never asked to be brought into this cold place so far from her home. A wave of love filled her heart for the pure creature that had done everything to survive and raise her young.

Then the Strix smiled and Lia understood how she had made the men desire her and protect her.

Before the Strix could read her intentions, Lia grabbed the bolt protruding from among the reddened feathers and shoved it deeper. The Strix threw her head back and screamed. A gout of dark blood struck Lia but she had clamped her mouth and eyes tight shut against it. The Strix swayed and fell forward. As if in slow motion, the metal end of the bolt came towards Lia's chest.

Ed flung himself between Lia and the Strix. The blunt bolt struck his shoulder, knocking it out of its socket. He voiced a snarl of pain and struggled to push the dead weight of the Strix off him with his good arm. Jasmine rushed forward and hauled the Strix backwards. Relieved of the weight of her body, Ed's injured arm hung loosely from his dislocated shoulder and he screamed.

Jasmine dropped the Strix and pulled Lia into her arms. Over her shoulder, Lia saw the young go quiet and slip down in the nest.

Ed was lying on his side, his face white.

Lia took her mother's hand and they went to him.

'Hello,' he said, his voice gruff with pain.

'Hello,' Lia said, smiling into his dark blue eyes.

Standing at the bow, Corvo saw the Strix leave the house alone. She had made others but they always died when her body died. As before, the spirit of the mother would live on. While he could, he would pursue her and search for a mortal who would take his place.

Strange how the world could look changed and yet be the same. The Strix was forever, a thread of blood from world's beginning to world's end.

Twenty-Eight

Do you believe in destiny? That even the powers of time can be altered for a single purpose? That the luckiest man who walks on this earth is the one who finds ... true love?

Bram Stoker, *Dracula*, 1897

Jasmine used her scarf to fashion a sling for Ed who had used a painful but effective technique to pop his shoulder back into its socket. Then they went downstairs and out of the house.

The storm was still violent, although from somewhere behind the clouds a grey light was filtering. Lia clung to Ed on his one good side, while Jasmine wrapped her arms around her. It took a long time to walk even a short distance from the house. Once they were back on the road, they had to hunker down beside the wall to shelter from the vicious gale coming off the sea. The air was full of the booming noises from the blowholes and plumes of foam were flying.

Lightning crackled all around them, forking continuously. There was a tremendous noise behind them and the wild air smelled sulphurous. Lia peeped over the wall, holding her breath against the wind.

The Hall was on fire. Lightning had struck. It was ablaze and sinking fast. The wind played with the inferno, spreading it instead of putting it out. Ed and Jasmine joined her and together they watched as the Hall sent the spirits of the lost into the dark sky in the form of smoke and flames. They bore witness to its death, waiting until it finally fell in upon itself, quenching the fire and leaving nothing but destruction and ruin behind. Except for one chimney that had run like a spine through the whole house, standing alone, a mutilated finger pointing blasphemously at the heavens.

Then, helping each other, they continued on their way. They stopped at the deserted Robin's Rest and quickly picked up their things. Lia hesitated, but slipped into the kitchen briefly. She looked around and, before she could rethink it, put the little carved robin in her pocket before rejoining the others. They walked into the village where there was both evidence of the storm's power and of the resilience of the people.

The Red Door opened to them and they found Mr. and Mrs. Glenn, as well as Matt, Becky and baby Francis, all shaken, but alive and safe. They waited together until it was finally safe to leave the island.

As the ferry, piloted by someone new, chugged towards the mainland, Lia looked at the remains of the Chimneys, destroyed by the storm, and circled by hundreds of screaming gulls, the great white birds wheeling against the sky.

The End